Patricia Frances
ROWELL

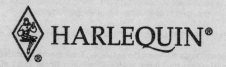

HARLEQUIN®

TORONTO • NEW YORK • LONDON
AMSTERDAM • PARIS • SYDNEY • HAMBURG
STOCKHOLM • ATHENS • TOKYO • MILAN • MADRID
PRAGUE • WARSAW • BUDAPEST • AUCKLAND

ISBN-13: 978-0-373-29500-5
ISBN-10:   0-373-29500-6

AN IMPETUOUS ABDUCTION

DON'T MISS THESE OTHER NOVELS AVAILABLE NOW:

#899 THE LAST RAKE IN LONDON—Nicola Cornick

Dangerous Jack Kestrel was the most sinfully sensual rogue she'd ever met, and the wicked glint in his eyes promised he'd take care of satisfying Sally's *every* need....
Watch as the last rake in London meets his match!

#901 KIDNAPPED BY THE COWBOY—Pam Crooks

TJ Grier was determined to clear his name, even if his actions might cost him the woman he loved!
Fall in love with Pam Crooks's honorable cowboy!

#902 INNOCENCE UNVEILED—Blythe Gifford

With her flaming red hair, Katrine knew no man would be tempted by her. But Renard, a man of secrets, intended to break through her defenses....
Innocence and passion are an intoxicating mix in this emotional Medieval tale.

This book is about family, and
it is dedicated to my first family—
My parents, Willard Houghton Moore and
Mary Edna Butler Moore and the best brother
in the world, John Willard Moore

And every time for the love of my life, Johnny

AND A WORD OF THANKS

To the kindest of all editors, Ann Leslie Tuttle,
my appreciation. You took a chance on me and
gave me the chance I needed. Thank you, dear.

Prologue

1796, Derbyshire, England

The little girl plastered herself against the wall, her gaze held fast by the long streamer of ribbon she twisted around her finger.

"Come now, Phona dearest." Mama smiled and placed an encouraging arm across her shoulders. "You want to play the game with the other children, don't you?"

A cold paralysis enfolded the child. Everyone was looking.

At her.

She pushed harder against the wall. Her mother pried the ribbon loose from her clenched hand. "Now, Phona, my love, you don't want to rumple your new frock. You must be perfect for your party."

Phona clutched her pristine white skirt with both hands and transferred her gaze to the tips of her white kid slippers. The immobilizing chill seemed to be taking even her breath.

She could not. She could not. She just could not.

"Phona." Her mother's smile faded as she jerked the fabric away from Phona's small hands and tried to smooth it. "This is the outside of enough. Come and join the game. The party is for you."

The little girl began to chew on her knuckle. Tears pushed their way out from behind her eyelids. She didn't *know* these children. She didn't know the other ladies. They were all looking.

At her.

Someone tittered. Mama seized her arm and pulled her away from the wall, yanking her fingers out of her mouth. "That looks very disagreeable." She was not smiling at all now. "Do not be such a baby, Phona. You are a great girl of five years. Big girls do *not* cry at parties."

A sob burst out of the child's constricted throat, but not a word could she utter. Someone else laughed.

Now Mama looked angry. "I went to a great deal of bother for this, and now you will not even play."

Had a pride of lions descended on her, Phona could not have, at that moment, moved. Could not have run away.

Her mother had on her scary face now. She gave the girl a hard shake and leaned the scary face close to hers.

"Persephone Proserpina! You are *embarrassing* me!"

She was dragged from the room in disgrace.

Chapter One

1811, Derbyshire, England

There he was again.

The stranger on the hill.

Phona reined her gentle bay mare to a halt in the lee of a small copse and patted her on the neck. "What do you think he is doing, Firefly? He has been there on that tall, awkward-looking horse four times this week. And many times in the last several months." She shaded her eyes with her hand. "I can't see his face under that brimmed hat."

The mare twitched her ears.

"No, he never makes a sound. I look up, and there he is, like an apparition in a penny dreadful. And like most apparitions, I suppose, he doesn't seem to see *me*. Do you think he is a shade, Firefly?" The mare shook her head, rattling her bridle and bit. "No, I'm sure you are right. He must be flesh and blood."

Between one breath and the next, the man disappeared again, leaving Phona to wonder if she and Firefly were wrong about his substantiality. "Did you see that? What *can* he be doing?"

The particular hill on which the non-apparition had appeared lay beyond her family's land, so heeding all the usual cautions and admonitions, Phona never rode that far.

Today, however, she would make an exception. "Come, let us go and see if we can discover what is so interesting about that specific hill—other than the rider who so often appears atop it."

Firefly sidled a bit. "Oh, stop that. I know that approaching him is completely improper. Today I have no patience with *proper,* nor with cautions and admonitions. None at all."

Whoever the man was, speaking with him would be better than talking to her horse. Which was far better than the conversation of Old Ned, her presently evaded groom. Which was *infinitely* better than going to the little party of young ladies and their mothers to which she and Mama had *not* been invited.

Mama would have the vapors. Again.

Except that Mama was *already* having the vapors over the *crushing snub* dealt her by Mrs. Rowsley. Phona sighed. "I love Mama, Firefly. You know I do. But sometimes I become very out of patience with her." And with cautions and admonitions.

Turning Firefly toward the distant hill, Phona gave her a tap of the crop and cantered across the rolling green landscape, enjoying the warm sunshine on her face and the crisp spring breeze streaming through her hair. She skirted scattered clumps of vegetation, drawing in the fragrance of early flowers emanating from them, and guided her mount around the numerous rocky outcrops. They jumped the drystone wall separating the Hathersage property from the neighbor's and pulled up.

Finding herself at the foot of a steep incline dotted with large boulders, Phona slowed her mount to a walk as they began the ascent. As she neared the top of the hill, strange sounds began to drift to her on the wind.

Clanks and thumps. The jingle of harness and the creak of cart wheels. Coarse voices calling to one another. What in the world? There should be nothing here but open countryside.

Phona reined in. What must she do about this unexpected development? She certainly could not risk encountering a group of rough men by herself. She should turn back. But what were they doing on the far side of that hill? Perhaps she could find a spot to peek over the ridge without being seen. Of course, if she did, they might—

How long her prudent self might have debated with her more adventurous one, Phona never learned. Suddenly the sound of hoofbeats erupted just above her. She looked up to see the stranger on the tall, rawboned black burst over the crest, galloping straight at her, wild hair flying from under the hat. A glimpse of a scowling, dark-bearded visage ended the argument in a heartbeat.

"Run, Firefly!" Phona tugged her mare's head around and kicked her sharply into motion. The steep slope forbade the pell-mell gallop her pounding heart demanded. A misstep on the rugged terrain would likely result in a broken leg for her mount or a broken neck for herself.

And certain capture.

Steady, steady. Every sense clamoring for precipitous flight, Phona forced herself to control her horse.

Oh, God. The noise of the chase was growing louder.

And closer.

He would be on her in seconds. She must find a way…

A copse of trees rose in front of her. If she could cut through them, perhaps she would gain some time, and even possibly lose her pursuer. Her little mare dived into the shelter as if she, too, feared for her life. They leaped over small bushes and fallen branches and careened between the trees.

Branches clawed at her face **and** raked her hat off her

head, the scarf all but strangling her before giving way. Seeking protection from nature's assault, she leaned closer to the mare's neck, keeping her body as low as possible. The sound of the following hooves faded a bit.

Could it be that the man hesitated to squeeze his big, ugly horse through the narrow spaces? Fortune was favoring her at last. Phona angled away from where she had entered the grove. If she could make her way back to her own land, the ground was easier, and she had known it for a lifetime. She could not imagine that he would hound her all the way to her home.

Phona and the mare emerged from the trees. She glanced to the right, and despair welled up in her. Whatever its deficiencies of appearance, the stranger's black must be a powerful beast. It had circled the grove in the time it took for her to go through it.

The next few minutes would be a head-to-head race. One which her small mare could hardly hope to win. Doubts notwithstanding, Phona turned down the hill and gave the horse her head.

The contest ended in moments. Thundering hooves pounded up alongside her, and a hard arm circled her waist. Phona fought to keep her seat, but found herself dragged, kicking and trying to scratch, onto the saddle in front of the stranger. His other arm wrapped around her, capturing her arms and clamping her tightly against him. A hand closed over her mouth.

An angry whisper sounded in her ear. "Listen to me and listen well. As you value your life, do *exactly* as I tell you."

Phona turned to look over her shoulder at the menacing face. All dark. Not only did a thick brown beard cover the lower portion, but a black patch hid one eye. She stifled a gasp.

A rough hand grasped her chin. "When I drop you, lie as you fall. Lie as if you were dead. Do not move! Do not even breathe until I return."

In the distance, Phona heard another set of hoofbeats closing on them. Oh, Lord! What now?

Her captor let out a roar and pulled her head sideways, his callused fingers sliding across her skin. And dropped her. As she hit the stony ground, Phona heard another voice shouting, "Is she dead?"

"Aye, 'ardesty, she'll talk to none." The dark stranger turned his horse back the way he had come, putting it between her and the other speaker.

Dear heaven! He had feigned breaking her neck! Who were these people? Phona took the hidden moment to shift her head to an awkward angle, then lay motionless.

Her attacker spoke again, in a Cockney accent. "Ye best get that load 'andled and get the 'ell out of 'ere before they come lookin' fer 'er. When her mount comes in without the chit aboard—"

The second man uttered a word Phona had never heard before and added, "These bloody hills will be swarming with searchers. Come, man. Move your arse!"

As they galloped away, Phona opened her eyes just enough to confirm something that she could hardly credit. The arm which had removed her from her mount so efficiently ended not in a hand, but in a sharp, black iron hook.

As he watched the departing convoy disappear into the next dale, Leo kept a wary watch. He could not quite see the girl where she lay on the far side of the trees, and he knew his confederates would leave a lookout in their wake to watch their back trail. He prayed he had frightened her sufficiently to keep her still. If she tried to run, the sentry might very well see her, and if he did, she would die.

Or the sentry would.

Or Leo would.

After an agonizing wait, he finally saw the scout ride away after his party. He eased his mount down the side of the hill and around the grove. The girl still lay where she had dropped, ringlets of auburn hair flung out around her, her head turned at a very strange angle. Ye gods! Surely he had not actually killed her!

Leo spurred to her and leaped out of his saddle. Going to one knee, he gently shook her shoulder. "Miss Hathersage?" She did not respond. Perhaps she had fainted from fright. He shook her a bit harder. "Miss! Can you hear me?"

Still no response. Just as panic was about to descend on him in full force, he noticed the infinitesimal movement of her breast, rising and falling as she breathed. Thank God! Sliding his left arm under her shoulders, he lifted her to a seated position, careful not to touch her with the hook. Her head lolled like a rag doll's. He used his good hand to feel the bones of her neck. They seemed sound enough—

At a rattle of stones below him on the hill, Leo sprang to his feet and yanked the pistol from his belt, dropping the girl to earth once again. This time he heard a distinct "Ow!" and glanced down in time to see her roll to her feet and bolt down the slope, making for the sound he had heard.

"God confound clever females!" Leo jammed the pistol back into his belt and gave chase. Now he could see that her mount, rather than racing off to her stable, had wandered quietly back to her mistress. Had it not kicked a stone in its path, he might never have known it was there. The aggravating wench had simply waited her chance to make a run for it.

And she was fast. For a girl. But there was nothing wrong with Leo's legs, and a girl in a riding habit was at a serious disadvantage. She had pulled the skirt up to her white thighs, but the train caught on every rock and bit of vegetation. Still, he barely caught her just as she seized the reins of the mare and was trying in vain to reach the stirrup of the sidesaddle.

She turned and struck at him, but he had expected no less and was ready for her. In a heartbeat he had locked his muscular arms around her from behind and lifted her off her feet. Her heels kicking against his shins made little impression on his booted legs. Fortunately, she was a tiny thing, and the back of her head slammed into his chest rather than his chin. A very game quarry!

"Miss Hathersage! Miss!" He leaned away from another crack of her head against his collarbone. "Ow! Damnation, woman, will you be still for a moment?"

Evidently not. She started squirming, desperately trying to wriggle out of his hold. Very well. If he could not subdue her with reassurance, he could resort to threats. He shifted his hook until the point of it just barely pricked her side. She stilled as if frozen in place.

Leo lowered his voice. "Be still or you will skewer yourself."

"You bloody bastard!" She gasped for breath.

"No, although you are not the first to make that charge." Her defiance made him grin. "But, tsk-tsk. Such unsuitable words from such pure lips."

"Cad! Blackguard!"

"Those allegations are closer to the mark. However, we have little time for character assassination." He cautiously allowed her feet to settle to the ground, carefully ignoring the sensation of her warm, firm body sliding down his.

Yet there was no denying the feelings invoked from the softness of her breasts against his arm. Leo forced the excitement of the chase and its incipient arousal back. He could not afford distractions of that sort. Not now.

Not ever.

She did not renew the struggle, so apparently the hook had done its work. It usually did. The mere sight of it terrified brawny men, let alone a girl barely out of the schoolroom. Perhaps he *was* a cad.

Her chest rose and fell in panicked breaths. Suddenly she took a longer breath and an ear-assaulting scream cleaved the quiet of the hillside. Leo jerked his head—and his ears—away from her.

"Good Lord, girl! Do not do that again. You will deafen us both." He jiggled the point of the hook ever so slightly to enforce this message. "No one is near enough to hear you. Save your breath and pay attention." He paused for a heartbeat to gather his thoughts before continuing.

"Your curiosity has come very close to killing the kitten, Miss Hathersage. I cannot allow you to recount today's experience to anyone. But neither do I wish to kill you to prevent it. In that I differ from the others in this venture. My associates would have done it in the blink of an eye."

The quietness that settled over her told him that she understood that assertion and the implied threat. She was giving him her full regard, trembling a little in his arms.

"Hence, I must constrain you to come with me for a time. What I am to do with you, I have no notion, but we will contrive something. Please believe that I intend you no harm."

She cried out and started to twist toward him, felt the prick of the hook, and checked. Leo sighed. "And I can see that you will not come compliantly. Therefore, as much a I regret it…" Leo pulled a leather thong from his pocket.

"No!" Suddenly she was struggling again, forgetting the hook in her panic.

"Damn it, woman! You'll hurt yourself. Don't you know when you are outgunned? Be still!" Leo looped one of her arms with the hook and forced her slender wrists together until he could tightly grasp both of them in his powerful right hand.

In spite of her frantic attempts to pull away, he looped the cord around her wrists and tied it with the agility of much practice, using the hook as a second hand.

Leo caught the reins of the mare and guided it close. Thanks be to his lucky stars that the bay was more docile than the lady. Since the hook prevented his lifting her by the waist, he grasped one of the girl's arms under the shoulder with his good hand and, slipping his other arm under her knees, attempted to wrestle her onto the sidesaddle. She refused to help him at all.

Her privilege, under the circumstances, but he was losing precious time. He must be away before her household missed her. "Miss Hathersage, please put your knee over the horn."

Her mouth firmed into a hard line and her chin went up. "I'll be damned!"

In spite of his frustration, a chuckle escaped Leo. "If you do not, I shall be forced to tie you facedown across the saddle."

He allowed her to contemplate traveling in that position for a moment. He was fast becoming exasperated enough to do it.

At last, she sighed, and he detected a defeated whisper, "Very well."

Yes, he definitely *was* a cad.

Fearing that she would try to slide off the horse, even with her hands tied, he used a second lash to secure her neat ankle and nicely rounded knee to the stirrup straps. That should make her fast.

He guided the mare back to his own mount and climbed into the saddle. Leading the bay and her passenger, he turned and started back up the hill.

"Do you have a name?"

The question, coming from behind him, startled him. "Yes, Miss Hathersage, I do. However, I fear I cannot share it with you at this time."

"You have the advantage of me, sir. What should I call you—other than those very appropriate sobriquets?"

He turned and gazed at her for a moment, then in spite of the troublesome situation, burst into laughter. "I believe, Miss Hathersage, that under these circumstances you should call me Lord Hades."

* * *

Lord Hathersage was at his wit's end. His adored wife had been having one fit of hysterics after the other for the last two hours. Nothing he said comforted her. He groped for words that might not set off another outburst, but was quickly disappointed. She spun away from the window out of which she had been staring and flung herself onto a settee.

"How *could* she do this to me?" His lady dabbed at her eyes and took the tiniest whiff of her salts. "She knows I worry about her—riding off who knows where by herself. Not even a groom in attendance. What people say of her I shudder to think." Suiting the action to the word, her ladyship shivered delicately, the creamy skin of her shoulders shimmering under her gossamer shawl.

Ignoring this distraction with the ease of long practice, his lordship chanced a cautious intervention. "Now, now. Demetra, my dearest…"

His dearest Demetra rolled on without pause. "But will she stay home just because *I* ask her?" She jumped to her feet and stamped her shapely foot. "Nooo! I am only her mother. If she had any respect… She *will* ride in the sun and get those horrible freckles. If she had any consideration for *me,* she would at least wear a large hat! How I am *ever* to interest a husband in her I have not the slightest notion. She comes in with her hair looking like a birch broom in a fright! And in the eyes of all, *I* have failed."

For once his lordship's patience with his adorable wife cracked just a hair. His lady tended to forget that Peresphone was his daughter, as well as hers. He had been astride a horse for many hours of the late afternoon, searching unsuccessfully for his lost child.

They had found not a trace of her, save for the prints where her horse had jumped the wall. Even now his men rode the hills with torches while he did his best to console her mother.

"Come now, Demetra. How can you concern yourself with that inconsequential drivel now? Phona might be lying somewhere—hurt or…"

"Oooh!" His wife threw herself facedown on the settee. "How can you be so cruel? You know I cannot bear to think of anything so terrible."

Lord Hathersage beat an immediate strategic retreat. He sat beside her and gathered her into his arms. She sobbed against his cravat.

Tears coursing down her cheeks, she choked out, "Oh, George, I couldn't bear losing her."

His lordship swallowed a sob of his own. "We will find her soon."

Lord Hathersage wished that he felt as sure as he sounded. Reason counseled that, had she been injured, they would have found her by now.

In spite of a tendency to indulge both his wife and his daughter, he was not an unworldly man—and certainly not a poor one. He recognized full well that everyone knew Phona stood to inherit his quite astonishing fortune.

And he knew what that meant.

How could he tell his poor, distraught wife that her daughter had been abducted?

The Hades reference could hardly be missed by anyone who had coped with the name Persephone Proserpina Hathersage for twenty years. And it told her a great deal about her escort. In spite of the fact that he looked like every child's image of a wicked pirate, the man must be well-educated.

How else would he know that in the Greek tale, Hades, Lord of the Underworld, figured as the abductor of Persephone, the daughter of Demeter?

Which also meant that, in addition to knowing that she was the daughter of the Hathersage house, he knew her full name. Which, in turn, must surely mean something. But what? Phona had certainly never met him before. She could hardly have forgotten a man who looked like *that*.

A chill ran over her.

Could she possibly escape him? At the moment Phona could not see how. She was rapidly becoming more and more disoriented. Dusk had begun to fall, gathering in the crooks and shadows of boulders, trees and crevices. Nothing looked familiar. Soon it would be dark, and she would never be able to find her way back.

Hades, on the other hand, clearly knew exactly where he was going. They had been riding steadily for hours, winding through the protection of small gorges and woodlands, never in sight of a trail, let alone a road. Obviously he had a destination in mind.

Phona cleared her throat. "Lord Hades? Where are we going?"

He twisted his broad shoulders toward her. "My apologies, Miss Hathersage. I fear I cannot tell you that."

What else did she expect? "Is it much farther?"

"Yes. I am afraid so. Are you tired?"

"A bit."

"You certainly should be, after *that* engagement. We will rest presently."

Phona made another try. "Where are we now?"

"In Derbyshire."

A decidedly unladylike snort escaped her. "I knew that much!"

"I was certain that you did."

The wretch! She could hear the smirk in his voice as he turned back to watch his path. She'd be damned if she spoke to him again!

The intensity of running and fighting with her intimidating adversary had faded, giving way to a discouraged weariness. Phona had been able neither to outrun him nor to outsmart him. She had been overpowered and dumped unceremoniously on the rocky ground twice each. Her neck ached from lying as if broken.

She could not slide off her mount and try to run without being dragged by the leg, and as he had so annoyingly pointed out, no one would hear her if she shrieked like a banshee.

As the warmth of the sun faded, she began to feel cool. Sweat from the chase had dampened her clothes and now sucked the heat out of her battered body. Dear heaven, she hurt all over.

Try as she might to suppress it, Phona shook with fright, fatigue and cold. How could she *not* be afraid? She could not get away from him, had no idea where he was taking her.

And what did he intend to do with her?

A knot began to tighten in her stomach. Surely, had he planned to kill her, he would not have taken the trouble to subdue her. But she could hardly afford to underestimate a man who called himself Hades.

Her captor had not yet deliberately hurt her, but he might prove more cruel than he now seemed. Phona knew a man might mistreat a woman in any number of ways.

Perhaps that was why he had taken her.

Chapter Two

When the sun had sunk completely and the lavender twilight had faded to black dark, Hades stopped in the shadow of a small wood and dismounted. He untied the thongs from her leg and helped her slide off her mare. Her legs wobbled from the long ride, and he steadied her with his good hand and led her to a boulder where she could sit.

"We will stay here and rest the horses until the moon rises. It is too dark to continue safely. Are you hungry?"

For a moment Phona's pride forbade her to answer. However, second thought made her realize that she could not allow herself to become weak with hunger. Now that he brought it to her attention, she felt starved.

And she had another problem.

She would have to speak. "Yes, I am, but I also need to…" She stopped in midsentence, the heat of a blush suffusing her cheeks, and gestured with her bound hands and her head toward the bushes.

"Ah." Lord Hades gazed at her consideringly. "Of course." He came to where she rested on the rock and knelt on one knee in front of her. He looked so intently into her eyes that Phona's face got even hotter. She studied her hands.

The man put a finger under her chin and lifted it until he could see her face in the faint starlight. "Do not mistake this for an opportunity to escape, Miss Hathersage. If I am forced to, I will keep watch on you every second. Do you understand?"

Phona pondered that declaration for a moment. She turned her head away from his scrutiny. "Sir, you are no gentleman!"

She thought she heard a wry amusement in his voice. "I believe we have already established that." The humor faded. "Miss Hathersage, I would give you all the privacy you need, if I could be sure that you will not try to hide or run away. You will not succeed, but I fear that if you try, you will get lost or injured. This is not safe county."

Every fiber of Phona's being longed to make the attempt, but her aggravatingly practical nature told her that the man was absolutely correct. And absolutely serious. He *would* watch her while she… Intolerable! Reluctantly, she nodded.

"Do you give me your word?" He continued to study her eyes.

Phona sighed and nodded again. "Very well. Word of a Hathersage. I will not use this as an occasion to escape."

Hades considered for a moment, then he nodded in turn. He obviously had not missed the qualification. But the assurance sufficed for now. With a few deft motions he untied her wrists. "Don't go far."

Little danger of that! The short trip into the dark bushes proved quite enough to make flight far less tempting. Mysterious small creatures rustled in the leaves, and she could imagine spiders as large as her hand dangling from the tree limbs.

She stumbled over every rock. Definitely not the time to try to lose Hades and make her way home. As soon as she could, she scurried back to where she had left him with the horses.

She found him rummaging in a saddlebag. He indicated with a motion that she should again sit and then followed her, carrying objects unrecognizable in the dim light. He made himself comfortable beside her and began to unwrap something from the folds of a white napkin. Phona's mouth started watering at the smell of a meat pasty.

Hades broke off a generous chunk and handed it to her, placing the remainder on the rock between them. "Plain fare for a lady, but sustaining enough."

"Thank you." She took a hearty bite and chewed appreciatively.

He broke a bite from his portion and popped it into his mouth, watching her from the corner of his eye. When he had swallowed, he took a swig from a jug which he had placed on his other side.

Phona eyed it enviously. The day and the pasty had left her very dry. He had almost set the bottle down again when he turned suddenly to glance at her. "Are you thirsty? I have only ale, and I doubt that young ladies care much for it."

"I have never drank any." She considered the jug. "But I am exceedingly thirsty."

"I doubt you will find it to your liking, but you are welcome to have some." He paused thoughtfully. "Just don't have too much. It will go straight to your head if you have never drank it." He handed her the bottle.

Phona sipped cautiously—and made a terrible face.

The man laughed. "As I thought."

"Don't be so hasty." She reached for the bottle as he took another swallow and set it aside. "I am quite parched." She managed a larger drink this time.

He grinned, his strong teeth glinting in the dark beard. "Pluck to the backbone."

Phona did not know how to answer that. She was not feeling very plucky. She ate her pie silently, occasionally sipping from the jug. The ale was not as strong as wine, but

Mama only allowed Phona a tiny taste of any form of spirits. Soon she could feel a pleasant warmth steal through her limbs.

She reached for the bottle again, but Hades moved it away. "I think not. We still have a long ride ahead of us, and I don't want you incapacitated." He glanced at the sky. "The moon is coming up, but so are the clouds. We must hurry."

He repacked the remains of the meal and disappeared into the bushes while Phona strolled about the clearing to stretch her muscles. And clear her head. The ale had, in fact, made her a bit dizzy. As well as bone-weary.

But for a strong application of resolution, Phona would have wept. The thought of more riding was almost more than she could bear, but apparently she had no choice. Therefore, bear it she would. And without showing any weakness to the rogue.

He was gone longer than she had expected, but made no explanation when he returned. She suspected he had scouted their back trail for pursuit. Evidently, he had found none.

Another disappointment.

He approached her and touched her cheek lightly. Phona jerked back, but he simply declared, "You are getting cold." Untying a roll from his saddle, he shook out a cloak and put it around her shoulders. He helped her to mount, and this time she did her part. If she became too much of a problem, he might leave her here, or even... Phona did not want to remain here alone.

Not alive, and certainly not dead.

Leo glanced back at the girl as they climbed the bank onto the old trail. She had uttered not a word, but he could see her swaying in the saddle. Her little mare looked no better. He felt very thoroughly the cad she had called him. A marauder, returning to port with his prize in tow.

And quite a prize she was. Beautifully made. Impressive

mettle. He found the task of making himself forget the feel of her warm, soft body struggling against his to be more than he could manage. As was trying to forget that he had her completely under his control. To remember that he *was* a gentleman. Leo did not feel like a gentleman.

Leo did not want to be a gentleman.

He sighed as a large drop of rain splashed on his forehead. The rest of the ride could only get worse. The wind whipped his cloak around the lady's small body, all but pulling her off her horse. Another drop followed the first, and suddenly the rain swept over them.

Hastily dismounting, Leo hurried back to his hostage. When he lifted his arms, she all but fell into them. "Come, we still must travel a bit farther. You will ride with me."

She stumbled, and Leo slipped an arm around her. She was shivering, her teeth chattering. If he didn't get her to shelter soon, she would be ill.

He made the mare fast to a lead rope, and with his help the girl managed to get herself onto the front of his saddle. Leo swung himself up behind her and flung the cloak over both of them. Cradling her against his chest, he tucked the cloak in well and pulled a fold of it over her head and face.

Leo tugged the brim of his hat low against the wind and rain and kneed his black into motion. The mare resisted for a moment and then, resignedly, followed. Thank God for his own stalwart mount, rawboned and homely, but strong as the capstan for which he was named.

Alone Leo might have made the ride back to his haven in half the time with naught more than moderate weariness, but the business with the girl had taken its toll—not the physical struggles with her so much as the sense of responsibility, the worry over her future.

And his, come to think of it. Even for him—nay, especially for him—absconding with a nobleman's daughter might have severe consequences if he were found out.

He guided his small cavalcade onto a track almost too faint to be seen. They wound their way up along the side of a steep, heavily wooded gorge. The stream at the bottom roared along noisily, full and fresh and joyous with the rain.

Leo himself might wish for a little less of it. The water trickled down the back of his neck and blew into his eye. Small branches swiped at his face and dumped their burden of droplets into his beard. At least the downpour would erase all sign of their passing.

Coming to a spot where the stream joined another, Leo urged his mount across the rising water and onto the point of land between them. The black put up a token protest, but splashed through and plodded upward along the trail, head held low. In the shelter of his body's heat, the girl had ceased shivering and seemed to be sleeping. Thank God for that.

Leo always felt a thrill as the stone walls rose out of the trees and rocks and dark. Tonight he also felt exceedingly thankful. They rode into the courtyard through the arch in the wall and across into the stable. At the sound of the horse-shoes clopping across the cobbles, the girl roused and sat straighter.

She gazed about her, craning her neck to look up into the oak-beamed rafters high above them. A horse whickered a soft, sleepy greeting. "Where are we?"

"In my stable." Leo pulled the cape free and swung down to the hay-strewn floor.

"I can see *that*," she snapped at him and tried to slide off the tall black and stand. Her knees failed to hold her, and she wound up in a heap in the straw. She swallowed a startled cry and, clinging to the stirrup, struggled bravely back to her feet.

The attempt again proved unsuccessful. Leo caught her as her legs threatened another collapse and eased her onto a box of tack. He quickly realized that would not answer, either. She began to list slowly to starboard, her eyelids fluttering closed.

He grasped her shoulders once again and was trying to decide how to proceed when a welcome voice spoke at the stable door.

"See to the lass. I'll tend the horses."

Leo gathered the girl into his arms, careful not to touch her with the hook, and carried her into his house.

No one had slept in the chamber in perhaps a hundred years, but when Leo had decided to use the place, they had cleaned it along with the rest of the ancient lodge and furnished it with new bedding.

The rotted bed curtains and other draperies they had burned, saving one fine, ancient tapestry which had defied the damp and dust. Other than that, only a low chest, a screen and a pair of heavy carved chairs remained to soften the stone walls.

Making the long climb up the stairs, Leo laid the girl on the tall bed. He next set about kindling a fire in the big fireplace, fumbling in the dark for the flint. Thank goodness they had already brought up wood against an emergency.

When the fire at last took hold, he walked back to the bed and gazed again at his guest, stroking his beard thoughtfully. Apparently asleep or unconscious, she was shaking again. No wonder in that; the room was little warmer than the rain-drenched night. Somehow he must get her out of her wet clothes.

That promised to be a harrowing experience.

Leo winced. Just cradling her in his arms had wakened feelings best left sleeping. Feelings that had been sleeping far too long. How could he…? Perhaps he could rouse her enough to accomplish the task herself.

Please, God.

The last thing he wanted was to be accused again of impropriety with a helpless young female. One allegation of savagery had been quite enough. Leo could easily imagine the fine uproar this one would make if she woke without her riding dress. Shuddering, he turned to go and find something dry for her to use in its stead.

As he closed the door, Leo took the precaution of twisting the key in the outside lock. He was fairly certain that she was too done up to try to escape, but he had not forgotten her earlier ploy of playing dead. No, he could not assume his clever miss was incapacitated. And she had given no pledge which applied to this location.

Leo went to his own bedchamber, down the curving flight of stone steps to the next level of the old house. Rummaging in his sea chest, he extracted a linen nightshirt and, after a moment's thought, a silk dressing gown richly embroidered in Arabian motifs. Either would swallow her whole.

He quickly blanked out the images of the young woman upstairs clad in either garment—the linen transparent across her high young breasts, the silk clinging to her neat curves, the robe falling open to reveal shapely legs.

Damnation! The job ahead of him would be difficult enough without his fancies intruding. How long had it been since he had held a woman close? And this woman…

Leo smiled. He admired her spunk. She was too young, too small, too inexperienced to be required to deal with this situation, and yet she coped with courage and resolution.

And he, maimed as he was, had no business even thinking about her lovely, fresh body. To her he would surely seem a monster. More important, she was in his care. He owed her protection and safety—even from himself.

Phona did her best to wake to the voice in her ear and the hand shaking her shoulder. "Miss Hathersage. Miss Hathersage, can you hear me?" She shoved at the hand, tried to turn away. The voice and the hand persisted. "You must get out of your wet clothing. Come now. Sit up."

An arm lifted her, but the darkness around her refused to

dissipate. Still, something pulled her relentlessly upward. Now a pounding started in her head. She mumbled, "G'away," but neither the voice nor the hand nor the pounding obeyed.

She thought she heard a heavy sigh. Someone began to fumble with the buttons of her habit. Lily? Her maid? It wasn't Lily's voice. It was a man's...

A man! Her buttons! She clutched the hand and pushed.

Another sigh. "Miss Hathersage, please. Can you unfasten your own dress? You must take it off. The rain has soaked it."

She nodded, and the hand moved away. Try as she might, her eyes would not open. Never mind. Blindly, she grappled with the buttons, but she could not prevail.

Her fingers refused her commands. Now her head throbbed with every heartbeat and fire shot through her bones. Someone groaned. Herself? It sounded like her.

"Let me help you." The voice sounded again. "Do not be afraid. I will only help you."

The hot skin of Phona's breasts cooled as her habit parted and the air found her damp shift. Then a hand rolled her from one side to the other, peeling away the wet riding dress.

"Can you remove your shift? It must come off, too."

Phona tried to nod, but her head hurt too much. She tugged at the ties of the shift. They came undone, but she could go no further. Her hands fell helplessly beside her, defeated by the ache.

She heard a soft whisper. "God help me." And then her shift was yanked roughly over her head.

Something soft and warm and dry immediately settled over her, and she was allowed to lie back against a pillow. The thunder in her head and the lightning bolts slicing through her bones eased just a bit. A smooth sheet and a warm cover were pulled over her body and tucked under her chin. She grasped them as firmly as she was able.

"Poor child. I shan't touch you." The owner of the voice drew the pins out of her hair and spread it across the pillow, running his fingers through the damp, tangled curls. "Not even a hat to protect your head. Such ill treatment for a courageous lady. I'm sorry."

Phona drifted away again into darkness, trying to remember who he was and why he was sorry.

The scream tore itself out of Phona's throat, rattling the shutters and setting the drums to throbbing in her head again. A skeleton leaned over her. Pale sunken cheeks, hollow eyes, a hairless head.

Bony hands reached for her.

She shrieked again and tried to roll, clawing her way across the bed. Running footsteps pounded into the room. The Pirate. Hades! He said his name was Lord Hades. Oh, God! Oh, God! Hades and a skeleton. The fire in her flesh. The flicker of a blaze leaping against the wall. The smell of smoke.

She was dead! She was dead and in Hell. Could she not feel the torturous flames punishing her body? Did she not see the fleshless shade?

Lord Hades had brought her to the underworld.

Why had she been sent to Hell? She had tried to be good. She treated everyone kindly. She always obeyed Papa, and she tried to obey Mama. But it was so hard.

Phona always disappointed Mama. She could not attract a husband. She always threw out a spot at just the wrong time. Her hair was too curly, too gingery, her dress too rumpled.

But were these mortal sins? God created her hair. It wasn't her fault! It wasn't fair. And it was too much. Far too much.

The wail escaped her in spite of her burning throat. "I want to go home!"

A papery voice responded. "Nay, now, lass. There's naught to fear."

The mattress sank as someone sat beside her and stroked her hair back from her face. A familiar voice. "What happened?"

"Like I told ye, me lord, this phiz o' mine scares women and little children."

"Not that much. Miss Hathersage…?"

Sobs choked their way out through her parched lips. "I don't want to be dead. I want to be alive again. I want to go home."

"Now, now, you are not dead."

"I am. I know I am." Phona gazed up into one bright blue eye. "You *said* you were Lord Hades. I should have known. You brought me to Hell. The Pirate killed me, and you brought me here. There is a skeleton!"

A cold, dry hand rested on her forehead, and the raspy voice said, "Fever dreams, me lord."

"Yes, she is burning with fever." A different hand, larger, warmer, cupped her cheek. "You are not dead, my dear, and I am not truly god of the Underworld. While this *is* my home, and I have brought you here, it is *not* Hell."

"I tried to be good. I did try." The sobs kept coming. Phona lay helpless as tears dripped into her hair. "Why must I suffer forever?"

Strong arms lifted her and cradled her against a hard, shirtless chest. Crisp hair tickled her nose, and she heard Hades' voice. "Come now, it will not be forever. The fever will go away. You are good and brave."

"I don't…" A sob. "I don't feel brave."

"Nay, as I know well, it is very hard to be brave when you are so ill, when nothing is as it seems." The big, warm hand pressed her head against the tickly hair. "Where do you hurt?"

"Everywhere. My head, my arms…" She coughed and croaked, "My throat."

"I feared this might happen." Lord Hades spoke to the Skeleton. "She has taken a chill."

"Aye, a hard ride for a lass. We best be gettin' some broth down her, and the tea, lest it get worse. She'll rest easier."

"Can you stop crying, little one? Can you take some soup?" Hades let her rest against the pillow again. Only now, several pillows held her in a sitting position.

Phona relaxed into their embrace and struggled to make sense of things. The Skeleton was holding a bowl and spoon out to Lord Hades. If she were not in hell, where had the Skeleton come from? If the Pirate was not Lord Hades, who was he?

She tried to take in a deep breath and stop crying, but coughing choked her. A large handkerchief wiped her eyes and nose. She tried again, and finally hiccuped into silence.

Hades extended a spoonful of broth. Phona drew back. "If I eat anything, I can never go home."

"What is she on about now?" the Skeleton inquired.

"It is an old story." Hades sighed. "I'll tell you later." He put the spoon back in the bowl. "Come, Miss Hathersage. You must have sustenance. You are not in the Underworld. You have my word."

"On your honor?" In a fleeting moment of clarity Phona glimpsed the irony of charging either Lord Hades or a pirate with his honor.

"Word of a..." He hesitated for a heartbeat. "Upon my family's honor."

He refilled the spoon, and after a moment Phona accepted a sip. If she was doomed, then she was doomed. She could do nothing to change it. The soup slid warmly down her throat, stinging for a moment. The second mouthful went easier, and after a third a welcome sort of warmth spread through her body, easing some of the fiery ache.

Her eyes began to close, but the two voices exhorted her to wait, to finish her broth. But Phona could not keep the darkness at bay. The bowl disappeared and a cup of bitter tea took its place. She managed to get down several swallows before trying to push it away.

"No, Miss Hathersage. You must drink all of this. It will

help you." She heard the firm voice through a fog, but opened her mouth again, thankful when he took away the nasty draught.

The Skeleton's voice asked, "The laudanum, do ye think?"

"Aye. It will help her pain."

Another pungent smell assaulted her nostrils, but this time Phona obediently opened her lips. Now perhaps they would leave her alone. Even as the extra pillows were removed, she was drifting away. And she did not care if she never returned.

Tired as he was, Leo could not bring himself to leave her. He had done this to her. Certainly it had been a better choice than allowing the others to kill her. Unfathomably better than killing her himself.

Better even than allowing to be destroyed all he had spent months setting in motion. Yet, the decision was his, and he bore the responsibility for it. He could only pray that her illness would not finish her after all.

Leo built up the fire, but the room seemed too cool for him to sit bare-chested, and he was loathe to leave the girl long enough to fetch a shirt. He lay beside her, atop the bed-clothes, and tugged a corner of the quilt over himself, rolling until he was well wrapped in it.

It seemed unlikely that she would even know that he lay near her, but still Leo moved as close to the far edge of the bed as the arrangement allowed, fearing that he might frighten her further should she unexpectedly wake.

She appeared to be lost in unconsciousness, tossing about and moaning now and again. Several times she started up, wild-eyed, her cry breaking the silence. Each time Leo placed a soothing hand on her shoulder and settled her back onto the pillows.

Each time he was uncomfortably aware of the heat radiating from her. Of the smoothness of her skin, the softness of her hair, the sparks of light from the fire caught in its waves.

What a surprising contradiction she was. So courageous and desirable in her womanhood. So vulnerable and child-like in her fever-induced pain and terror of Hell. Leo smiled into the dark. Little had he known how far his Persephone would take *that* jest.

He pitied both her pain and her fear. Leo knew what it was to lie in helpless agony, prey to delirious images, terrified, not only of the enemies in one's dreams, but of the helpless-ness. The fear that gangrene and the surgeon would take the rest of his arm. Too weak to resist.

A hand plagued him with phantom tortures, yet was no longer his to command. Was no longer there at all. The image of it as it disappeared in a spray of blood and grape-shot. Hell.

She had the right of that.

Just as the light of sunrise began to creep through the shutters, his patient flung the bedclothes off. Leo reached for them to protect her once more, but realized that she was sweating. A hand to her forehead confirmed that, while she still felt too warm, her excessive fever had broken.

It would no doubt increase again later in the day, but Leo gave thanks for any sign of improvement. If they could prevent the lady developing an inflammation of the lungs, they might pull her through.

Leo had been almost two days without real sleep. Now that she slept more deeply, he would have gone to his own bed, save that he feared she would be frightened if she awoke alone.

And he feared even more that the sight of his bare stump would cause her further distress. Last night, when he had heard her scream at the sight of Aelfred, he had just removed his shirt and the straps which secured the hook to his body. He had raced up the stairs without a thought for his repulsive deformity.

Now, in the light of day...

Aelfred solved this dilemma by slipping stealthily into the room and handing Leo a shirt. "How fares the lass?"

"A little better, I think. She is sweating."

"Aye, a good sign. Ye'll find coffee and porridge in the kitchen and a bath drawn by your fire. I'll sit with her until she wakes. Mayhap in the light I won't scare the bejabbers out of her." His thin lips quirked. "Or mayhap the light'll be worse."

Leo clapped Aelfred on the shoulder. "Come now, man. Her fever caused that alarm, as well you know. I must sleep now. Thank you." He paused by the bed a moment, gently touching the girl's cheek. "She feels cooler now."

She looked so vulnerable lying there that he could not leave her uncovered. He tucked the quilt around her and finally brought himself to take his leave.

Phona drifted to the surface of consciousness from an unfathomable depth. She wanted to open her eyes, but the growing light hurt, even if she squeezed her lids tightly. Eventually, they adjusted a bit, and she risked a peek.

The light came from a window. A window in a strange room. Rain beat upon the glass of the casement in an uneven tattoo. She closed her eyes again and tried to think.

Rain. She remembered rain. And riding. And riding and riding. A man—a pirate? And a skeleton? Surely she had been dreaming. But where was she? Phona squinted again through aching eyelids. She still lay in the strange bed in the strange room.

Between her and the window someone sat in a chair . She could not make out his features against the glare, but he was working on something in his hands. She tried to raise herself on her elbow. The person in the chair glanced up and rose.

A tall, lean man walked to the bed and looked down at her. "Morning, miss." He held up a restraining hand. "Now don't ye go raising another screech. I ain't much to look at, but I ain't no skelyton nor no boggart, neither."

No, he could not be called a skeleton, but the skin stretched so tightly over the bones of his face that he appeared cadaverous at best. Above his deep-set eyes rose a shining, bald dome of a head, and his lips seemed but a slit in his narrow face. Phona gazed up at him. Was this the bony apparition of her dream?

The alleged apparition announced, "I'm called Aelfred. I keep things in order here." Before she could ask where *here* was, he continued. "I reckon ye be needing some porridge and tea. Won't be a minute." The man disappeared through the door. Phona heard the unmistakable sound of a key turning in the lock.

He had locked her in!

A moment of panic swept over her. She couldn't stay here locked in! She flung back the bedclothes and tried to put her legs over the edge of the high bed, struggling to sit. This attempt was met by a wave of dizziness, and she fell back on the pillow with a thump. Dear God, she was weak as a newborn filly!

When her head quit spinning, Phona glanced down at her body. She was wearing a... Yes. A man's nightshirt enveloped her from shoulders far past her feet, one made of soft, translucent linen. She could see the details of her person right through it. Good grief!

She yanked on the covers. It proved all she could do to deal with the voluminous garment, but she prevailed at last. Exhausted, she lay back, motionless. Dealing with the locking in would have to wait.

After a few minutes she felt able to look around again. She had seen a pirate. He had chased her. Caught her. Forced her to come with him. Now Phona remembered riding on the saddle before him, wrapped in his cloak and his strong arms.

Was this his lair? It certainly *looked* like a pirates' lair, the furnishings very old, the walls of rough stones, a huge fireplace.

At the sound of footsteps, she quickly pulled the quilt up to her chin. Aelfred opened the door and came in carrying a tray. He set it on a low chest beside the bed. Lifting her to a sitting position, he stacked the extra pillows behind her and proceeded to spread a large napkin under her chin.

He offered her a bite of porridge. She tried to take the spoon from him, but her arms felt too heavy to bear the weight. She almost knocked it to the bed.

"Oh, I'm sorry." Tears pricked behind her eyelids.

"No matter, miss. Ye passed a hard night. Little wonder ye feel a mite feeble this morning." He gave her several more spoonfuls and then picked up a teacup. "Here ye go. This will put ye right."

She wrinkled her face at the bitterness. The taste recalled something else. Someone sitting on the bed last night. Offering her the bitter cup. "Who else was here last night?"

"Just his—my master."

"The Pirate?"

"Pirate? Nay… Well, mayhap, in a manner o' speaking." Oh, Lord! He really *was* a pirate!

Chapter Three

By the time she saw him again, Phona had lost much of her interest in her host's piratical calling. Her head and limbs had begun to ache fiercely once more, and her eyes burned unbearably.

Aelfred brought gruel and nasty brews, saying that his master would visit her when he awoke. When finally the turning of the key in the door announced the presence of this personage, Phona could hardly believe her blurry eyes.

She could not mistake the man who walked through the door for anyone other than her assailant of yesterday, yet he looked very…different. The black patch still covered one eye, but the wild, dark hair and beard had been combed and trimmed, the long mane neatly restrained at the nape of his neck by a black ribbon. No hook appeared at the end of his left arm.

Nor did a hand.

The sleeve of his fine linen shirt simply ended, folded over and tightly fastened with a pair of buttons. He wore a black leather vest, but no coat or cravat. Nor was yesterday's scowl visible on his face—a face constructed of strong features, chin square, nose prominent.

He stopped at the foot of the bed and smiled. The flash of fierce, white teeth within the beard reminded her of his grinning like that in the dark woods. In the night she had not seen the brightness of the single blue eye that now twinkled at her.

He still looked like a pirate. A slightly civilized pirate. Very slightly.

But when he spoke, the Cockney voice she had first heard was not in evidence. "Good afternoon, Miss Hathersage. I hope I find you feeling better?"

Phona glared at him. "No, I am *not* better."

"I am sorry to hear that." The Pirate's smile faded. He strolled around the bed and, without a by-your-leave, rested his hand on her forehead. "You *are* very feverish. I had hoped for more improvement, but at least you are lucid."

She moved away from his hand. "No thanks to you for it."

"Au contraire, Miss Hathersage. Had I not brought you here, improvement would be beyond the realm of possibility." He pulled the chair vacated by Aelfred nearer the bed and sat facing her.

"You mean that I would be dead."

"Dead in fact, rather than in fancy. Do you remember last night?" He propped his feet comfortably on the chest by the bed.

"Very little. Only extremely strange dreams."

"In your delirium you thought that I, as Lord Hades, had abducted you to the Underworld."

"Oh, my." Phona felt the heat rising in her face. "How foolish of me."

"Nay, not foolish. You were quite out of your head with fever. You'd had a very hard passage. But would you prefer to call me by some other name? Perhaps Hades is a little *too* apt." He stroked his beard and peered questioningly at her.

"Lord Cad, perhaps? Lord Blackguard? We agreed yesterday, I believe, that those were suitable designations." Phona raised her eyebrows and returned the inquiring gaze.

"Ha!" A short laugh burst out of him. "I see you have recovered both your memory and your spirit. A fierce little kitten challenging a wolfhound. You must be better, after all. But I believe I might prefer some other appellation."

"Lord Hades will do well enough. It certainly fits the situation. But how did you know *my* name was Persephone?"

"Persephone Proserpina. Poor child, christened in both the Greek and the Latin version of the myth." He chuckled again. "I make it my business to know everything that might affect an enterprise before I embark upon it."

"This most recent enterprise appears to be one of piracy." Phona folded her arms across her chest and stared at him severely. "And you, sir, give every appearance of being a pirate."

"I did once have a career upon the sea." He nodded thoughtfully. "But you hardly expect me to confess to you that I am a freebooter." His grin flashed. "Unless, of course, you wish to call me Lord Blackbeard instead of Lord Blackguard."

"I believe I shall stay with Lord Hades. And no, I do not expect you to tell me your felonious business. I can see that it is not to my advantage to know it."

"Quite right, Miss Hathersage."

"I only wish to know how long I must stay…wherever it is that I am. I don't suppose that you will tell me *that*, either."

"Perceptive as always. My apologies." He smiled again. "Our whereabouts are one of my better-kept secrets." Sobering, he added, "As to how long you must stay, I cannot be sure. For now, you will stay in that bed until I am satisfied that you are in no more danger from your illness. After that…we will have to see how long it takes for me to complete my present…uh, felonious business. One cannot rush these things."

In alarm, Phona tried to sit up. "But I must go home. My parents will be frantic. Mama has by now fallen into strong hysterics. You cannot so cruel as to keep me here."

"Therein you are mistaken, Miss Hathersage. I can, and I shall. But I do not intend cruelty. I have already written to your family to relieve their minds. The letter will be delivered within a day or two."

"But what—" At that moment Aelfred interrupted the conversation by opening the door and shoving a cot into the room. Hades rose and helped him muscle it to a place near the bed.

Phona gazed at it askance. "What is *that* for?"

"For me, should we be fortunate and the watch uneventful. You did not expect me to leave you here alone and delirious throughout the night, did you?"

Panic rushed over Phona. She could not sleep in the same room with a man…with *him*. "But…I don't need…"

Lord Hades grinned at her in his most piratical manner. "Do you prefer that I share the bed with you as I did last night?"

Heat rushed to Phona's face, and she covered it with both hands. "You did *not!* You *could* not."

The blue eye twinkled. "I could, Miss Hathersage, and I did."

As shame suffused his guest's lovely face, Leo immediately regretted his words. He hastily sat on the edge of the bed and gently drew her hands away from her face. "No, no, Miss Hathersage. Forgive me for teasing you. We did not share the sheets. I lay atop the quilt." He smiled. "Had I a naked sword, I should have placed it between us, as did the knights of old."

She wrinkled her nose. "That sounds both very dangerous and very uncomfortable."

Leo could not help but laugh. "Indeed, it does, however virtuous and romantic. But have no fear. Your honor is quite intact."

"If anyone ever learns of the fact, that will make no difference at all. My reputation will be in tatters. If Mrs. Rowsley ever gets wind of it…"

"No one will ever hear a word of it from me—I swear to you."

"Word of a...?"

Leo laughed aloud. "Clever minx. Do you suppose you will find me out that easily? I swear on my family's honor."

"A conveniently anonymous family." She turned her face.

Leo paused. Had a man questioned his heritage in that manner, violence would certainly have ensued. But this was not a man. This was a woman, a very sick woman, one with a genuine grievance. He moved from the bed back to the chair and took a steadying breath. "Just so, Miss Hathersage."

Perhaps the expression on his face warned her that she had gone too far. She looked at him again, started to speak, subsided once more. Finally, she closed her eyes and sighed.

Once again Leo felt a complete brute. How was she to know that at one time his parentage was a very tender subject with him? And she looked so pulled and pale. What was he doing bullying a lady too weak even to respond?

He leaned forward in the chair. "My dear, I assure you I meant no harm. You were so very ill. I could not leave you, yet I was weary and cold to the bone. If you can but seal your own lips, the matter is forgotten."

Without opening her eyes she muttered, "You are not acquainted with Mrs. Rowsley."

Leo chuckled and leaned back as she drifted into sleep. "Thank God."

If the previous night had been Hell for his guest, the next night exceeded that condition for Leo. She tossed and moaned. One moment she clutched the quilts to her chin, her teeth rattling in her head and chills racking her small body. Minutes later she flung them away, revealing the sweat-soaked nightshirt clinging to every feature of that well-molded form.

Leo tried to do the noble thing and avert his gaze from high, round breasts crowned with firm nipples peeping through the damp linen. From perfectly formed legs unveiled by the rucked-up hem.

By midnight he had developed a very strained view of nobility. A lovely lady lay in his bed, and that constituted a major improvement over recent months. He would never lay a hand on a helpless woman, but she would be well again someday and still in his bed.

Might she stay there willingly?

Angry with himself, Leo shook his head in frustration and firmly tucked the quilt around her. He was doing it again, letting his self-imposed deprivation make him vulnerable to misconduct. He must muster his self-discipline. He would not put himself in the wrong again.

True, he should have smelled the trap when he found Celeste in his bedchamber. He should have known that no innocent maiden would put herself in that position, accepting forbidden intimacy with a mutilated wreck of a man.

But he never, *never* should have taken a virgin.

Or so he believed her at the time. How foolish she must have thought him. How she must have laughed as she wrapped herself around him.

He had not ventured to approach any woman since his maiming—not since the first one had backed away from him, horror on her face. But Celeste had enchanted him, and he had been made weak with need. He had gone against his principles and made love to a woman he believed to be an innocent.

Had Celeste truly been a virgin, he would have married her, of course. But that did not answer to his conscience. The real bite of some of the accusations that had been fired at him later was that they bit too close to the bone.

He had failed his own standards. He had given up his discipline. He had broken his own rules.

What disturbed him the most was that, for once in his life, he had thoroughly enjoyed doing it.

When Phona awakened again, it was daylight. As promised, Lord Hades lay sleeping on the cot, his long form stretched the length of it, and his feet hanging over the end. Locks of hair, escaped from the ribbon, curled around his face and made him look younger and…yes, less ferocious. He was snoring just a little.

What a difference in his aspect! Did snoring make everyone seem harmless? Phona had only seen Hades as big and threatening. Commanding and enforcing obedience. Brooking no resistance.

Piratical.

Now he looked… Well, human. She supposed even brigands had to sleep sometimes. But clearly, this man had not always been an outlaw. Not only his knowledge of the classics, but—except for the few words spoken to the man called Hardesty—his speech and address marked him an educated man. How could he have come to this?

Phona rested her eyes for a moment. They still burned and felt blurry. When she opened them again, a single blue eye regarded her steadily. Just that suddenly his humanity dissolved. He became once more the indomitable force.

"Good morning, Miss Hathersage." He swung his feet over the side of the cot. "Apparently we both slept at last. How do you feel this morning?"

"Better than yesterday evening." Phona tried to sit up, failed and fell back against the pillow. "Not well enough."

"That is to be expected. You had developed a very high fever before I could get you out of the rain and cold." He rose to his feet. "Forgive me if I leave you for a while. I'll let Aelfred know you are awake. He will bring you something to eat."

She wrinkled her nose. "I am confident that gruel is on the menu."

"No doubt, at least once before the day is out. And several cups of nasty medicine. I will come again this afternoon after I have slept. Try to do the same. Your rest last night was badly disturbed." He grinned, and again regained a hint of the human. "And obey Aelfred while I am absent."

Phona grimaced, and he laughed aloud as he went out.

During a dismal, foggy day, Phona dutifully slept, ate as much as she could and drank from the bitter cup. In spite of the fog in her mind and the fire in her limbs, she suddenly noticed that she was eating from silver implements and sipping from fine china. Now where in the world would a man like Hades come by those niceties?

Unless, of course, he stole them.

After breakfast Aelfred brought her a fresh nightshirt. "We'll see to changing the linens as soon as you are able to sit in the chair, miss," he assured her. Phona could hardly wait. The sheets had become damp and sticky with perspiration.

The day dragged on interminably. She still had trouble staying alert. Sometime after a light nuncheon—which had included a slice of bread with her gruel—she woke abruptly from a doze to find Lord Hades sitting in the chair beside her bed, reading.

He set aside the book. "Good afternoon, Miss Hathersage. What is the report now? Any progress?"

Phona coughed and cleared her throat. "Well, I am no longer beside myself. That must be counted progress, I should think."

"Yes, indeed. That is a terrifying condition." He rose and picked up her wrist. "Hmm. Still much too warm and your pulse is a bit tumultuous."

He returned her arm to her own keeping, and Phona hastily hid it under the covers. Something about his touch, his nearness, created an unfamiliar unease. She heaved a small sigh of relief when he sat again.

"So…" He leaned back in the chair, rested his elbows on the carved arms and cupped his right hand over the folded left sleeve. "Tell me more about the dreaded Mrs. Rowsley."

Phona thought he might have steepled his fingers, except, of course, that he had no fingers on the left hand to steeple. The thought gave her pause. How awful to lose a limb! And an eye. She quickly looked at his face.

But he had already caught her staring. He started to move his hand to his lap, then instead, resumed the position and gave her a tight-jawed look. "Does my lack of a hand distress you, Miss Hathersage?"

His voice held a hint of ice, a challenge. Phona looked steadily into the cool blue eye. His oddity did unsettle her a bit, but she refused to be intimidated by it. Or by his manner. "No, my lord, but surely it must distress *you.*"

"It does so no longer. But let us return to Mrs. Rowsley."

Phona heard the lie in his voice. His loss still distressed him very much. But she had no strength to deal with the subject. Let him deal with it himself!

"Yes, well, though it is sometimes hard to credit, she is Mama's bosom friend. Yet the least thing puts them at dagger-drawing. They are so envious of one another. The day I first encountered you, she gave a small party and did not invite Mama and me. Mama was quite distraught."

"Over an invitation to a party?" He shook his head in disbelief.

"Mama is much given to the vapors." Phona sighed. "I suspect she enjoys them."

"Very likely. But you do not?"

"No! No, indeed." She shook her head. "I had ridden out to escape them. It is always somehow my fault, you see."

Lord Hades raised an eyebrow. "And how did this omitted invitation come to be laid at your door?"

"I said something—well, *untactful*—about Mrs. Rowsley's future son-in-law. I should not have, of course, but I had heard so much of how the very *young* Suzette Rowsley has already captured a fiancé, whereas I… It wears on one to have one's shortcomings held up too often."

"I should imagine so. And Mrs. Rowsley overheard your remark?"

"Oh, no! I would never say that in her hearing, but what must Mama do but repeat my 'clever' remark. So now we are all out of charity."

"But if your Mama repeated it…?"

"It is my fault for having said it in the first place."

His lordship—did Hades qualify as *his lordship?*—shook his head. "I will never understand women. What was this disastrous remark?"

Phona flushed. "That he looks as much the bantam cockerel as he sounds."

Hades threw back his head and a roar of laughter erupted.

Phona scowled with what defiance she could muster. Then she, too, began to laugh.

She laughed until exhaustion caught up with her and tears of weakness began to escape. She wiped at them angrily, swatting at the big, linen handkerchief that appeared before her face. "Give me the handkerchief. I can do it."

"I have no doubt you can, but today I shall do it." Hades moved her hands away firmly and wiped her eyes.

"Stop it! I am not a child!" Phona sank wearily into the pillows.

He returned the handkerchief to his pocket. "No, my dear, you are not. Believe me, I am well aware of that fact."

Now what in the world did he mean by that?

The footman brought the note directly to Lady Hathersage's sitting room where she and his lordship had sought seclusion. Demetra's breath stopped, and she grasped her throat with both hands. Dear God in heaven! Please let this be news of her dearest Phona.

Her husband took the letter, dismissing the footman with a nod. Demetra sank back into the cushions of her chaise and clutched the pillows in both hands. A sound squeezed past her lips. "George...?"

He unfolded the paper, his face grim.

"What...? What...?" Demetra leaned forward, willing him to speak. Instead he looked puzzled. She slid to her feet and tried to read over his shoulder.

He handed her the letter. "I don't know what to make of this. On my life, I don't."

"What does this mean?" She raised her gaze to his. She could not make it out without her eyeglasses, and she refused to wear them.

"I was expecting a demand for ransom." He took the note from her trembling fingers and perused it again. "And this makes no mention of it."

"Is she alive? Is she hurt?" Demetra reached again for the letter, but this time George did not relinquish it.

"Yes, she is alive. He says that she is well save a case of *la grippe.*"

"*La grippe!* I told her it was too cool to ride that afternoon. But did she listen...?"

"Enough, Demetra! That is hardly the point." Lord Hathersage scowled.

Recoiling in astonishment, Demetra took refuge behind a lacy handkerchief, and sank onto the chaise. Fresh tears filled her eyes. George *never* growled at her.

He continued, "This scoundrel says that he must keep her with him for her own safety. He suggests that we put it about that she is exhausted and has gone to Bath to take the waters."

A delicate snort erupted from the chaise. "Phona exhausted? *Phona* drinking the waters? No one will believe *that.*"

His lordship gave her another look, and Demetra subsided. Her husband continued to read. "He assures me that as soon as the danger is past, he will return her to us unscathed."

"Unscathed? Does he mean that he will not…? Or…oh, my God, George! What if he already has!" Demetra's hands flew to cover her face. "Oh! She will never marry. I will have failed her completely."

"Damn his bloody soul to hell! He'd best not have. If he is trying to force a marriage with an heiress, I shall pull him limb from limb! I shall cut off his bloody…" He glanced at her and broke off.

Dear heaven! Demetra had never seen him so angry. For a moment she feared apoplexy. Then her own anger welled up in her, almost choking her.

"No, George. You will hold him, and *I* shall wield the knife!"

Chapter Four

As the days passed, the unimaginable oddness of the situation began to fade. The men cared for her as Lily and Nurse might have, and Phona found herself accepting their ministrations. She even found herself looking forward to another chat with Lord Hades each afternoon.

Just to break the monotony of the day, of course.

She had slept better the previous night than before, allowing his lordship to do the same. But even though he probably was not sleeping this morning, she had not seen him since he'd left his cot.

When he did appear, Phona found herself alternately elated and dismayed. He came in with Aelfred, bearing a small table and basin, while his henchman was laden with clean sheets. Hades set his burden down near the fire.

Aelfred laid his linens on a chair. "Back directly with the water."

Phona rejoiced. She was to have a bath and a clean bed.

With them as attendants.

Oh, no!

"Lord Hades, I... Uh... I..."

He turned to her and grinned. "Be of good cheer, Miss Hathersage, your modesty will be preserved."

He pulled a chair into place near the table with the basin, then wrestled the heavy, carved screen from the corner of the room to shelter them. Hades turned and looked closely at her. "Why, Miss Hathersage, you are blushing."

"I am not!" Phona turned her face away.

Hades came to the bed and, with a hand on her chin, pulled it toward him. "Yes, you are." He smiled. "But it is a very becoming blush. It makes you appear very... innocent." He paused thoughtfully for a moment. "Just as you should."

She thought he might have said more, but Aelfred came through the door carrying a can of hot water. He poured part of it into the basin and put in a cautious finger.

Which he quickly jerked out. "Too hot, me lo...er, sir. Best wait a bit."

"That is just as well. By the time I get our lady situated, it will no doubt have cooled."

Phona gazed at him warily. He advanced on her, purpose in his eye. She grabbed the bedclothes and pulled them to her chin. "Um, one moment, my lord. Perhaps I can..."

Hades began to laugh, firmly seizing the covers. "Miss Hathersage, you have not even the strength to raise yourself on the pillows successfully. Here, let me have the quilts."

He separated the quilts from the sheet and pulled them back. She clutched the sheet desperately to her chin. He shook his head. She need have no worry. The last thing he wanted to deal with was the sight of her nubile body. The temptation hovering in the air was burden enough. "Are you ready?"

She nodded and gamely lifted her chin. "Yes. I *would* like to be clean. Proceed, sir."

"That's my brave lady." He tucked the sheet around her and lifted her off the bed. He carried her to the chair behind the screen and settled her into it. For a moment Leo feared she would not be able to sit, but she rallied and straightened.

"Thank you, sir. I can manage now."

"Not so fast, Miss Hathersage. I am not sure of that at all." Leo tested the water again, stirring it with his finger. The fragrance of lavender wafted into the room. "It is still too warm. I don't want a burn to add to your miseries. Shall I brush your hair while it cools?"

"You don't mind playing the lady's maid?"

"Not at all." In fact, he relished the idea of feeling the silky warmth in his hand. He retrieved a brush he had thrust into his back pocket, and set to work.

"My hair must be very nasty after lying on the ground." The lady sighed. "Yesterday I could barely manage the comb."

"Not that bad." Leo flicked a dusting of soil from the sheet. "But you still have a few leaves and twigs caught in the curls."

"How humiliating! These hateful curls!"

"What?" He quit brushing and leaned over to look at her face. "I cannot allow that, miss. Your curls are delightful."

"You are very kind, sir, if untruthful. I own a mirror."

Leo resumed brushing. "Apparently a very poor one. I must bring you one that shows your beauty accurately."

"How gallant you are! Who would have thought it?" She chuckled softly. He liked her laugh. He had not heard enough of it.

"Even rogues can speak the truth." He closed his hand around a cluster of ringlets. "You are quite lovely." Before that remark could linger, he added, "There. All done. Let us see about the water. Ah, just right. I shall be within call."

Suiting action to the words, he stepped around the edge of the screen and waited. Hearing no sound of water sloshing, he ventured a question. "Miss Hathersage, do you need help?"

Her voice sounded near to frustrated tears. "No. It…it is just that I can't get the sheet off."

Deciding that meant she was still covered, Leo went back to the fireside. She slumped a bit to one side, leaning her elbow on the arm of the chair, a ghastly pallor draining her color. She would not last much longer. "I fear we must take the bull by the horns, Miss Hathersage. I will help you remove it—and the nightshirt."

"Sir…Oh, dear. I suppose…" She rubbed her brow.

"We'd best just do it." Leo took hold of the sheet.

"I am so tired. Perhaps I should just go back to bed."

"I promise not to look." He covered his mouth to hide a smile.

She gave him a suspicious glance. "How can you not? Oh, very well. Why should I draw back now? I have come this far. Close your eyes."

A laugh escaped him. "Yes, miss."

He dutifully closed his eyes, peeled away the sheet and tugged the nightshirt over her head.

"Are your eyes closed?"

He strongly suspected that her own were squeezed tight. "Yes, Miss Hathersage, they are quite sealed." He dropped the sheet to the floor. Blindly, he inched backward a few steps, groping behind him for the edge of the screen.

And promptly tripped right over it. It crashed to the floor with a resounding clatter.

So did Leo.

The lady shrieked.

Leo cursed.

Hell and damnation, he could not separate himself from the blasted screen! It had fallen on top of him. As he tried to find his feet, his eyes flew open. Working frantically, he finally shoved the screen away and stood.

Miss Hathersage would be beside herself once more— this time with outrage. Leo risked a quick glance. She was reaching in vain for the sheet. He took a step toward her.

"Would ye be needing assistance, sir?" Aelfred spoke from the door, his voice carefully neutral.

Leo dived for the sheet and whipped it over the lady's white form. He also carefully controlled his voice.

"Just right the damned screen, please, Aelfred."

Leo stood, silent, holding the sheet while Aelfred set the shelter back up. His henchman's face revealed not a single thought. Leo knew he was suppressing laughter. At Leo's expense. He clenched his teeth and kept firm hold of the sheet.

Aelfred finished his task and vanished through the door. Leo knew he had stopped on the staircase, awaiting further emergencies. He sighed. "Well, let us move on before you tire completely. Call when you need me to help you dress."

"Thank you, sir." He thought he detected a small giggle. "But I think we should make the next attempt with your eyes open. I shall try to restrain my maidenly blushes."

Leo's laughter burst out of him. "Don't do that, Miss Hathersage. I should very much miss your lovely blushes."

She had surely blushed aplenty when his lordship returned to hastily slip the fresh nightshirt over her. Her whole body burned with it. But he had accomplished the task so quickly she felt sure his gaze had not lingered on her nakedness. Perhaps he was, after all, a more civilized pirate than she had previously believed.

Hades set her gently on the bed and pulled the cover up to her chin. He lowered himself into the chair with a plop. "My God! I'm as tired as though I had hauled canvas in a storm. Who would have thought giving one small lady a bath would be so exhausting?"

"You must think me a complete ninny, to create such a fuss." She gazed up at him, grateful for the crisp feel and sunshiny smell of the clean sheets. Still blushing, she knew.

"Not at all, Miss Hathersage." He propped his feet up on

the chest. "Inexperienced, yes. Innocent, yes. Pure. But a ninny? No. You are bearing up amazingly well under the circumstances. One would expect you to be in strong hysterics."

"I never have hysterics. It is just that no one has ever seen me... That is..."

"No man has ever seen your body, you mean. This must be very difficult for you."

"Yes." Phona sighed. "Of course. I don't mean to seem unappreciative for the care you have given me. But if you had not..."

"If I had not brought you here in the first place, it would not be necessary. I have already explained that, but I understand your anger. Do not repine. I will take you home as soon may be."

She closed her eyes and nodded. "But how will I go on once I am there? I feel that I will see eveything differently after this experience. Matters that once seemed important..."

He looked at her thoughtfully. "Yes, I would imagine that you will have a very different point of view. But how did you go on before? I know you rode nearly every day. Did you go to parties often?"

Phona wrinkled her nose. "Not if I could avoid it. As I said before, I *loathe* parties. It is all I can do even to be polite. I always feel so...inadequate."

"You? Inadequate? I can hardly credit that." He raised a skeptical eyebrow.

"Well, only at parties. I do other things very well."

"What other things do you do?"

"Mama does not like seeing to the household and the estate, so I do much of that. I enjoy it, especially visiting the tenants. Mama..." She had to think a moment about it. "Mama does not know how to talk to them as I do, whereas at a ball she knows just how to captivate everyone. A nod here, a touch there, a word to the favored few."

He chuckled. "Yes, an apt description. I have seen your mother in action."

"Have you?" Phona tried to sit up. "Where?"

"At a ball."

She fell back. "You won't tell me, of course." It was a statement, not a question. She let it pass and continued, "I have never been able to do that. I sit by the wall, tongue-tied, wearing unbecoming colors and feeling ugly and awkward while my hostess brings young men to introduce to me and my hair works its way out of the pins. I dare not dance. It would all fall to my shoulders. I can't even move my head. And I blush. So they think me very stiff and a great bore. And then, of course, there are the freckles."

He smiled. "Blushing, your hair fallen to your shoulders. Now *that* would be a truly captivating sight. All the young men would trample one another to make your acquaintance."

"You are teasing me."

"No, indeed. I am completely serious. But why do you wear colors which do not flatter you?"

Phona sighed. "Because Mama wants to drape me in maidenly white at all times—at every ball, afternoon parties, certainly all *al fresco* occasions. I hate it, and it doesn't suit me."

He gazed at her, a twinkle in his eye. "You are not qualified for maidenly white?"

Her cheeks flamed. "My lord! How dare you?"

"Forgive me, Miss Hathersage." He laughed aloud. "You are delightful to tease." Leo sobered. "But you seriously underrate yourself. You will make a fine wife." He looked thoughtfully into the fire for a moment. "Yes, a very fine wife. Beautiful, in spite of your distorted vision of yourself, accomplished in the needs of an estate. And both courageous and ingenuous." He seemed almost to be talking to himself.

Before she could answer, he stood. "And right now, very weary. You should nap. I will return at supper time to keep you company. You will be happy to know there will be no gruel tonight. Aelfred has promised to make you a panada. Rest well."

As he went out the door, Phona, already half-asleep, had a dreamy vision of herself dancing at a ball, around and around and around, her skirts swirling, her curls flying loose.

Dancing…with whom? She could see… Yes.

A man with a beard. A black vest.

And a hook.

This was a dangerous state of affairs!

She was beginning to be attracted to this man: a nameless rogue, a brigand—a maimed *thief*? Unbelievable.

Yet she looked forward to his visits every afternoon. Felt relieved when he appeared after supper to keep watch over her through the night. A wave of warmth spread through her whenever he touched her forehead to gauge her fever and a subtle, smoky scent rose around him.

This would not do at all. Phona had gone from the spit right into the heart of the flames. She resolved to guard her emotions more carefully. Each resolution lasted until the next time he sauntered into the room and her heart raced in her breast.

What a goose! Mama would shriek the house down if she knew.

Phona's strength had gradually increased as her fever receded. Aelfred now brought her baked eggs at midday and boiled chicken and onions and a bit of cheese for dinner in place of the insipid, if highly nourishing and digestible, gruel.

Every afternoon Lord Hades lifted her into a chair, wrapped in a man's huge silk dressing gown, while he sat nearby, keeping a sharp eye on her. While it provided a pleasant change to sit, Phona always returned to her bed with a sigh of relief. Would she never feel vigorous again?

Hades did so many things for her now. This afternoon he had again played the lady's maid, helping her wash the still-lingering grit out of her hair.

Phona badly wanted a real bath in a real tub, but her host had shaken his head with a wry grin. "But nay! I should peek around the screen to find you sunk to the bottom, and then I should have to fish you out. With my eyes closed."

Phona wrinkled her nose, then broke into a giggle. "I must agree the last attempt ended in complete disaster."

"You have no idea how great…" He had broken off, leaving Phona wondering what he intended to say.

This evening as she sat up against the pillows, clean and combed, awaiting dinner, Aelfred came into the room and set the small table and two chairs tête-à-tête near the bed. "Good evening, miss. His… My master thought ye might be able to eat at table tonight."

"Why, yes, thank you. I would enjoy being out of the bed."

As she spoke, Hades arrived, looking his most civilized. He carried something green in his hand.

"What do you have there?"

He smiled. "A wreath for my lady's freshly washed hair." He held it up for her inspection. It was twisted of small, pliable branches of spring leaves and tiny white flowers. "When I noticed the leaves in your hair the first time I brushed it, I thought it somehow suited you—the daughter of a fertility goddess."

Phona laughed. "Mama is hardly a fertility goddess."

"No, hardly. But her namesake, Demeter, was." He laid the circlet over her curls and stepped back for a better view. "Charming."

"I doubt that, but thank you. You are very thoughtful." Strange how even a little bit of frippery made her feel more attractive, more feminine.

He held up the silk robe. "Are you up to a proper dinner?"

"I should love one."

He picked her up and transferred her to one of the chairs. "Tonight you shall have venison and a small glass of red wine."

"Wine? I am quite astonished."

"We need to build your blood. I do not like this lingering weakness. Ah! Here is Aelfred."

They dined on venison and potato pie, a bowl of apples, and, as promised, red wine. Phona sipped cautiously. She was barely accustomed to wine of any sort. Nor did she care much for the sour stuff. She had drunk about half of her portion when Hades moved his chair around the table nearer to her own.

From somewhere on his person a sharp blade appeared as if by legerdemain. Phona blinked and leaned away from him a bit. If he noticed, he gave no sign of it. He reached for an apple, set it on the table, and, steadying it with his truncated left arm, began to make careful slices. When he had cut half the apple, he set down the knife, plucked a piece from the pile and, without warning, slipped it between Phona's lips.

"Oh!" Startled, she drew back again. He had been helping her eat for many days, but there seemed something different about this. The simple gesture sent a wave of sensation through her.

Perhaps it was the wine.

Or perhaps it was the way he was gazing at her, a crooked smile on his lips and a warmth she had never seen in his one twinkling eye.

She blushed.

He laughed softly. "Have a bite of apple, my lady."

"Uh… Thank you." Phona swallowed, and he fed her another slice.

"And another sip of wine." He handed her the glass.

She took a tiny sip and set it down. "I am not very fond of wine."

"I know, but you need it. And apples are very healthful." He popped another slice into her mouth.

His fingers never touched her lips, but somehow Phona had felt their warmth. In fact, she could feel the warmth of his whole body as he sat next to her. Could sense that subtle scent. It created a response down deep inside her.

Looking amused, he picked up the uncut portion of the apple and took a large bite, white teeth gleaming. The heat blossomed.

It *must* be the wine.

Phona glanced at the man beside her. He took another bite, looking steadily at her as he chewed. Phona all but gasped.

It could *only* be the wine!

Leo had taken a distinctly wicked satisfaction in his modest seduction of Miss Hathersage. Her inexperience with dalliance made flirting with her a pleasure. He liked the flush that crept from her breast to her cheeks. Liked her response to his play with the apple.

Liked the fact that she had been aware of him as a man.

It pleased him to think she might respond to him. He had barely restrained himself from kissing her when he lifted her into his arms to return her to the bed, from lying down beside her and teaching her the delights of being a woman.

But he must not unleash his passion now, must not let those impulses take him too far. He had begun to see the shape of the future that he knew must inevitably follow this situation. It could not be kept secret forever, and the consequences of exposure were certain. Only one honorable course would be open to him.

But Leo could not yet approach that future. He still had the "felonious business" to complete. A strong chance existed that he would not survive it. And the truth was, even as much as he desired her, he would avoid a future with her if honor allowed it.

The kissing, the holding, the teaching—

Sheer fantasy.

He would never expose his scarred and crippled body to her artless gaze.

She would have to be more careful of spirits.

The sensations she had experienced last night while drinking the wine frightened her. She must keep firmly in mind that she was in the company of an outlaw. She could not afford to see him as anything else.

Just as Phona was making these resolutions anew, Hades walked into the chamber. One glimpse of the strong neck revealed by his open collar and her resolve crumbled. She had never seen a man like him. All of the other gentlemen of her acquaintance wore tall cravats and long coats.

If he could be described as a gentleman at all.

Which she doubted.

This could *not* continue!

He was carrying an inkwell in his hand and had a sheaf of paper wedged under his arm. "Good afternoon, Miss Hathersage." He laid the items on the table. "I thought you might like to write a letter to your parents."

Phona blinked. "A letter? I did not think… That is, I did not expect…"

"You did not believe that I would allow it." He came and stood by the bed, gazing at her seriously. "But aside from the fact that you are not at liberty to leave, you are not a prisoner here. You are my guest."

Phona could not restrain a wry smile. "Now there, my Lord Hades, is a nice distinction. In just what way does a guest who is not allowed to leave differ from a prisoner?"

For a moment he looked startled. Then he threw back his head and roared with laughter. "You have me there, Miss Hathersage. Hoist by me own petard!"

His laugh was infectious. Phona could not helping joining

him. She cocked her head and gazed up at him, thinking of the locked door. "I am sure I don't know what a petard may be, but I am eager have the answer to my question."

Still smiling, he said, "Hmm. That is a cant phrase, and you should *not* know what it is. I was at fault saying it in your hearing. As to the question—I must consider it for a moment."

He tipped his head to one side, apparently thinking. At last he said, "I believe the difference must be in my view of the situation as opposed to yours. In any event, you are quite at liberty to write to your parents, although I must ask you not to describe me in any way, nor your present surroundings. My life and yours, as well as Aelfred's, depend on that."

"Great heavens!" The implications of the restriction chilled Phona. "In *what* are you embroiled?"

"Dark doings, my dear lady, not fit for your unworldly ears."

A shadow seemed to fall over the day. Phona had for some time considered her gravest danger to be her own feelings with respect to her…uh, host.

She had felt physically safe here. But she should have remembered the original circumstances that had precipitated her capture. The very air had been awash in violence.

"Very well. I will make no such description. I will simply assure them of my improved health and send my love."

He studied her soberly. "Thank you, Miss Hathersage. I appreciate your good sense."

Phona sighed. "I am ordinarily quite famous for good sense."

"You sound as though you are not happy with that assessment." He pulled a chair closer and sat.

"Well, you must admit it sounds very dull. I always face matters sensibly—except parties. I never faint. I never indulge in the vapors. I never weep. Well, not where anyone can hear."

"That sounds very pleasant to me." His forehead creased. "Except that I do not like hearing that you weep alone. What occasions these episodes of sadness?"

Phona gazed into the fire for a long moment. "It is considering my future."

"And is it so bleak then?" His frown deepened.

"Perhaps not. But let us consider the facts. I am twenty years old. I have already had two spectactularly unsuccessful seasons in London."

"Ah. And the Shelf looms?"

"Indeed it does. And that would not be so bad, perhaps. I enjoy the life I lead on the estate now, and I know Papa will provide well for me. But…I will not even have the opportunity to dwindle into an aunt. I have no brothers or sisters, you see."

He raised an inquiring eyebrow. "You see yourself caring for your mother—forever."

"I feel very selfish for not wanting to do so, but I do not." She might as well be honest with this man. She would probably never see him again. "I would much prefer my own establishment."

"Not selfish. Very natural. Your mama sounds rather difficult to care for."

"Yes, she is. But she does try to do her best for me, to find me a husband. She is also beautiful and charming and…helpless. I feel…"

Lord Hades snorted. "Your mama is approximately as helpless as an Indian tiger."

Phona frowned. "What do you mean? She falls into helpless hysterics at the smallest misfortune."

"And thereby gets precisely what she wants."

"Well, yes. There is that."

He sighed. "Ah, me. Your poor papa."

She had to chuckle at that. "He adores her, you know."

"It is a very good thing that he does. Otherwise, he would have strangled her long ere now."

Phona had never looked at the matter in that light. Yes, Mama must be very difficult for Papa at times. As she was for Phona. All she could answer was, "Papa would never do that."

The corner of his mouth quirked. "I admire his discipline. But if she wishes so much for you to marry, why does she insist that you wear an unbecoming color?"

"I do not believe she *intentionally* leads me astray. Although she is very competitive with other women and might not wish for me to be as lovely as *she* is, she does want me to be more beautiful, accomplished and poised than anyone else's daughter." Phona tried to shed more light on the situation. "For she must be a perfect mother, you see, the most devoted mother of all time."

"Like her namesake, Demeter."

"Yes. Just so. Therefore I must be the most perfect daughter of all time, else she has failed."

"Egad! What a ghastly fate."

"Indeed! I feel very angry with her at times, but that is pointless. You see, she does not really *look* at me. She has her own ideas of what is perfectly impressive or perfectly fashionable or perfectly suitable—and I must live up to that perfection. But you see, she also *must* be perfect in every way at all times."

"An even worse fate." He shook his head. "But what can the bachelors of the *ton* be thinking? Are they both stupid *and* blind?"

"What do you mean?"

He gestured toward her. "Here they have a woman of both beauty and fire, and they can't see her? And she is an heiress to boot?" He leaned back in the chair and shook his head.

"Well, they are hardly beating a path to my door. Except, of course, Lawrence Hudders." Phona sighed.

Hades raised an eyebrow. "I take it that you do not find Mr. Hudders to be a suitable suitor."

"Indeed, no. He is not quite right in the upper story, you know. Even Mama does not encourage him. She does truly want the best for me." After a thoughtful pause she said, "And Papa is very careful to keep fortune hunters away."

"One of which he most likely believes I am."

"And are you?" Phona leaned forward and gazed seriously at him.

"No, Miss Hathersage, I am not." He sounded just a bit annoyed. "But if I were, I would take care to steer clear of your father."

There it was again. Another hint that he knew her family. "Lord Hades, how do you…"

He stood and held out an arm. "Come, I will help you to the table where you can write more easily."

And that was the end of the conversation.

Phona ventured not another word.

The swish of the stone against the knife blade filled the room. Finally the man wielding it said, "So you can't find him."

His companion took a long pull from his tankard of ale. "I said I haven't found him. Not the same thing."

"It comes to the same sum." He moved the stone to the other side of the blade. Swish. Swish.

"Not at all. It is only a matter of time. How many gentlemen are there who have but one hand?" He sipped thoughtfully. "However, I do know of one rogue who…"

The steel caught the light for a moment. Swish. Swish. Slower now. Swi-ish. Swi-ish. Slow. Sensual. Loving.

Swi-ish.

Its owner glanced at the other man. "If you don't find him soon, there will be another."

Faster than a striking asp, the point buried itself in the wood of the table.

It almost missed the skin of his companion's wrist.

Chapter Five

"Is that from *him?* Is she…? Does he want…?" Clutching her shawl to her breast, Lady Hathersage half rose from her couch as her husband stepped into the room. She wore a wrinkled wrapper. Her silky golden hair fell in a tangled mass, and there were deep circles under her lovely blue eyes.

Lord Hathersage's heart sank. For Demetra, the woman who felt compelled to be perfection itself, not to consider her appearance meant she was in desperate case indeed. He handed the letter to her. "Good news. It is from Phona. She says she is well and unharmed."

"Here… Wait." She rummaged in a pocket and withdrew her spectacles. She put them on and took the paper. "Yes. Yes, she says she is better. But, oh dear God, she has been very ill." Lady Hathersage sank to her couch. "Oh, George! She might die."

"Now, my love, she says she is improving."

"Yes, but still very weak." She cast the eyeglasses aside and rocked herself, her arms held tightly around her chest.

George took the note from her. "The important thing, Demetra, is that she confirms that she has not been harmed in any way."

His lordship sat beside her, taking her chin in his hand. "You must not fall into a decline. For her sake, as well as your own." *And certainly for mine.* "Now come. Call your maid and have her brush your hair and put something cool on your eyes. You must not let yourself become unkempt."

"Unkempt! Oh, George." She snatched a mirror off the side table and gazed into it. "Oh, dear! I do look a positive *fright!*"

"Never to me, my love," George murmured diplomatically. He gathered her in his arms. "But I need you, for myself and… Both Cook and the housekeeper are asking questions I can't answer."

Pushing him back a bit, Demetra began running her fingers through her snarled hair. "I doubt I shall know the answers, either. You know that Phona always—" She broke off and sat straighter. "But I shall try."

She got to her feet and rang for her maid. Then she leaned against George's chest. "I shall try to bear up, dearest. It is my duty, I know."

"Duty be damned!" He kissed her warmly on the lips. "Do it for me."

Thank God his guest's health continued to improve. After several more days her skin had regained a hint of pink. The pretty little freckles no longer shone so brightly across her dainty nose. With his help, she could now walk a few steps. He had brought her several books, and she moved by herself to a chair to read them.

Leo needed to arrange another transfer soon, but he would not depart until she was on her feet. He would not leave her immobile and trapped in the tower room.

When he entered the bedchamber, Phona was sitting on the edge of the bed, the silk robe over her nightshirt. She had a determined look in her eye.

"Good morning, Miss Hathersage." He strolled around the end of the bed. "Were you thinking of going for a walk?"

"Good morning, Lord Hades. Yes, I have resolved to walk to the window today."

She smiled up at him and something inside Leo quivered. He tried to frown disapprovingly, but could not quite accomplish it. He gave it up and returned her smile. "An excellent ambition, my dear lady, but better achieved with my help."

"Well, you were not here, you see. Surely I can walk ten steps alone." She grasped the bedpost and stood.

By greatest effort, Leo resisted the temptation to seize her elbow and steady her. If she was set on doing it by herself, he must not allow himself to interfere. He watched anxiously while she carefully gathered the too-long nightshirt in one hand and took a tentative step. Wobbling a bit, she took hold of the arm of the chair, and then, after another step, the back of it.

She glanced at him over her shoulder. "You see, I have covered half the distance."

What Leo saw was that she looked ready to collapse in a heap. However, all he said was, "Excellent, Miss Hathersage."

He moved a bit closer. She straightened and gamely released her hold on the chair. She took another pace. Begin to waver.

Leo came to her side, but she motioned him away. "I must do this, my lord."

He nodded. Leo understood her determination. And admired it. He had been in the selfsame situation—weak, alone, afraid. "Take all the time you require. I am here beside you."

"Thank you, my lord." Her newly regained color had slipped away from her face. The freckles again held sway. She took two more quick steps, swayed a little, then in a rush, crossed the remaining distance and grasped the window casing in a desperate grip.

"You see! I have done it." She cast him a triumphant glance.

"Huzzah!" Leo hastily slipped an arm around her waist. "Always the brave lady." He eased her sideways until she could look out the window.

"My goodness! I did not know we were so high." Phona tried unsuccessfully to see the bottom of the building. "Would you be good enough to open the casement? I have been wanting to look out for days."

"Hmm. I suppose so, but only for a minute. You must not get chilled." Hades unlatched the window and opened one side. Phona peered over the sill, acutely aware of his strong arm bracing her.

She took in several long breaths of fresh air. How she had missed it! Her room had been made very comfortable, but there was always a hint of wood smoke in the air.

She appeared to be in a tower behind which lay a deep, wooded gorge. She could hear water running through it. The walls of the building extended downward almost out of sight to the bottom of the ravine. Straight ahead she saw only the opposite side of the defile.

To her left the house stepped down a level. The tower extended upward for some distance. She craned her neck, but could not see the top.

"It seems that we are very remote." Phona felt a pang of discouragement. Her growing strength, added to her fascination with Lord Hades, had caused thoughts of escape to begin bubbling up in her mind. Every moment in his presence saw her more wrapped in his spell. She could not allow it to continue.

And there was also pride. Pride urged her to resist being held captive, which in spite of his mincing of words, she was.

He had no right.

However, even if she had the strength to escape, she now sensed that, in fact, she would never find her way home, even in the daylight. If, in fact, she could actually muster the courage to run away from the handsome rogue in whose house she languished before she fell completely in love with him.

If, in fact, she had not already done so.

Hades turned her away from the window and closed the casement. "We are very remote. In that fact lies our safety."

Again the undescribed threat. Phona's knees began to tremble. She leaned against Hades' shoulder and willed her legs to work. Dear heaven, they were so tired. But she had made it to the window.

Tomorrow, the door.

And on the morrow, to the door she had walked. Around the bed. In front of the fireplace and across the floor to the door. With Hades standing between her and fire, guarding her against a tumble.

The next day the clean nightshirt brought to her by Aelfred had been shortened, so that she might not trip. So each day thereafter she had walked around the room, from bed to window to door. And then several times each day.

Until the day she thought to try the door and found it unlocked. An oversight? Or did her "host" believe her too infirm to leave the room?

Phona pulled the door open and peered cautiously out into a small anteroom. A flight of stairs descended to a landing, then turned and disappeared. How far down lay the next floor? She felt much stronger today. Even though the stairs were quite steep, surely she could gain the lower level.

There was no handrail fastened to the old stones. Never mind. She would be very careful. Phona braced one hand against the wall and tried the first step.

One by one, she conquered the stairs until she had achieved the first landing. At that point she had no choice but to sit and rest. The large steps had proved exhausting to descend with no handhold, and the cold, rough stones wore the skin of her bare feet almost raw.

Dare she try the next flight? Just as she stood to make the attempt, Phona heard the sound of boots coming up the lower flight toward her. For some reason she did not fully understand, she turned, almost in panic, and started back up.

She must not be found out of the bedchamber. She did not want him to know. He might—

Might what?

She made three steps before her right knee began to shake. As she lifted her left foot and placed her weight on the right, the knee buckled. Her hand clutched frantically at the wall. The nails skittered along the stone, finding no purchase. Oh, God, she would break her neck!

Phona shrieked.

Went over backward.

And landed in the sturdy arms of Lord Hades.

Having expected to land on the back of her head with an agonizing crash, all Phona could do was tremble with relief. She could say nothing.

His lordship chose to say nothing, as well. He carried her up to the tower room without a word. All Phona could think of was the subtle masculine scent he exuded. The power in his arms.

Foolish woman that she was.

Hades laid her, too spent to move, on the bed, and stood over her, his hand stroking his beard. Finally, he spoke. "Sometimes, Miss Hathersage, you suffer from an excess of courage. It is not good for the health."

Phona drew in a long breath. "But I have been feeling so much stronger."

"Obviously not strong enough to negotiate stairs at speed."

"Obviously." A flush of embarrassment crept up her neck. Why had she felt the impulse to flee?

The answer was not that difficult to fathom. She had been feeling guilty for even considering escape, and he seemed to suspect her motives in trying the stairs. "Forgive my foolishness, my lord. And thank you for saving me from a bad fall."

He sighed and sat in the nearest chair. "You frightened me, Miss Hathersage. Had I not come around the corner of the landing…"

"I know. I frightened myself." There existed one thing she could say with honesty. "I am very tired of being in only one room."

"I understand your desire for new surroundings. Tomorrow I will aid you in getting down the stairs. You may sit in the study to read. It is a very pleasant room, and Aelfred and I pass through it at intervals. I feel sure you have been lonely up here. But please do not attempt it alone again."

"I shall not. But tell me—is this place a castle? It has every appearance of one."

"More of a fortified estate or hunting lodge. Not as large as a castle, as you will see later."

"It looks very old."

"It is."

"How did you…" Phona broke off, not knowing how to phrase the question tactfully.

He grinned at her. "Believe it or not, Miss Hathersage, I came by it honestly."

Phona flushed again. "I did not mean to impugn—"

"My honesty?" He laughed without humor. "But Miss Hathersage… Have we not agreed that I am the blackest of brigands? A cad? A blackguard? What honesty did you expect?"

He rose and left the room.

Turning the key in the lock.

She had tried to run from him.

A dart of pain ran through Leo's chest. Why the devil had she done that? Obviously he had caught her in a surreptitious attempt at the stairs. The clandestine behavior must mean that she was exploring the possibilities of escape.

Escape? She had no need of escape! Had he not promised to take her home in due time? Perhaps his flirtation with the apple had frightened her. Leo cursed himself for a fool. He should have known better. Of course, she had been frightened. He was a big man, roughly groomed and dressed.

One who wore an eyepatch and a hook.

One who had no hand under the hook.

Another small twinge tugged at something inside him, a bit of anguish that he refused to acknowledge. Leo cast himself into his chair in the study and gazed morosely into the fire, thrusting the feeling away, searching for his usual discipline.

Did his touch revolt her?

She had never given any indication that it did, except for glancing at his wrist. Of course, as long as she was too weak to stand, she had no choice but to accept his help. Leo always took care to keep the stump covered, and he thought she was accustomed to his hand's absence.

Evidently not.

Leo rose and, seizing the poker, gave the fire a vicious jab. He had made a mistake in coaxing her to be aware of him as a man. In that context, what woman could tolerate being touched by him?

He would not touch her in that way again.

She had wounded him. He had acted like a man hurt and angry. The way she had seen Papa behave when Mama made her most outrageous accusations. He knew she was testing the notion of freeing herself.

And that wounded him. But she could not afford to fall in love with an outlaw, be he ever so kind and seductive. When he did take her home, she would never see him again.

Never again enjoy his dry wit. Never gaze on his strong body. Tears gathered in the corners of her eyes.

She wiped them away angrily. Where was her pride? Must she surrender her heart to him like a prize of conquest? He had no right to bring her here. To make her love him. She needed to get away from him.

Yet she must marshal her famous good sense. Obviously she could not make her way home alone. To do it, she must find a way to abscond with Firefly. Even so, the chances of finding the track which had brought her here must be vanishingly small.

Besides, he would find her.

And bring her back.

The next time Phona saw the stairs, a rope had been arranged to act as a rudimentary handhold. Hades came to her room bearing a pair of soft deerskin slippers, neatly made with black ribbons for the ankle. The ribbons looked very much like those worn by Hades to hold back his hair.

He laid them beside her as she sat on the side of the bed. "Aelfred made these for you. He is very clever with leather."

"How kind of him! And how lovely they are. He must have known that the stones rubbed my feet."

"Anyone who has spent time here knows that these stone steps chafe bare feet." He went to open the door.

Phona descended the stairs with one hand on the rope and Hades walking before her. She arrived, breathless, in a large, paneled room which in the past must have been the great hall of the house.

Converted to a comfortably masculine study, it featured a huge recessed fireplace with two padded, carved chairs resting on a faded Oriental rug before it. Tall windows let in warm light, reflected off wood floors worn smooth with the passage of countless feet.

Two walls held books on a broad selection of subjects.

Hades allowed her to explore, read titles, gaze out the windows, peer down a second set of stairs. When she looked into an adjacent room, he simply said, "My bedchamber."

Phona hastily retreated.

"The kitchen is down those stairs, along with Aelfred's quarters." He pointed at the steps she had examined. "The double doors ahead of you lead into the courtyard. They have a long stair, so I fear you must wait a little longer before getting out-of-doors."

"This will do nicely for a while." Phona selected a book and settled on a cushioned bench under a window. "When I can see out now and again while I read, I will feel much less confined."

"Excellent! Now, if you will excuse me, I have chores in the stable. Aelfred is capable of astonishing efficiency, but I try to do my part."

"The two of you have a quite remarkable number of accomplishments between you—nursing, leatherwork, horse-tending…" Phona gave him a cheeky grin. "Even playing lady's maid."

Hades laughed. "Men of the sea must develop many skills. All sailors can sew. As to nursing, there is no doctor to be called at sea, save the ship's surgeon, and often, after a battle, he has more work than he can do. One must care for one's mates."

"Oh, my." Phona covered her mouth with one hand. How horrible the consequences of a sea battle must be! A mental picture of bloody carnage formed in her mind. The decks awash with gore. Men lying dead and burned, maimed—

"But that is not a subject to concern a lady." Hades paused beside her for a moment. Hesitated. Then swept his hand before her eyes. "Put away the distressing images I see reflected on your lovely face."

Leaning across her to point, he directed her gaze out the window. She leaned forward, and her ear brushed against his chest. "Rather, think of how that single ray of sunlight makes its way through the trees. Do you see it? Every leaf in its path glows like fairy fire. A much more suitable vision for a sweet lady to store in her mind. Think of that, Miss Hathersage."

Phona kept her gaze on the shining leaves, willing away the grim picture that had invaded her. She felt his hand rest briefly on her shoulder before she heard his footsteps cross the room and go out the double doors.

A gentle ploy from a man who had survived brutal horror.

Chapter Six

Save the fact that Hades' ability to cause her to desire him frightened her half out of her wits, the days passed in pleasant leisure. She could ascend the stairs now with no difficulty, so Phona partook of her nuncheon in the study.

At times Hades joined her. At others he went about his own business, sometimes leaving the manor astride the big, awkward black horse. But he always returned in time to have dinner with her before the fire in the study.

Phona had learned to sip the red wine slowly, and Hades had fed her no more apples. He stayed on his side of the small dining table, and she remained on hers, a much more comfortable arrangement.

If somewhat lacking in excitement.

She penned several more letters to her parents, keeping the notes reassuringly vague. How the missives reached their intended destination—or if they reached it—she had no idea. She could only guess that Aelfred somehow posted them.

One night at dinner she announced to Lord Hades that she felt ready to conquer the out-of-doors. He agreed and the next morning Aelfred brought her riding dress to her bed-chamber. She could not ride yet, of course, but the thick velvet would protect her from any chill that might be lingering in the air.

The habit had been brushed and pressed, but still looked much the worse for its last outing. Most of the dirt had come off with the brushing, but her charge through the woods had left several small tears.

A button had been torn off and replaced with one that did not match, and the train had been pinned up for ease in walking. After their noon meal, Phona retired to her room to don it.

As she came down the stairs, Hades glanced at it askance, a frown wrinkling his brow. "I am allowing my guest to go about looking like a ragamuffin. A poor host, indeed."

"Hmm. Another interesting question." Phona arched her eyebrows. "Exactly what responsibility for wardrobe does a *host* have toward a *guest* who may not leave?"

Unabashed, he smiled and offered his arm as they started for the carved oaken doors to the courtyard. "Alas, that is too difficult a point for a mere brigand to puzzle out. I will assure you, however, that if I were fortunate enough to have so lovely a lady always in my care, she would not wear battered finery."

Suddenly, Phona felt angry. "I am your *guest,* not your mistress."

His expression turned grim. "No, certainly not that, nor will you ever be."

Of course not. Who would want her awkward self as a mistress? Why did she blurt out such a nonsensical thing? A little ache grew in her heart.

He opened the heavy door and turned to face her, his voice becoming serious. "It pains me, my lady, to see you clad thus, especially knowing my part in the matter. I would much prefer that you had become my guest in some other way."

Not knowing how to answer that declaration, Phona silently allowed him to escort her out into the sunshine. Who was this man? Who had he been… When? Before his injury? Before some fall from grace? She would never know. The little ache became a deeper ache.

As he had told her, past the double doors a set of steps, both long and wide, led down to a cobble-paved courtyard. He backed down the steps in front of her. "Take care, Miss Hathersage. A fall would result in an unimpeded roll. I should have to scrape you off the bricks."

Phona laughed, forgetting her pique. It felt *wonderful* to be out of the house. "I do not believe it will come to that, my lord. The steps are broad and shallow."

They strolled across the yard to the stable. The friendly smells of stables everywhere wafted out to meet her—hay, horse, and the other inevitable accompaniments of animals. They walked into the shadowy space.

"Oh! There is Firefly. How I have missed her." Phona hastened to her mare. The bay turned in her stall and whickered softly, looking plump and prosperous, her coat shiny. She laid her head on Phona's shoulder.

Hades smiled. "A loyal mount and true. She never abandoned you."

"No, she did not, did she?" Phona glanced at him over her shoulder as she stroked the horse's neck. "I should have brought her a treat. She loves carrots."

"So I have discovered." Hades opened a wooden box and withdrew a shriveled carrot, the end of last summer's crop. He handed it to Phona, and she passed it on to Firefly, who munched contentedly.

"You have pampered her." Phona smiled at her host. "Thank you. I appreciate your care of her. And…of me. I fear I have not shown you the proper gratitude."

He smiled down at her, his expression warm. "It has been my pleasure, Miss Hathersage. I shall miss you when I have restored you to your proper home. Which brings up a subject we must discuss."

He pointed out the stable door, and they walked together across the courtyard to the wide, arched door in the walls. Someone had set a wooden bench just outside the gates. An errant ray of sun slipped through the trees of the gorge to warm the seat. He indicated it with a nod, and Phona sat. Hades stood facing her, one boot propped on the bench.

"The sunlight is caught in your curls." He reached his left arm forward to touch her hair. Then, as if remembering his lack of a hand, suddenly withdrew it and moved back a bit.

"Miss Hathersage, I must go away for a few days. Aelfred will be here to look after you. I am hoping that this trip will settle my—" He grinned at her. "Felonious business. If it does, I shall take you to your parents straightaway."

"I see." Somehow Phona did not feel the relief she should have. Something inside fell with a tiny bump. "How long will you be gone?"

"I can never be certain. At least four days." His expression became serious. "I must have your promise that you will not try to leave while I am away. Look around you."

He swept his arm in a wide circle. "The terrain here is very difficult. It becomes more so as you descend the gorge. You might be seriously injured if you attempted it. And certainly lost. I do not wish to be compelled to have Aelfred lock you in your room."

"Oh no!" Alarm pierced Phona. "Please do not do that."

"May I have your word that you will not go farther than this bench?" He smiled, eyebrows raised in inquiry. "Word of a Hathersage?"

Phona considered for a minute. Pride insisted that she make no concessions to the enemy, that she make every attempt to evade any captor. But pride once more must go down in ignominious defeat. Good sense carried the day. She sighed and nodded.

"Very well. Word of a Hathersage."

It was not until they had returned to the study that she

realized that, through the whole outing, he had never offered her his arm. Nor had he done so since she became liberated from the tower room.

How unlike him.

Dinner that evening had been rather quiet—Phona still wrestling with conflicting emotions, and Hades lost in his own thoughts. Both had gone to bed with only a cursory good-night.

Thinking him gone on his way, the next morning shortly after Aelfred brought her porridge, Phona was surprised by a polite tap on the bedchamber door announcing Lord Hades' continued presence.

As he came into the room, Phona could not restrain a gasp. Her hands flew to her mouth, and she had to force herself not to leap out of the bed and run.

For this was not the gentle man who had cared for her through illness and recovery. This was the ruffian with a hook who had pursued her, overpowered her, who had brought her here as a captive.

"Forgive me, Miss Hathersage. I did not mean to startle you." He stood uncertainly by the door.

"I—I—" Phona took a deep breath and steeled her nerves. At least his voice was the same. "Of course. Come in, my lord."

As he came around the end of the bed, Phona took a longer look. No ribbon now graced the nape of his neck. His hair and beard had been somehow roughed up, making them stand out from his head in a bushy mane, and he wore a crude frock coat and dirty buckskin britches.

And he smelled.

Phona wrinkled her nose. For the first time since she had known him, Hades looked abashed. "Your pardon, Miss Hathersage. I know I am unfit for the company of a lady, but I wanted to say goodbye."

"Good heavens!" Phona shook her head. "You did give me a turn. You are quite disguised. Until you spoke I would hardly have known you."

He smiled at last. "That is the purpose of a disguise."

"Yes, I suppose it must be." Phona chuckled. "Where are you going?"

He answered with a wry smile.

She sighed. "Yes, I know. If I ask no questions, I shall be told no lies. Or more likely, I shall hear nothing at all."

"My apologies. I am all repentance." His teeth flashed in a grin.

"Oh, yes, you look the very soul of repentance." Phona shook her head. "And very much the brigand."

"Good. I am happy to hear that." Sobering, he held out his good hand, keeping his hook close to his side. "Be well until I return."

A lump rose in Phona's throat as she took his hand. He was going into danger. They both knew that. He might, in fact, *never* return. She cleared her throat with a cough and sniffed. In spite of herself she felt a tear form in the corner of her eye.

Hades gazed at it, his expression grave. "Forgive me if I rejoice at this tiny tear, Miss Hathersage. Perhaps you hold me in some small esteem."

She must not let him see that. It would only make her more vulnerable to his charm. She should not care if she never saw him again. Phona quickly blinked her eyes. "Take care, my lord, wherever it is you are going."

He leaned over as if to place the chastest of kisses on her forehead, then halted himself and straightened. "God guard you, my lady."

Phona hated the fact that she missed him.

Somehow the days stretched out long and empty ahead of her. And the only thing that had changed was that Lord Hades no longer shared them. What an idiot she was! Falling in love with a man apparently as damaged in reputation as he was in body.

He must at some time have been a naval officer. It was the only logical explanation. True, he looked like a pirate now, but no pirate would be so erudite, so well-spoken. Certainly not so kind and respectful to a captured maiden.

And now, to her chagrin, the maiden was lonely for him.

So, on the second day, she sought comfort in the kitchen. Stepping carefully down the stairs, Phona emerged into a low-ceilinged room fully as large as the great hall. Here the floors as well as the walls were stone, and the recessed fireplace held not only a spit large enough to roast a carcass, but a large kettle from which enticing aromas emanated.

Phona suspected that one of the barnyard fowl had come to a tragic end in the depths of the pot. "Soup for nuncheon?"

Startled, Aelfred turned from where he stood working at a table of wide boards, worn into a dip in the middle from the preparation of innumerable meals. "Why, good day, miss. Ye gave me a right turn, ye did. Was you needin' aught?"

"Only someone to talk to. I am heartily sick of my own society, and I am certainly tired of eating in solitary state." Phona spied a low stool and pulled it over to the table.

"Aye. Too much of yer own self can be wearisome." Aelfred picked up one of two china bowls already set out in saucers on the table and carried it to the pot, where he ladled a steamy portion into the bowl and set it before her. "Would you be wantin' tea? Or a dram of ale?"

"Tea, thank you." Phona wrinkled her nose. "I have never acquired the taste for ale."

"It do take some time." He winked, and his thin mouth moved in what, for Aelfred, passed for a smile. "And a large quantity of ale."

Phona laughed and blew on one of the hot dumplings she fished from the broth. Aelfred set the tea to steep and filled a bowl of soup and a tankard of ale for himself. They ate in companionable silence until Aelfred got up to pour her tea.

He set the cup on the table and rubbed his chin thoughtfully as he sat back down. "Miss, there's aught I'd like to ask you, an' you don't mind."

"Well." She sipped the hot tea and smiled. "I don't *think* I will mind."

"What is this old story you and my master are on about? Why do you call him Hades? Be you cursing him?"

"Oh, no. At least, not now. He will not tell me his proper name, you see. As for the story, it is a myth told by the ancient Greeks which the Romans later adopted. It concerns the goddess of fertility, Demeter, and her daughter, Persephone. My mother's name is Demetra, so she named me Persephone."

"Hmm. That's a mouthful."

"Even worse—my middle name is Proserpina, the Latin version."

Aelfred looked taken aback. "Per... Pros... Hah! Plumb breaks my teeth to try and say it."

"Just so." Phona sighed. "But to make a very long tale shorter, Hades—the god of the Underworld—admired Persephone and abducted her to be his wife."

"Here now! Ain't been none o' that in this house." Her companion glared at her sternly.

"No, no! Lord Hades has been the very soul of a gentleman."

"Aye, or I'd have combed his hair with a joint stool, and no mistake." He took a pull from the tankard. "But why wouldn't you eat?"

Phona took another spoonful of soup. "Well, you see, Demeter missed her daughter so much that she could not maintain the earth's fertility. All she could do was weep. The crops stopped growing, and it turned cold."

"Aha. Like winter."

"Exactly. At last, an agreement was reached so that Persephone might return to her mother for six months of the year. She had eaten six pomegranate seeds in the Underworld, you see."

"Huh! Don't make no sense to me. Ain't that much food. And why would eating it…? But never mind. I collect that her Mama was pleased, and that's why we have summer and winter."

"Or so the ancients say." Phona scraped up the last of her soup. "How long do you think he will be gone?"

"Couldn't say, miss." He picked up her empty bowl. "Ye never can tell with his—with him."

Aelfred knew who the man was—or had been. Phona was sure of it. He had almost said *his lordship,* and he had done so before. Her host had fallen far indeed. Phona's curiosity as to who he had been was raging, but she couldn't ask his loyal man that.

So instead she asked, "Do you know how he lost his hand?"

"Well, aye, miss." Aelfred glanced at her over his tankard. "But it ain't my place to talk his business."

"Of course not. Forgive me." Her inquisitiveness was putting the man in a bad position. Soon he would not speak to her at all. "I'll ask you no more questions about him. Except…do you think he is in danger?"

Aelfred gazed at her shrewdly, and Phona blushed. "I don't think there's no doubt about that, miss." He rose and gathered up the dishes. "But don't ye worry yerself. He'll be back. Soon or late. He always is."

Phona sighed. With that less-than-comforting thought she would have to be content.

Even though she should not care at all.

Leo made his way home through the night, swearing under his breath every foot of the way. This business was not going well. The man he sought had not appeared. Had, again, only sent his lieutenant, Hardesty. Damnation! Leo knew who the little fish were, had known from the beginning. He wanted their master.

He was convinced that when he tracked down the leader of the thieves, he would find his enemy—the shadowy scoundrel who had blackened his name, questioned his parentage and attempted to have him taken up for a capital crime.

Who had even tried to kill him.

Leo was terrified that at the end of the hunt he would find the heir to his position, his cousin, Rob. With all his soul he did not want to find him there.

Rob had been orphaned very early. They had grown up together, running through the fields of his home, climbing trees, learning to hunt. He had already lost his older brother, Percy. His heart broke at the thought of also losing Rob. At the thought that his much-loved cousin might turn against him.

He needed to know soon. The pain of suspicion had gone on much too long.

Leo guided Capstan through the byways and gorges with one part of his mind, while with another, he attempted to puzzle out a more successful course of action. Somewhere between the two, a small sound intruded. A very small sound. A pebble rolling against stone.

In an instant, Leo forgot everything but the sound.

Pulling up in the shelter of a rough-faced, giant boulder, he bent every sense toward identifying the direction from which the sound had come. Above? Only an empty silence greeted him. He cast about in the dark for some sign of movement, quietly sweeping his gaze from right to left. Nothing there.

Nothing that he could see.

He eased his mount forward a few slow steps, as though

satisfied that he was alone. One step away from the boulder, two. Three. Four. Abruptly, he wheeled back toward the rock. Something flashed silver in the starlight, hissing past an inch from Leo's back and crashing into the brush ahead of him.

Leo vaulted from his horse and rolled under its belly just as the boom and the muzzle flash of a pistol flared from the top of the great stone. Capstan galloped away into the woods. Damnation! He had almost allowed himself to be taken in ambush.

Drawing his own pistol as he rolled, Leo came to his feet pressed close against the rock. With luck the slight overhang would protect him from another shot. Or another knife. He braced his back against the stone and waited.

It did not take long. Two figures dropped silently out of the black sky and landed where Leo had fallen only a second ago. He did not give them time to come fully upright. He fired at one and dived into the other, bearing him to the ground. His empty pistol flew away into the gloom as his opponent reared up and threw him on his back.

They thrashed in the dirt, each staking his life on control of the other. Where the devil was the man at whom he had shot? God grant he was wounded mortally. If not, Leo was lost.

The man straddling him had a second knife. Leo grasped the wrist of the arm wielding it with his good hand and slashed at his adversary's midsection with the hook. The man roared in pain as the hook ripped through his skin and flesh. He pulled back, trying to get to his feet. Leo came up with him.

Leo had learned that fighting with only one hand could prove a bit awkward. He must reach across both bodies to stop his adversary's weapon-bearing right arm with his own right hand—his *only* hand. But he had trained well to make the contingency an asset. Maintaining his hold, he surged to his feet and used his momentum to force his assailant's knife arm back over the man's shoulder.

Leo took one step behind the other man and pulled the arm backward. Rather than feel his shoulder break, the man fell against him. Leo went down again, taking his adversary with him to the earth. Now Leo lay on the ground with his opponent's back against his chest.

His grip still tight on the knife hand, he wrapped his left arm around the man's head and fastened the hook in the flesh of his neck. A quick jerk, and blood spurted over both of them. The man flailed, but Leo held him fast. It took only a minute until the attacker lay still, a dead weight on top of Leo.

Leo wiped blood out of his eyes and got carefully to his feet, the assassin's knife now ready in his hand. Crouching, every muscle tense, he looked around him. The other assailant must, indeed, be dead, otherwise he would have joined his partner. But where was he?

Just as the question came to mind, another shot roared out. A searing pain sliced through Leo's thigh. Bloody hell! The rascal had dragged himself into the bushes.

Leo dismissed the pain. He must eliminate the fellow before he got off another shot. Now following sounds of uncontrollable coughing, he charged in the direction from which the report of the pistol had come. He slowed as he reached the bushes. The coughing seemed to be coming from the earth in front of him.

He knelt and felt about. His groping hand encountered a bundle of cloth, sticky to the touch. A limp hand struck at him weakly.

"Ye bloody bastard." A cough. "Ye've done fer me." A few more choking breaths and then a chilling silence. The bundle of cloth lay still.

Leo got to his feet and whistled for Capstan. A river of blood ran down his own leg. The pain suddenly leaped up at him like the teeth of a predator. Now his enemy, whoever the hound was, had tried to kill him twice.

And this time, he might have succeeded.

Chapter Seven

As the fifth day dragged into night, Phona lay in the big carved bed and tried to sleep. For the last two nights she had sat at the kitchen table with Aelfred, playing with a cup of tea, peeking under the cloth at the rising bread and occasionally stirring the ever-present pot of soup, while he calmly mended a spare leather harness.

Pride, that undependable commodity, had returned and kept her from asking Aelfred—many times an evening—if he thought his master was safe. There was no answer to the question, and she didn't wish to figure as the abandoned maiden. Didn't wish to care what the answer was. Now she lay awake asking the question of herself. And still getting no answer.

Until she heard the thump.

She sat up in bed and listened. Nothing. No more thumps. No footsteps. No voices.

Only a burned log collapsing into the grate. Phona flipped over in the bed and pushed her pillow into a new shape. She closed her eyes. Looked behind her eyelids for sheep to count. Found only the face of her missing host.

At last, sighing, she gave it up, slid over the side of the

bed and felt with her feet for her slippers. She tied them and, taking the bedside candle to the fire, lit it at the coals and made her way in the dim light to the stairway.

She was *not* investigating the thump. She was merely going to the study to fetch her book. Perhaps reading a bit in bed would help her sleep. She had no interest in that thump.

Nonetheless, Phona took the stairs carefully, peering around the corner at the landing before descending to the bottom. The study was pitch-dark. She saw nothing untoward. Nothing moved. No one spoke.

As it should be. She started across the room to the window seat where she had left the book, candlestick held high, squinting to see ahead of herself in the small puddle of light.

And tripped over something lying on the floor.

Phona went sprawling. The candle hit the floor and flickered out. The thing on the floor said, "Mmph!"

Phona choked back a shriek. She sat up and felt cautiously behind her. A hand grasped her wrist. The shriek exploded, echoing off the stone walls.

"God, don't!" The hand jerked her down, and Phona found herself wrapped in strong arms, her scream stopped by a warm, demanding mouth. She tried to pull away, but a hand captured the back of her head and held her fast. An odor wafted around her, not a pleasant odor, but one she had smelled briefly five days before.

Hades!

And he was kissing her.

Soundly.

New feelings flooded Phona's body. The heat of his mouth. The roughness of his whiskers. A warmth in her lower belly. She hesitated, then in a rush, gave her whole self to the kiss, savoring every sensation.

Suddenly the hand dropped limply away.

Phona sat up. "My lord? Lord Hades?"

A muffled growl answered her. "Whom were you expecting?"

She began frantically searching around for the candle, moving her hands over the floor. One hand knocked into his lordship.

"Aaa!"

Wet and sticky, Phona jumped back. "My lord! You are injured!" Dear heaven, he needed help. She must find the candle. Just then, to her prodigious relief, a pale glow developed in the kitchen stairwell. "Aelfred! Come quickly. His lordship is hurt."

The light rapidly grew brighter as the sound of footsteps hurried up the steps. A moment later, Aelfred's tall form folded itself down beside her. He set his candlestick on the floor and immediately began to examine his now-silent employer.

Phona finally located her own candle and lit it from Aelfred's. Placing it on the opposite side of the fallen man, she knelt beside the two of them.

"Me lord, can ye hear me?"

"Aye." The answer sounded faint, his breathing rough.

"Where're ye hurt?"

Hades roused and tried to sit. He managed to lay a hand on his thigh before falling back. "Here."

Aelfred glanced at Phona. "More light."

Springing to her feet, she raced across the room and seized the candelabra from the table. She put it on the floor by Hades' feet and used her candle to light all the tapers. The new light revealed a figure covered in blood from head to foot.

Phona gasped.

Even Aelfred seemed taken aback. "Gor! Where—?"

"Just my leg," Hades whispered.

"Thank God." Phona leaned across him to peer at the wound. She could now see a rough bandage tied around his leg and a small pool of dark liquid forming under the thigh. She looked up at Aelfred. "He is still bleeding."

The serving man quickly gazed around them. "Me lord, are they close behind ye?"

A ragged breath. Then a murmur. "Nay."

Aelfred gestured with his head. "Best bar the door, lass, all the same."

Phona jumped up and ran to the big doors. Only one stood partly open, and she pushed it to and struggled to get the heavy bar in place. Then she raced back to the two men. "It is cold in here. We should get him to his bed."

"Right ye are, lass." Aelfred slipped an arm under Hades' shoulders and lifted him to a sitting position. "Can ye help me, me lord?"

Hades nodded and tried to come to his feet. The attempt was doomed to failure. He wobbled, but did not rise far. Phona knelt and pulled one of his arms over her own shoulders. Aelfred did the same on the other side and together the three of them got Hades standing.

He mumbled, "'Ware the hook."

Suddenly Phona realized that the arm she held ended in the fearsome implement. She took a firmer hold on the arm and moved it a safe distance away from her body.

Aelfred seized a candle in his free hand, and they walked Hades into his bedchamber and let him sink to a sitting position on the bed. Aelfred kept a firm hold on him, while Phona lit all the candles in the room. Then she grabbed the poker and stirred up the coals, adding enough wood for a blaze.

By the time she had completed these tasks, Aelfred had gotten Hades' filthy, blood-soaked coat, shirt and boots off. The hook had disappeared, and Hades had thrust his left wrist under the extra pillows.

"Yer that nasty, me lord. We'd best get the britches off, too."

The answer was faint but clear. "I'll be damned."

"Nonsense, my lord. We must clean the wound." Phona marched to the bed, laid a hand on his shoulder and gave him a firm push in the direction of the pillows. As he toppled backward, Aelfred grasped his legs and heaved them onto the bed.

Hades sucked in a sudden breath and uttered another word that Phona had never before heard. Then, through labored breathing, he muttered something that sounded like, "Your pardon, Miss Hath…"

Aelfred took the knife from Hades' belt and, starting at the ankle, began to cut open the leg of the buckskins which housed the injured leg. Hades muttered something else that sounded like, "Don't ruin…"

His henchman ignored him and, carefully cutting around the wound, continued through the waist of the britches. When that side was loose, he nodded at Phona. "I'll lift him a bit, miss, and ye pull the other side off."

Hades' good hand clamped down on the waistband of his violated apparel. "No! Miss Hather—"

"Don't be ridiculous, sir." Phona took firm hold of the britches. "They must come off."

She gave a strong tug. Hades resisted. Phona braced herself and pulled harder. Suddenly the leather slipped through his weakened fingers. The britches came off over his foot all at once, and Phona landed in a heap on the floor.

"Yer lucky, me lord. The ball missed the bone. Went clean through. Ye've lost a good deal of blood, I'll warrant. We want some hot water and the brandy."

Aelfred made for the door, leaving Phona in charge of their patient. She got to her feet, tossing the tattered britches aside.

At which point she *saw* something she had never before seen.

For a moment she could only stare. She had grown up on

a farm, after all, and farm animals could hardly be depended upon to behave discreetly. Despite Mama's vigilance, Phona had often witnessed scenes that had caused her mother to hustle her away. So, of course, she knew the basic structure.

But she had not expected it to be so…so…

Beautiful.

Lord Hades' body was quite beautiful. Curling black hair covered a sculpted chest and formed a narrow line down his taut stomach. It sprang thickly from his groin. From it jutted a thick male member. Phona drew in a sudden breath. Oh, my!

The object of her admiration groaned, bringing Phona back to a consciousness of the situation. She folded the coverlet over one side of him, discreetly covering what modesty required. He clutched the fabric to him and growled.

Phona ignored the growl. "Are you cold?"

He shivered slightly and nodded, murmuring, "I bled like a butchered pig."

She folded the cover over his exposed chest and placed a hand on his forehead.

"We shall soon have you to rights, my lord." Not knowing what else to do for him, Phona covered the hand clinging to the coverlet with her own. It seemed he started to pull back, but then relaxed with a sigh.

Aelfred returned with a can of steaming water and a bottle of brandy. Phona fetched the washbasin from its stand and set it on the bed table. The manservant pulled several cloths out of his pocket, and they set about washing as much blood off Hades as possible.

It must have been hurting him dreadfully, but aside from an occasional flinch, Hades bore the cleaning stoically. They tactfully forbore to wash any areas of his person which, in Phona's presence, would cause him distress. She felt a small prick of disappointment. Then she flushed with shame.

What was she thinking?

"Ye ain't going to care much for this part, me lord." Aelfred brandished the bottle. "But I got it to do."

As quick as lightning, Hades snatched the bottle and, lifting his head from the bed, took two long pulls. Then he returned it to his henchman. "Now! Do your worst, damn you."

His man wiped away the seeping blood and carefully tipped the liquor into the wound. Hades drew in a hissing breath and let it go with a loud, "Damnation!"

Aelfred continued, undeterred, flexing the flesh to open the swollen channel. Phona slipped a cloth under the leg to catch the excess. Hades arched his back, fists tight in the bed-clothes, but all he uttered was a long, "A-a-ah."

How could he endure it?

"There. All done, me lord." Aelfred set the bottle aside. "Now we need to bind it. That's got it bleeding proper again."

When the bandange was tight, Hades lay breathing in labored gasps, conscious but fading. Aelfred lifted part of Hades' weight off the bedclothes, and Phona pulled the bloody coverlet away from the bed and tugged the sheets and quilt from under him. They tucked him in, and he settled back with a sigh.

Aelfred gathered up the soiled fabrics. "I'll fetch him some soup and ale. He needs them."

Phona nodded. She found a chair and drug it nearer the bed. "Good. I shall sit with him."

He looked frighteningly pale, his long hair wild and dark on the pillow. She thought him sleeping or unconscious, but he fumbled his hand out of the covers and laid it near her. She took it in her own.

A ghost of a smile flitted over his lips, and a blue eye regarded her. "You are, indeed, an intrepid little kitten. I am glad you are with me."

It was only then that Phona realized that an hour ago she had experienced her first passionate kiss.

Wearing a man's nightshirt.

* * *

Lord Hathersage was a worried man. Worried, of course, about his missing daughter. The vague letters of reassurance she had sent had failed notably in their purpose. He was *not* reassured. Rather the opposite.

Surely the bloody scoundrel who had taken her was forcing her to write them. George could not allow himself to dwell for more than a minute on what else the blackguard might be forcing her to do, lest his rage threaten to overpower him.

He himself had looked high and low for her. Afraid of mounting an out-and-out search for fear of forever destroying her reputation, he made visits, sending out subtle feelers to his friends, giving them an opportunity to mention that they had seen her.

No one did so.

He went to London and spent hours in the coffee room of his club, listening for some hint. He had even gone to Bath and drunk the execrable water. He heard a great deal of gossip, as always, but none of it about Phona.

He had ridden to York and to Bristol. He even made inquiries at Gretna Green. No one had seen her. In desperation, he had hired the Runners to make discreet inquiries, but so far those worthies had had no better results than he himself.

But he worried also about her mother. Never had his lady been so subdued. She did not laugh. She did not chatter. She did not flirt. She did not even have the vapors.

She simply went about the business of the household quietly—a word to the cook, a conference with the housekeeper, an instruction to a footman. His home enjoyed perfect management.

But it was as though winter had descended prematurely on the house.

Phona sat with Lord Hades until the early hours of the morning. She reminded herself again and again that it wasn't because she loved this man. She could not afford to love him. She was simply returning his kindness in keeping vigil with her when she was ill. That was all.

I am glad you are with me. His words echoed in her heart. Phona repressed them ruthlessly. They were not an expression of affection. Of course he was glad to have someone with him.

Anyone.

And neither did the kiss mean anything. He must have been delirious with pain. It could not possibly indicate that he had missed her as she had missed him. She must keep that firmly in mind. Her own silly feelings were trying to lead her astray. To lead her into hope. And she had nothing to hope for.

Even if he returned her regard there could be no future between them.

Only when Aelfred relieved her of the watch did she wearily climb the stairs. She pulled the now-bloody nightshirt over her head, dropped it on the floor and fell into bed. The fact that she had worn only the thin linen garment in the company of two men never crossed her mind.

Artificial strictures did not matter here.

She slept the sleep of the just until shortly before midday. Thinking to relieve Aelfred at Hades' bedside, she dressed and combed her hair. She lacked a mirror, but she could feel her curls fluffing out around her head in a soft cloud. Mama would shudder if she could see it. Another thing that did not matter here.

She found his lordship in much better condition than she had expected. He sat up in his bed, propped on several pillows. His hair had been combed and his beard trimmed. A clean nightshirt now covered his chest and fresh bedclothes covered everything else.

Phona forced down a rush of feeling she refused to put a name to.

He held a tankard of ale and an empty bowl and spoon rested on a tray beside him. "Good morning, Miss Hathersage." He took a swallow of ale and set the tankard on the tray. "Have you recovered from the alarms of the night?"

"I would think, sir, that a better question is, have *you?*" Phona drew the chair nearer to the bed and sat. "You were in sad case when I discovered you last night."

Hades grimaced. "I am sorry you saw it. It must have been very distressing for you."

She shook her head. "Only in that I was very frightened for you. So much blood…"

"Nay, now. Do not think about the blood. I lost a little, but was mostly a bit weak from pain and exhaustion."

For a moment all Phona *could* think about was the blood. If only a small part of it belonged to his lordship, then to whom had the balance belonged?

She sensed that it was that very question that he did not want her to consider. He must have killed the man who shot him—and at close quarters. He did not want her to realize that.

Indeed, it did give her a strange feeling. Phona glanced at him again. She had never thought about him as capable of killing, although she felt sure that he had been in a naval battle.

One never thought of the killing, the blood, when one considered military heroes. Only of the bravery and the daring. Handsome young men in dashing uniforms.

A handsome brigand in tattered clothes.

Clothes soaked in blood.

She would not think of that now. She gazed into his face. "All that signifies, my lord, is that you have returned to us safely. We will soon have you mended."

"Ah, the brave lady. Pluck to the backbone." He took another sip from the tankard and relaxed against the pillows.

At that moment Aelfred came in with another bowl of

soup on a saucer. He replaced the empty one on the tray with it.

Hades regarded it askance. "Aelfred is trying to drown me in soup and drink."

"Just what ye need to set ye right, me lord."

"Yes, well… I do seem to have a thirst today." He lifted the bowl and blew on the steaming liquid.

Aelfred nodded at Phona. "It's glad I am to see yer awake, miss. His lordship needs red meat. I need to hunt a hart for the pot. If ye could get yer own meal—"

"Of course." Phona got to her feet. "By all means, go. I'll take care of his lordship's needs."

From the bed came a low mutter. It sounded rather like, "I sincerely doubt it."

"Sir?" Phona turned back to him. "Were you speaking to me?"

She was greeted with a crooked grin. "No, Miss Hathersage. I was merely thinking aloud."

Leo waited until she had finished her soup, but he found himself unwilling to wait any longer. He had promised himself this scene hour after hour on the long, difficult ride through the night. Through the painful hours before dawn.

Since the moment last night that she had voluntarily taken his hand in hers.

Before she could pick up her book and settle in the chair, he pointed across the room and asked, "Miss Hathersage, do you think you might bring those saddlebags nearer the bed?"

She considered the bulging bags and nodded. "Of course. Do you need something out of them?"

"Just bring them near your chair."

The bags were heavy, but she managed to get them across the room. "There, my lord. Shall I open them?"

"Please."

Kneeling beside them, she worked at the buckles for a

moment. When they were open, she asked, "What do you want?"

"Just start emptying them."

Giving Leo a puzzled glance, she shrugged and lifted out the first item. It was the napkin in which Aelfred had wrapped his chicken pasties. She set that aside with her empty dish and reached in again.

"Oh, how lovely!" This time she pulled out a hand mirror with a heavy, embossed silver frame. She looked at herself and made a face.

"Here now!" At the sharp tone in his voice, she turned, startled. "Never let me see you make such a face again when you look in that glass. I promised you I would bring you a mirror that would show your true beauty. Whenever you look into this one, you must smile."

To his satisfaction a spontaneous smile blossomed on her face. She looked into the glass again. "But my hair…"

"No buts, Miss Hathersage." Leo leaned forward, reached for a handful of curls, then quickly stopped himself. "Your hair is like a mist with firelight shining through it."

Damn! He could hardly keep his hands off her. Just because she was kind enough to comfort him, he must not assume that she welcomed his touch.

She set the looking glass in her lap, and smiled into his eyes. Warmth spread through his heart. Seeing her smile like that had been worth all the risk and the all the lies he had had to tell to extract a few items from the treasure hoard—even though he had every right to them. He reined himself in before the warmth made its way any lower.

"Oh, Lord Hades. You are flattering me, sir." She blushed beautifully and put the glass aside, but continued to smile.

"What else is in the bag?" He rested against the pillow again. Damnation! He felt weak as a cat.

"Oh, my lord! Silk stockings?" She pulled them out, a look of wonder now gracing her face.

"For the lovely lady that you are. Continue."

Now she peered eagerly into the bag. She drew in a quick breath. "Ah!"

Next in the bag lay a dinner gown. A soft green silk that he thought would set her off to perfection. She pulled it out and held it up to herself. "My lord, you brought all this for me?"

He nodded. "I told you I would not suffer a lady in my care to dress like a street urchin—even if she is *not* my mistress."

As much as it had galled Leo to sit idle while his leg healed, the situation had manifested sundry advantages. In the first place, his lovely guest insisted on waiting on him hand and foot and catering to his every need.

Well, perhaps not *every* need. Still…

Had it been anyone else, her attentions might have driven him to distraction. As it was, he relished the proximity the little tasks required. It allowed him to inhale her womanly fragrance, to enjoy the touch of her gentle hands, to glance discreetly at her feminine curves.

All in all, hardly an unbearable affliction.

It had become obvious that his present course of action would not bring the enemy he sought close enough for him to lay hands on. Or, as he would have preferred, to lay hook on. So far the scoundrel had proved himself too canny even to be identified.

The attack on Leo clearly indicated that his clandestine position in the gang of thieves had been compromised. Leo could no longer serve as their guide to the caves. He would be obliged to find another way to reveal their leader—the man he believed to be his most dangerous enemy.

He had, instead, concluded the present affair with a few well-placed letters to his contacts in the Home Office. Just today Aelfred had found an answer waiting for him at one of the many village post offices he used to obscure his where-abouts. It was done. The scheme was finished.

He had, at least, exacted vengeance on Hardesty for his role in the rape accusation. What kind of man would use his own sister in such a scheme?

Leo now sat before the fire in the study, awaiting the arrival of his dinner companion. Aelfred had set the small table between the two big chairs and furnished it with the best the house had to offer. This was to be a farewell dinner, after all.

At the sound of his guest's light tread on the stone steps, Leo looked up, his heart racing a bit. She rounded the landing and walked gracefully down into the candlelight, like the original Persephone entering the domain of the Lord of the Underworld.

Seeing him waiting for her, she flashed her engaging smile. "Good evening, my lord."

She wore the second of the two dinner gowns he had been able to fit into his saddlebag, a soft rose silk with the skirt pulled into a drape that showed her rounded hips to advantage.

And a bodice cut very low. Much lower than her protective mama had allowed her wear, he would dare swear, but much to his own liking. He knew the gown had been created for a married lady.

In fact, he knew exactly which lady.

Still uncertain about touching her, he rose and extended a hand. Without hesitation she rewarded him with her own and ducked her head shyly. "You look exquisite this evening, Miss Hathersage. As ever you do."

"And you, my lord, are ever the flatterer."

"Not at all. I simply report the discernment of my own eyes." Or perhaps he should have said eye. What a remarkable woman she was, daunted by neither hook nor eye patch. "I particularly like your hair arranged that way."

She had combed it away from her face a bit and secured it with a ribbon sacrificed from the gown. The back fell in a soft cloud of ringlets, brushing against her white shoulders. The effect robbed him of his breath.

He held her chair for her and reclaimed his own. "I have news today which I am sure you will be happy to hear." He could only hope she would not be *too* happy. He watched her face closely. "I am now able to escort you back to your parents."

One expression after another flitted over her face—surprise, joy, and then, to his great relief, disappointment. "Why...Why... That is indeed excellent news, my lord." She forced a smile. "When will we set out?"

"Tomorrow, I think. My wound has healed sufficiently for me to ride, and there will be a full moon."

"A full moon? Will we go by night, then?"

"It will be after dark by the time we arrive, which is just as well." He cast a wary glance in her direction. "Discretion indicates that I restore you to your proper home without being discovered doing so."

"Oh. I see." She suddenly devoted her attention to cutting her roast venison.

"I really would prefer not to be immediately arrested, Miss Hathersage. Nor shot by your father."

"Oh, no! Of course not." She quickly looked up into his face. "It is just...I find I am a bit sad to be leaving. It is hard for me to think of you now as...anything but a friend."

"Do not look so downcast, dear lady. We will meet again. You may depend on it."

She did not answer that. Leo could see that she did not believe him, but he was not yet ready to explain the situation to her. He let the matter drop, and they made only desultory conservation for the rest of the meal.

When they had finished their apples and cheese, Aelfred came and took away the dishes and moved the table, leaving the bottle of port at Leo's elbow. As his guest rose to excuse herself, he held out his hand to her. "Please stay, Miss Hathersage."

"My lord?" Her eyebrows rose in inquiry, but she stepped toward him and allowed him to take her hand. A positive sign. It felt tiny and vulnerable within his own callused grip.

Leo could hardly have said what his purpose was. He wanted her. That he knew all too well. And he also knew that he would not take her. She trusted him not to do so. Still…

He hoped that she would be able to tolerate him, to allow him to feel her warmth and soft curves against him for a space without drawing away.

He pulled her toward him, then with his arm, invited her to sit on his knee. She stiffened for a moment, but eased herself down carefully. "My lord, are you sure you wish this? Your leg—"

"Be damned to my leg." He drew her a little closer. "I find I am not quite ready to relinquish you. Will you sit here with me for a while?"

"I…I am quite sure it is completely improper." She made as if to get up, but he captured her again and held her lightly.

"Allow me this one small indulgence. We have managed to remain above reproach, Miss Hathersage, even though nothing we have done during your residency here has been quite proper."

"It certainly has not." She relaxed a little in his hold. "If my parents have not been successful in their charade, I will find myself a fallen woman when I return."

"And I shall deal severely with anyone who dares say so."

"You will not know of it." She spoke very quietly, her gaze on her hands.

"I shall hear."

She shook her head, then rested it against his shoulder. "I may have to run away to sea."

"I trust that will not prove necessary." He smiled at the

image. "Never fear that I will abandon you to the wolves, Miss Hathersage." Wanting to change the subject, he lifted the glass of port to her lips. "Have you ever tried port?"

She took a cautious sip. "Oh, I like it. It is much nicer than claret."

"Much sweeter, yes, but also much stronger. Be careful of it, lest you wake with a headache." He offered her another taste.

She took a swallow. "I would never drink port at home. What a remarkable experience this has been."

Leo took a long pull of the wine. "It certainly has, Miss Hathersage."

He set the glass on the table and wrapped his arms around her, pulling her closer. Throwing caution to the wind, he slid his hand into her hair and drew her lips to his. They tasted of the wine, sweet and rich, warm against his mouth.

For a moment she yielded, sinking into the kiss, delicate and fragile in his embrace. He drank her in, his senses awash with her.

Suddenly her eyes snapped opened, and she moved back. "My lord! We cannot. We simply cannot." She jumped up and stood before him, breathing heavily. "I…I'm afraid—"

Leo came abruptly to his feet. Did his mutilated body revolt her after all? "Afraid of me, Miss Hathersage? Or repulsed?"

He took a step toward her, and she backed away. "No. Not…" She put up a hand, as if to fend him off. "Please, Lord Hades."

All at once a completely unreasonable anger engulfed Leo. She dared back away from him after all his constraint, all his care, all his unrequited desire?

"So I am Lord Cad again, am I, Miss Hathersage?" His jaw tightened. He took a longer step, trying to close the distance between them. "Lord Blackguard, the dismembered brigand?"

"No! Not that. How could I— Please don't!" She continued to retreat. Leo could see tears running down her cheeks.

Oh, Lord. Now he had made her cry. Suddenly the anger evaporated, leaving him guilty and ashamed. He *was* a cad. She stepped back again and turned toward the stairs.

"Miss Hathersage, wait!"

He lunged for her and grasped her wrist. She gave her hand a sharp tug, pulling him forward. The toe of his boot hung on a fold in the rug. Already off balance, Leo tried to free his foot from the carpet. He stepped forward on his injured leg.

It chose that moment to fail him.

He went down, taking his lady with him. She swallowed a small shriek as she fell, and he twisted to get between her and the floor. She sprawled on top of him, his body cushioning her impact.

There was nothing, however, to cushion his. Leo hit the backbreaking wood with her weight on top of him. He uttered a loud groan and lay motionless for a heartbeat.

After a startled moment, she tried to sit up. "My lord! Your leg!"

"The devil with my leg." He had never let go of her wrist. Leo used it to pull her down on top of him. Folding his arms around her, he drew her into another kiss, this one quick and fierce. He release her and glared.

"Do not back away from me, Miss Hathersage. Appalling though I may appear, whatever you do, do not back away!"

Chapter Eight

It had taken quite a while to sort themselves out and regain their feet. Leo immediately dropped his accusations and begged forgiveness for his ungentlemanly conduct. His guest had granted it with lowered eyes and, without further discussion of the issue, had hastened to her bed.

Leo felt like a fool. What had possessed him to coax her into his lap? He should have known that could only end in disaster.

Lord Idiot!

Now they rode single-file down the gorge, much as they had come up it. Only now Leo rode to give up his prize. Riding thus prevented easy conversation, but perhaps that was just as well. He wanted to tell her the truth, but he restrained himself.

He would not give her any knowledge that would endanger her, now or later. Until he was certain that those who might threaten her were, in fact, safely in the toils of the law, Lord Hades he must remain.

At least she rode home in the soft blue velvet habit he had provided her from the stolen treasure. He could not have abided bringing her to her parents in the tattered wreck she had worn on the previous journey.

As dusk fell, Leo called a halt to his little party in the same glade where they had rested before. He went to her instinctively to lift her down, but just as he was about to reach for her, he stopped himself.

His pride had taken a beating the evening before. He wasn't sure his battered confidence could tolerate a rejection. Seeing his hesitation, she tried to dismount by herself. She came tumbling off her horse onto legs that were too tired to hold her.

As she stumbled backward, Leo flung an arm around her waist and kept her on her feet. "Are you completely done up, Miss Hathersage?"

A sigh whispered against his chest. "I *am* rather glad to stop for a rest. How much farther is it?"

"A good distance, yet." Leo conducted her to the big stone they had used before. "Sit, or walk about, if you wish. Whatever you think will rest your legs."

"I'll do a bit of both, I believe. Have you made this ride often?" She arched her back and stretched her arms.

"Many times. It is easier with only myself and Capstan." He opened his saddlebag and extracted the meal that Aelfred had prepared for them.

"Are you going all the way back tonight?" She looked at him quizzically and began unwrapping the food.

"No. Not tonight." In fact, he was not returning to the lodge in the gorge at all for a while. His henchman had spent the day quietly closing it and packing up their clothing. He would meet Leo at quite another place. "But look—Aelfred has packed you a bottle of port. You will not have to make do with ale."

"Oh, my!" Her giggle sent a quiver of desire through Leo. "I shall not be able to ride at all if I am not careful."

He laughed. "Not to worry, my dear Miss Hathersage. I shall get you home, even if a trifle foxed."

They sat on the rock to eat, sharing morsels and sipping

carefully. When they had finished, Leo spread a cloak on the ground beside the rock. "Come, Miss Hathersage." He sat and leaned against the stone, holding out his arm. "Sit with me, and let us watch the moon rise."

She lowered herself to the ground beside him and leaned against the boulder, but she did not touch him. Just as well. He hardly relished the risk of a repetition of last night's scene.

Leo handed her the bottle. "Enjoy a few more sips. We have but little time to spend savoring the night. Let us make the most of it."

A long sigh reached his ears. "I fear this is last time we shall spend *any* time together. So yes, let us make the most of it."

She turned in his arm and offered him her lips. He dipped his head and tasted them briefly, resisting the impulse to devour her.

He lifted his head and gazed into her eyes. "Alas, my lady, we must not tempt fate." *Or me.* "If I start down this road, I fear my desire for you will carry us both to the end of it. I will not do that to you. You came to me pure, and you will part from me in the same condition."

He heard a tiny sniff. "I am sure you are right."

She leaned away from him. He wanted to comfort her, but did not dare. It would stretch his already strained willpower too far. But deep inside himself, he exulted. He was not alone in his desire.

She had invited his touch.

As a woman to a man.

Several hours later, in the small hours of the morning, he finally brought the lady home, riding before him on his saddle, exhausted, a trifle tipsy and half-asleep. He carried her into the stable and deposited her in a deep pile of hay. She regarded him through half-open eyes.

"Enjoy your homecoming, my lady." Leo leaned over her and placed a swift kiss on her forehead.

Then he turned and slipped silently into the night. Alone.

* * *

Phona opened her eyes to great hubbub and commotion.
"It's her! It's her, me lord!"

She could hear Old Ned, her groom, shouting as he ran.
Behind him pounded heavy footsteps she took to be her
father's, and Mama calling, "Ned, is it she? Is it truly
Phona?"

She was home.

Safe.

Alone.

Phona sat and unfolded the heavy cloak that was wrapped
warmly around her. Hades' doing. It smelled of his scent. But
she had only a moment to feel the heaviness of her heart.
Within seconds Papa burst through the stable door, pulling
Mama along by one wrist.

"Phona! Phona, my baby! Oh, Phona, Phona!" Her
mother threw herself into the pile of straw beside her,
wrapping her arms around Phona and rocking her, sobbing.

"Oh, Mama." Phona returned the embrace, tears running
down her own cheeks. "I am home. Do not cry. I am here
and well. I have suffered no harm. None at all."

A heavy arm fell around her shoulders. She turned her
head to see her father, down on one knee beside her, his own
face wet. "Ah, Phona, my girl." He sniffed loudly.

Mama's words were lost altogether in her sobs. Phona
could even hear Ned clearing his throat. She gave up trying
to be brave, and let her own sobs mingle with her mother's.

She cried for joy at being home again, for hearing her
parents' grief and relief, for missing them and, at last, for the
man she would never see again. But all tears come eventually to an end. She and Mama each finally choked to silence
and regarded one another.

"Oh, Phona. You have straw in your hair." Mama plucked
at the prickly wisps, sniffing.

"Here, lass, let's have a look at you." Papa placed hands

on each of her shoulders and turned her to face him. "You are well? You have not been hurt?"

"No, Papa. I assure you. I have been treated with nothing but kindness." Phona leaned over and kissed his cheek.

Her father scowled. "I want the truth, my girl. Look me in the eye. I must know."

"I promise you, Papa. No one offered me any offense at all. Word of a Hathersage." Phona smiled, thinking of the last time she had uttered those words.

"Well… Humph. Well, I suppose we will have the whole story soon enough." He got to his feet.

"Oh, George. Don't bother her now." Mama took the hand offered by her husband and also stood. "She has just been returned to us."

Phona took her father's other hand and followed them to her feet. She saw Old Ned standing a little apart, wiping at his eyes. She crossed to him and clasped his shoulders, kissing him lightly on the cheek. "I'm home, Ned. All is well."

"Aye, but if I'd o' kept a better eye on you…"

"No blame falls on you, Ned. It was all the result of my own foolishness. If I had not avoided you and ridden off our property, it would never have happened."

And I would never have met him.

Phona wiped her eyes. She would not ruin her homecoming for them all with a long face. They would believe then, after all, that he had raped her. She would never convince Papa otherwise if she moped about. Turning back to her parents, she took her father's arm. He offered his other one to her mother, but she insisted in escorting her daughter, an arm around her waist.

"Where did that riding habit come from, dear? It is rather handsome, though a bit crushed." She wrinkled her nose. "And smelling of horse, of course."

"I should think so." Phona smiled. Depend upon Mama

to think of clothes at a time like this—or at any other time. And to find fault with them. "I have ridden quite a long way."

"Why did the blackguard leave you in the stable?" her father growled. "Did he dare not show his cowardly face at the door?"

"Well…" Phona searched for just the correct words. It would not do to defend Hades. Her shrewd father would become suspicious immediately. "I believe he had need for…a bit of discretion. And I was fast asleep when we arrived."

"What the devil do you mean by 'discretion'?"

"How could you ride while sleeping?"

Both her parents spoke at the same time. Phona chuckled. "He mentioned that he wished to be neither shot nor arrested. I found that understandable. And as for riding, he carried me the last few miles. I was quite done up."

"Oh, my poor baby! We must get you to the house. A nice warm bath is what you need, and a nice cup of tea, and some of Cook's fresh scones." Mama gave her an assessing glance. "I'm sure you have lost weight. Your cheeks are quite hollow."

"That sounds wonderful, Mama." And it did. Home, her own clothes, a bath and some of Cook's fine pastries. Mama's complaints. Wonderful.

If only she did not miss him so.

On consideration, Phona concluded that her own clothes, while comfortably familiar, were not all that wonderful, after all. Why had she so defiantly chosen such dark colors? She missed the lovely rose and the green dinner gowns that Hades had brought her. Too bad she could not bring them home.

But that might have set off all manner of speculation on the part of her family. The dresses were far more revealing than any she owned. Until she could persuade her mother to plan a shopping expedition to London—no difficult task, that—she would have to make do with a surfeit of white.

Since arriving home a week before, she had endured interrogation after interrogation from both her father and her mother. Papa's, at least, were straightforward, if delicately phrased.

Was she sure she had *suffered no insult?* What was the name of her abductor? Where had she been held prisoner? Phona had, of course, felt completely unequal to explaining to her father the difference between a prisoner and a guest who was not allowed to leave. So she did not try.

Even trying made her miss Hades all the more.

She might have given a more complete description of Lord Hades' appearance, but while she would not lie to Papa, she gave a deliberately vague account. After all, he did cut a rather distinctive figure. She would not contribute to his arrest.

"Evidently I know something about the affair that you do not. Just a week ago a band of thieves was apprehended exactly where you describe. Quite a commotion."

Papa leaned back and blotted his lips on his serviette. "Apparently, they had been robbing the homes of noblemen for some time and hiding the booty in caves on Pointeforte's land. I thought it must have been them who had taken you."

He cleared his throat. "Gave me quite a turn to think those outlaws had you. Brought in a young upstart who was seen about the *ton* last season. Hubert Hardesty. Shocking."

"Oh, yes! But what could you expect of *that* young man." Mama leaned forward, relishing her next revelation. "His sister, Celeste, was not at all the thing. Behaved appallingly with both Lord Pointeforte and his cousin. And she actually wore stolen jewels to a masquerade! Can you imagine? They were recognized, of course. I don't doubt that led to the downfall of all."

"Now, now, my love," Papa chided gently. "That does not work out. Celeste Hardesty's arrest occurred *last* season. She has been transported—as her brother soon will be, I don't doubt."

Mama waved a dismissive hand. "Clearly her fault."

The veteran of many such discussions, Papa shrugged and returned his attention to his beef. Phona sipped from the tiny glass of wine Mama allowed to be set by her place at table and smiled.

What would Mama say if Phona revealed that she had developed a taste for that manliest of all beverages, port? Or that she had worn nothing but a nightshirt in the presence of two men? That one of them had helped her bathe. That it had not mattered.

Phona could see that she had been correct, weeks ago. Nothing was the same anymore. Oh, it looked the same. Mama appeared a bit drawn, and yes, even a bit older. But she still dismissed logic with cheerful abandon. She still loved the frivolous. She still corrected Phona's deportment and suggested endless adjustments to her hair and clothes. Mama would never accept her just as she was.

Phona sighed. If she did not succeed this year as a debutante, it would not be for lack of effort on Mama's part.

No, Mama was the same as she had always been. She would not accept her daughter for who she was.

It was Phona who had changed.

Nonetheless, it was her mother's interrogations which most disturbed her. Mama saw into her woman's soul in a way that Papa could never do. Her questions, oblique and innocent-sounding, cut closer to that which Phona most wanted to keep hidden.

How foolish she would look to her ambitious mother if she admitted that she had fallen in love with her kidnapper! An outlaw. A man with no eye and no hand. No future.

And yet… Phona knew that Mama knew. And Mama

would not rest until she knew how far that love had taken her daughter.

Thank God Phona had no reason to flinch when she looked her mother in the eye.

Well, here she was again. At a ball.

In maidenly white.

They had arrived in London late for the Season. Phona had been obliged to insist that she had quite recovered from her *ordeal,* as Mama insisted on calling it. Ordeal, indeed! But she could not protest the description too much, lest her wise and suspicious parent interpret the protest with complete accuracy.

Phona was glad now that she had come. The shopping and parties and balls served as a welcome distraction, not only keeping her from dwelling what she had lost, but deflecting some of Mama's scrutiny. Mama loved the Season and dived into its entertainments wholeheartedly.

They had even arrived at an accommodation regarding fashion. Phona had quickly seen that a refusal to wear white this year would immediately be perceived by Mama as an admission of ineligibility, so she had been obliged to compromise. She had their favorite mantua-maker, Madame LeBlanc, to thank for the successful negotiation.

Standing with a swath of blindingly white silk draped across her bosom, Phona had stared at the mirror and wrinkled her nose. How could she possibly avoid wearing it? "Mama, don't you think that it makes me look just a little pulled?"

"Now, Phona. I know you dislike white, but…"

"If I may, my lady, I believe that particular shade may not be the most becoming choice for Miss Hathersage?" The modiste whisked away the offending fabric and signaled to her assistant. Immediately a new bolt appeared, white, yet not quite so dazzlingly so. "Here, you see. A little softer tone."

Phona saw her chance. "I like this much better, Mama. It would make a perfectly ravishing ball gown." Ravishing? Surely she had never before used so outrageous an adjective to describe a garment, let alone a white ball gown.

Mama stepped back and gazed at her consideringly. "I do believe you are right, Phona. The effect is more delicate, and it will match the white kid gloves to perfection."

Wonder of wonders! Mama actually thought she was right.

Heaving a sigh of relief, Phona leaped into the discussion of styles. Eventually, while the gown was by no means as revealing as those she had worn with Hades, she and Madame LeBlanc between them had prevented Mama from wrapping her to the ears with folds of white fabric.

And while Mama seemed in an agreeable mood, Phona had seized the opportunity to become rapturous over several other swaths of subtly toned materials, taking care to include a dusty rose and a soft green.

Having never seen Phona in raptures over any form of clothing, Mama was filled with delight at her interest, so they had placed orders for a whole new wardrobe.

"And if you should form an alliance this Season, these may form part of your trousseau, so the expense will be quite justified."

Phona could only wonder if Papa would think so.

So here she was again. Whitely maidenlike.

And utterly eligible for it.

But tonight she was determined to dance. She had worn her thick curly hair in the style favored by Lord Hades, held a little back from her face with a ribbon, loose ringlets falling to her shoulders.

Mama had taken one look and shrieked for her own maid. "Phona, dearest! You cannot wear your hair in that style to a ball. You are too old, and it looks very…untidy. Do let Halby pin it up for you."

But tonight Phona was determined to go as herself, whether Mama approved of her as she was or not. "Mama, your hair is *so* lovely in a smooth chignon. But, alas, you know mine will not stay, and I want to enjoy the dancing."

In the unlikely event that I am asked.

Mama sighed in turn. *What am I to do with this awkward girl?* writ large upon her angelic face. "Very well, but, Halby, could you possibly…" She waved a resigned hand. "Do…do…*something?* And, Halby, if you please…the freckles."

Halby had not become a highly paid lady's dresser without possessing a large measure of diplomatic sagacity. Without voicing her opinion, she dabbed a bit of powder on the offending freckles. Then she added an abundance of flowers to Phona's hair, tucking them around the ribbon and scattering them amongst the dark auburn curls.

In her own way, Halby was an artist. Regarding herself in the mirror, Phona decided she looked like a wood nymph in a romantic painting. For once she had not allowed Mama's despair to dismay her. What did she care for the opinion of the *ton?*

One man thought her beautiful. He had told her so. If only she had the mirror he had brought her, perhaps she would believe it, as well. Phona blinked back tears. He would not see her tonight.

He would never see her again.

To her absolute astonishment, Lord Hades had been proved correct. Blushing as usual with her feelings of awkwardness, her flower-decked hair flowing untidily to her shoulders, Phona had become an immediate success.

Her hostess had been kept busy presenting young men who had requested introductions, all of whom asked her to dance, plied her with lemonade and invited her to stroll in the moonlit garden. All of whom seemed hopelessly insipid.

How could she help but compare these would-be gallants to the stalwart Hades? How could they but fall short?

Still, being a success at a ball was ever so much nicer than sitting by the wall. Phona loved the dancing, and she found that she was not required to offer much to the conversation. The insipid young men all had a great deal to say about themselves.

Was this to be her fate for the rest of her life?

Listening to insipid men? Heaven forfend!

During a pause for the musicians to rest, Phona had managed to slip away to the ladies' withdrawing room for a moment to collect herself. She found that her spirits swooped and dived liked swallows. One moment she was in alt; the next she was fighting tears.

The new attention was heady stuff for a wallflower of such long standing. Yet the face of each new gentleman reminded her that he was not Lord Hades. That she would *never* dance with Lord Hades.

Sometimes Phona would think she saw him in the throng, then the man would turn toward her and the illusion would disappear. Now, as she stood in the door to the ballroom, she had that impression again.

A tall man, wearing black, with dark hair curling over the edge of his collar. Something about the set of his broad shoulders... In spite of herself, Phona's heart quickened.

Then, once again, the man turned toward her. Two functional eyes glanced in her direction. In his left hand he held a glass of champagne. His right shook her father's hand. Apparently, an acquaintance of Papa's.

Phona sighed. She really must desist from seeing him everywhere, in thinking of him all the time. She moved through the crowd, back to the spot where Mama held court. As always, gentlemen of all ages surrounded her mother. Phona decided it was not worth the effort to force her way through. No one would notice her.

Just as she was looking about for an empty chair, her father appeared at her elbow. Detecting a very subdued hint of excitement in his demeanor, she raised an inquiring eyebrow. The gentleman she had seen earlier with Papa stood beside him.

"Phona, my dear, may I present Lord Pointeforte? My lord, my daughter, Persephone."

She gazed up into twinkling blue eyes—two of them. Phona glanced to his left. Yes, he *was* holding a glass. She looked again at his face and frowned. No beard, but… No. Surely not. She was doing it again. He bowed.

"Leopold DeBolsover, at your service, Miss Hathersage. Would you honor me with this dance?" Without giving her a chance to respond, he gave his glass to a passing servant and rushed her into a forming set.

On hearing his voice Phona stumbled over her own feet. "Hades! It… It… It *is* you!"

"I believe so." Grinning a familiar grin, he caught her deftly and righted her before she fell. "Be careful in exclaiming *Hades,* Miss Hathersage. People will think you are cursing."

The dance parted them. Phona tripped over the feet of the partner to whom Hades passed her. Muttering apologies, she was whirled back to… To whom? Hades? *Pointeforte?* Could it be?

"Take care, Miss Hathersage, or I shall have to carry you."

"Beast! How could you do this to me? My heart almost stopped when you spoke. But your eye—"

"The eye is true, the patch false."

"But you never removed it! Not the whole time I was—"

"No, and the dratted thing itched like the devil."

"How can you—"

The dance once more swept her to the next gentleman. He received her with a certain degree of caution with respect to his footwear. Phona was once again obliged to hold her tongue, smiling stiffly, until the steps brought her back to…to…

Oh, bother!

Leopold DeBolsover claimed her as she came through the figure. Bowing to the others in the set, he drew her out of it and propelled her hastily out the French doors to the terrace. "I believe, Miss Hathersage, that we could both do with a breath of air."

Ignoring the glances cast in their direction, he guided her out and into a deep patch of shadow. They had barely cleared the door when she rounded on him.

"And your hand! How could you have concealed *that?*"

For answer he offered both gloved hands to her, then firmly grasped the left with the right. The fingers collapsed into an unnatural clump.

Phona turned away, looking out over the papapet. "How did you lose it?"

"At Trafalgar. Why have you never asked before?"

"You would not have told me, and…and everything about you was so mysterious. It seemed all of a piece. But I felt sure it happened during a sea battle. Are you truly the Marquess of Pointeforte?"

"Yes. Miss Hathersage, please look at me."

Turning, she stared into his face. Studied its contours. The slight tan of its upper reaches. The blue-black shadow cloaking the jaw. The hitherto hidden cleft in his chin.

Similar, but not the same. A very different man.

Phona lowered her gaze to his hands. Somehow he had straightened his fingers into a normal appearance. "Why did you wait so long to reveal yourself to me? Why choose such a public place?"

"For the first, I have been obliged to finish the business which first brought us together. I would not allow it to place you in harm's way again." He seemed to be thinking for a moment. At last he said, "As for the second, I wished to be presented to you publicly. I do not want our acquaintance to appear clandestine."

"Acquaintance? You seem such a stranger now."

"Strangeness may be corrected through association. I am still the same man, Miss Hathersage. And I would like for us to be friends."

Friends. He wanted merely to be friends. Phona lifted her chin. She must not let him see her hurt.

Just then they heard a voice at the gallery door. "Phona? Phona, dearest."

"It is Mama."

"So it is." He raised his voice slightly. "She is here, Lady Hathersage." He led her back to her mother and bowed. "Miss Hathersage became overly warm with the dancing. I thought it best to bring her outside for a moment."

Mama flashed her most dazzling smile. "You are too kind, my lord. Persephone is not accustomed to so much dancing."

Thus neatly returning Phona to her proper place.

Swish. Swish. The stone caressed the blade. The man holding it slowly ran his tongue over his lips. Swish. Swish. "Well, do you think you can find him now that he is at the end of your arm?"

His companion prudently kept his hands off of the table. The slice in his wrist had almost healed. "I have already found him once, hiding right in the midst of us, the bloody traitor. I thought he was dead, but now I fear the bastard has killed two of my best assassins."

"Yet his lordship continues to live." The man cautiously ran his finger along the knife, smiling at the drop of blood forming on his finger.

The other man scowled. "You know I have been...otherwise engaged."

His only answer was a nasty laugh. The man with the

knife regarded the blood running down his hand with loving attention. Then he began to lick it off his finger, running his tongue from the base to the tip. "And now I will have to tend to it—as you are...otherwise engaged."

His companion hastily rose and left the room.

Chapter Nine

Leo repressed a small twinge of disappointment. The fun of surprising her had not quite lived up to expectation. On seeing her, he realized that he had missed her a great deal, but the lady had seemed very cool.

Perhaps she had been *too* surprised. Disoriented by his change in appearance. Angry about the deception. Or dismayed by the grotesque crumpling of his left glove.

She had turned away from it.

Away from him.

Leo shoved the hurt away. What had he expected? Any woman would be revolted. Had he really believed she would be different? He only hoped the story of their stay together never came out. If it did, there would be only one course of action open to them. He prayed she would not be forced to marry him.

Still, they needed to appear to the world as friends and neighbors. He must renew their acquaintance gradually. If he could dodge her lady mother long enough, they would have a longer talk. In private. But for now, there was her mother. And—

"Leo, by Jove! Where have you been hiding yourself?"

Leo suppressed a grimace. "Good evening, Rob. Lady Hathersage, Miss Hathersage, may I present my cousin, Robert DeBolsover?"

Rob bowed deeply to each woman. "My lady. Miss Hathersage. I am completely at your service." Turning back to Leo, he grinned. "Depend upon you, cos, always to be in the company of the loveliest ladies."

Leo raised one eyebrow. "Indeed. And where have you been? I have not seen you since I came to town."

"Oh, I've been rusticating," his cousin answered carelessly.

A bit too carelessly, Leo thought. "You expect me to believe that you find the attractions of Maplewood superior to those of London during the Season?"

Rob grinned. "Perhaps I am gaining wisdom with age. Miss Hathersage, may I have this dance?"

She flicked a glance at Leo. "Why, yes, thank you, Mr. DeBolsover."

Leo watched in annoyance as she walked away on the arm of his dratted cousin.

When had he become so possessive of her?

And when would his suspicions of his deeply loved cousin be put to rest?

Lord Hathersage, clad in his dressing gown and slippers, sank onto the sofa in his wife's boudoir and propped his feet on the footrest with a sigh of relief. She had sent her maid away and sat at her dressing table brushing her own silky golden hair.

As always, the sight of her started the stirrings of desire. Almost forty years old, and by Jove, still an established beauty. He counted himself a lucky man. "Did you enjoy the ball, my love?"

She turned toward him and favored him with a seductive smile. "Oh, yes, indeed. I found the music delightful and the company quite congenial."

"Phona seems to have been quite the success this evening. I believe she danced with every gentleman in attendance."

His wife's brow puckered. "Little wonder. With her hair arranged in such a way, she appeared quite wanton."

"Oh, come now, Demetra." Lord Hathersage rose and came to stand behind his wife's chair. "Phona? Wanton?"

"Oh, no. But perhaps the gentlemen thought—"

"Nonsense." He took the brush from her and began to run it through the luxuriant mass. "Phona looked the very picture of virginal innocence—all in white with the flowers in her hair. It was that which attracted the gentlemen, you may be sure."

Demetra leaned back against him and sighed. "If you say so, my lord. You would know better than I."

Her lord set the brush down and clasped her hand, pulling her to her feet. "Sometimes I do not understand you, Demetra." He led her to the sofa. "You spare no expense, no effort to make Phona a success, but you are never satisfied. Why, even Leo DeBolsover could not keep his eyes off her!"

"Exactly." She leaned against his shoulder.

He peered down at her. "Exactly what?"

"I cannot be pleased with Pointeforte as a suitor for Phona's hand."

"For God's sake, woman! Why the devil not? The man is a marquess—and rich enough to buy an abbey. Every mother in the room but you was throwing her daughter in his way." He pulled his lady a bit closer. "Come now, my love. What is it that troubles you about him?"

"His reputation is not what I could wish for Phona. There are allegations that he was not Pointeforte's true son, you know."

"Poppycock! Leo was born but seven months after his father's death."

She snuggled closer. "Many children are born of a seven-month pregnancy. And Lady Pointeforte *did* take up with Lord Alborough as soon as she was delivered of him. One must wonder."

"But she reared him with his brother and cousin at Darkwood Park, just as she should. With Aldborough's help, I admit, but that claptrap was started earlier by his uncle and, I'll warrant, revived by his cousin after Percival died. He wanted that seat for himself. But Parliament ruled in favor of Leo these three years ago."

"And then they say he *did* rape that young person. And she was badly beaten, I'm told."

He gave her a sharp look. "Demetra, what ails you? We know that tart's brother to be a thief and a conniver. And Leo's cousin's admitted the girl had been his mistress. Clearly another unsuccessful ploy to gain the marquessate. I have known Pointeforte since he was a lad, and I've not known a better one. You have never before taken those allegations seriously. In fact, you were hot in his defense at the time."

"But he is mutilated." She shuddered slightly against him.

Hathersage sighed. "There is that. Perhaps revolting to a young lady in spite of his cleverly wired gloves. But if he approaches me about Phona, I shall see that she knows about the amputation. She must make her own decision."

"I cannot believe she could tolerate it. I could not."

His lordship favored his wife with a speculative glance. "But, if I know you, and I do, you have yet to come to the point. Out with it."

"Well, then…since she has returned from her abduction, she has been…well, different. We would not want to offend a man as powerful as Pointeforte."

"My God!" Hathersage leaned forward to gaze into her face. "Never tell me that you believe, after all, that the bastard who took her dishonored her."

She lifted her face to his. "No, George. I believe that she fell in love with him."

* * *

The bouquet of white roses almost filled the foyer of the Hathersage town house. Their fragrance could be enjoyed even upstairs in Phona's bedchamber. Although bouquets of flowers from all the insipid young men she had danced with last night sat on every available table in the house, the roses quite overwhelmed all the rest.

Hades had sent them, of course, though the card read Pointeforte. Phona was finding Pointeforte to be just as overwhelming as his flowers. But had she not found Hades to be so in the early stages of their acquaintance?

The second she had recognized him, her wits and her coordination had flown. She had lost count of the number of toes she had bruised in the dancing.

How in the world could it be possible that the dashing outlaw in whose house she had stayed was none other than her noble neighbor? She could not remember meeting him before, but there was little wonder in that. He had been away at sea for several years and, she had heard, had become reclusive for a time after his injury. If he had come to visit her parents before he went to sea ten years ago, she would have remained firmly in the care of her governess.

But more than anything, Phona felt stunned by the change in his appearance. This man *sounded* like Hades. He *moved* like Hades. But he looked proper and stylish and…and…

It was all so confusing. She was—had been?—so in love with Hades. Pointeforte seem quite a different person. Hades lived a life of rebellion and danger. Pointeforte lived a life of… Of what? Apparently a life of deception and danger.

Had Hades deceived her also? She could not say that he had. He had simply refused to explain who he was or why he had brought her to his house in the gorge.

But could she say that Pointeforte had actually deceived her? Yes, by God! By becoming Hades. And he had then bereaved her by taking Hades away. She felt as if Hades had died.

Drat it! This was one man, not two. She must now deal with Pointeforte, whoever that might be.

He, at least, could not be called insipid.

The next afternoon as she sat with Mama in the drawing room receiving a seemingly endless parade of callers, Samuels, the butler, came into the room with a note in his hand. He started toward Phona.

Mama spoke sharply. "You may give that to me, Samuels."

The butler checked, turned in his tracks and was about to extend his hand to her when Papa spoke from the doorway.

"Samuels."

The butler turned made another about-face—and marched to Papa. Papa took the paper from him and read it while Samuels beat a hasty retreat. Thereupon, Papa strolled across the room and handed the note to Phona. A speaking look flew from her mother to her father.

Oh, dear. That little exchange would surely provide for a bout of recriminations later. Phona opened the note and had just time enough to peruse its contents when Mrs. Rowsley and her daughter were announced. Papa hastily bowed and made his excuses.

Mrs. Rowsley sniffed and wrinkled her nose. "My dear, your house smells like a florist's shop."

"Well, yes. Pointeforte's roses, you know." Mama bestowed a restrained peck on her friend's cheek.

"He sent me flowers, too, of course." Suzette Rowsley glanced around the bedecked room, her expression assessing the number of floral offerings.

Phona declined to enter the competition. This situation called for distraction. She patted the sofa beside her. "Do come, Suzette, and tell me how you enjoyed last night's festivities."

"Oh, amazingly well!" The young lady launched into a description of the delights she had experienced, then flowed without a halt into the marvelous additions to her trousseau she had recently acquired. From long acquaintance, Phona estimated that would take up the rest of the visit. She listened with one ear and considered how best to get away.

Her mother and Mrs. Rowsley had their heads together, buzzing like a hive of bees. A few words drifted across the room.

"It must be true. That girl… She was his cousin's mistress, too, you know."

"His mother… Lord Aldborough…"

"I was never so shocked, my dear, indeed…"

At half after four Phona stood. "Mrs. Rowsley, Suzette, I beg that you will excuse me." An imp of mischief tickled her for a moment. Yes, in spite of her confusion, she would greatly enjoy delivering *this* announcement. It should create quite a flutter.

"I must change. I am to drive in the park with Lord Pointeforte at five, and I do not wish to keep his horses standing."

She swept out of the room, three pairs of eyes boring into her back.

Leo arrived at the Hathersage establishment precisely at five o'clock, driving a matched pair of shiny blacks harnessed to a black curricle with the wheels picked out in silver. He consulted his pocket watch and, satisfied, nodded to Aelfred. "Take their heads. I shan't be a moment."

He jumped to the ground and bounded up the stairs. The butler opened to his knock, and Leo found himself being shown into a small parlor. He declined the offered seat, and prowled around the room while the lady was notified of his arrival.

Why was he feeling so anxious about this encounter? It was not as though he and Miss Hathersage were unacquainted. And he was *not* courting her. He simply wanted to explain what had happened. What was so difficult about that?

Besides the chilly reception he had received the previous evening.

He had only time to pace around the room twice before the lady came in. She wore an ensemble the precise green of the dinner gown he had brought her. Soft ringlets peeked from under her hat, framing her face. She was blushing.

She looked perfectly delectable.

Leo quickly put the thought aside. "Good afternoon, Miss Hathersage."

"Good afternoon, my lord. I hope I didn't keep you waiting."

"Not at all." He opened the door and ushered her out into the foyer, careful not to brush against her with his left glove.

The butler showed them out, and they emerged into the sunshine.

"It *is* a lovely day for a drive." Miss Hathersage gazed down the steps. "Oh! We are to ride in your curricle. I love sporting carriages, although Mama says they are not at all the thing for ladies."

"Do you drive?"

"A bit. Sometimes Papa allows me to take the ribbons— Is that Aelfred?"

"Have a care. You cannot appear to know him."

"But…but he has been my friend. How can I…?" She turned to him, frowning.

"I know. He wanted to see you. You will be able to speak to him once we are under way."

"Oh, dear. I am not good at deception."

"One of your more endearing traits, Miss Hathersage." He handed her into the curricle. Vaulting up, he took up the reins, whereupon Aelfred hurried to the rear of the equipage and climbed onto the groom's perch. Leo gave his horses the office to start, and they set off up the street.

Phona twisted around to look over her shoulder. "Oh, Aelfred! How happy I am to see you. Are you well?"

"Aye, miss, but don't turn when you speak. It don't look seemly."

"But…" She let out an exasperated-sounding sigh and faced front again. "I don't like this. I liked it much better when we could converse as we liked."

"Perhaps you will have another opportunity." His lordship paused while he negotiated passage around a knot of carriages in the crowded street. "I requested your company today because I feel certain you have many unanswered questions."

"Yes. I do indeed." Phona frowned. Started to speak. Hesitated. Then blurted out, "My lord, were you in league with the thieves?"

"For a time, yes."

Phona drew in a short breath.

He glanced sideways at her. "Nay, do not look at me in that suspicious way. We got on well enough when you believed me, without a doubt, to be one of them."

Phona ducked her head and chewed her lip. That was true enough. Why did it now seem reprehensible?

Before she could answer, he added, "I was aiding the authorities in apprehending them, Miss Hathersage."

"Oh." Phona's thoughts were whirling. She looked up into his face. "This is all very odd. Before, I simply accepted who and what I thought you were. Now I find—"

"That I am someone and something else entirely."

"Yes, someone who is—or at least should be—eminently respectable."

"As I hope I am." He returned her gaze seriously. "Am I less acceptable in my respectable persona?"

Phona considered carefully. Had she succumbed to the romantic notion of falling in love with an outlaw? Had she been so immature? God forbid.

Until she was able to answer those telling questions, however, perhaps it would be best to equivocate. She cocked her head to one side and studied him. "Well... I do miss your lovely beard."

Pointeforte laughed aloud. "And no doubt my patch and my hook."

"As to that— They were part and parcel of who I believed you to be."

"I see. So...?"

"So I think I will have to get to know you again." Phona was quiet for a moment, thinking. Then she asked, "Why did you embark on such a risky venture?"

He easily guided his horses through a tangle. "That's a long story."

Phona glanced at him expectantly.

Pointeforte took a long breath and finally said, "I have an enemy. One who attacks from hiding. To date he has stirred up doubts about my paternity and my right to the marquessate. He has attempted to have me hung for rape—"

At Phona's gasp he turned and gave her an assessing look. "Surely you do not believe me guilty of *that?*"

"No. Oh, no! How could I? With me you were the soul of delicacy."

"I am relieved to hear it." His mouth quirked on the corner. "It required considerable effort."

Memories and feeling flooded Phona. "Always a gentleman."

His expression softened. "You see—I am quite respectable, after all."

"So you are." Phona smiled. "But please continue the tale of how you came to be an outlaw. You have an enemy...?"

"Yes. In addition to the previously mentioned offenses he has tried at least twice to have me killed."

"Oh, my!" Phona's hand flew to her mouth. "When you returned to the lodge wounded—"

"That was the second time. Although it is possible that the assassins were trying to steal the goods I took from the cave."

"Those lovely gowns." Phona sighed. "I do wish I might have brought them home with me."

Pointeforte chuckled again. "Probably not wise. Having once belonged to my sister-in-law, the dowager, they would certainly be recognized."

"Indeed? How curious! They had been stolen?"

"Straight out of my own home while I played quartermaster to the marauders." He shook his head at the irony. "And the mirror once graced a dressing table at Darkwood Park. But you shall have that back."

"And your sister-in-law?"

"My older brother, Percival's, widow. She remains at the estate, in the dower house with my grandmother and my great-aunt."

"But I still do not understand. How could becoming an outlaw—"

"Address the situation with my unknown enemy?" She nodded, and he continued. "I thought him involved with the ring of thieves who had been pillaging noble houses for over a year. You see, the young woman he sent to entrap me for rape was later arrested wearing stolen jewels."

"How foolish!" Phona shook her head.

His lordship's expression grew grim. "Yes, very. I believe she now resides in Australia. But I find I cannot lament her fate. Had she had her way, I should have found myself dangling at the end of a rope."

Damn it all! She had given Aelfred a warmer welcome than she had given him. Not that it mattered.

Leo guided his pair carefully through the congested drive of the park. Riders and carriages clogged the way as people paused to greet friends and gossip. He patiently touched his hat to the ladies and exchanged a few words with the gentlemen of his acquaintance, all the while chafing at the restraint.

As much as he enjoyed escorting the prettiest lady present, it was all he could do not to drive across the lawns and abduct her once more. She sat beside him, smiling shyly at those who greeted them. Her sweet scent drifted up to him through those of horse and human.

Suddenly, to his great annoyance, he glimpsed Rob coming toward them, though still some distance away in the throng. His cousin hailed him and waved, indicating by gestures that they should attempt to close the gap which lay between them.

Ha! Not likely. He had seen that gleam in his relative's eye before. His interest lay not in Leo, but in the lady at Leo's side.

"Isn't that your cousin riding the tall bay?" Miss Hathersage waved back at Rob.

Leo growled, "Yes, I believe it seems to be," and allowed his carriage to be crowded back a space.

"I believe he wants to visit with us."

"Hmm. Possibly."

Miss Hathersage gave him a puzzled glance. "Do you not wish to speak with him?"

Leo shrugged.

She turned toward him, frowning. "He was ever so pleasant last evening. I enjoyed dancing with him."

"That, Miss Hathersage, is exactly what concerns me." Again, Leo let a rider come between them and his troublesome relation.

Her brows came together sharply. "You are making fun of me."

"Not at all." He returned the frown. "I know when my cousin is interested in a lady."

The frown deepened. "And why, my lord, does that cause you vexation?"

"I?" He raised one eyebrow. "I am not vexed."

"Eh, me lord, and who do you think to gull?" Behind Leo, Aelfred laughed aloud. "I been knowing you and Mr. Rob many a year, and I ain't never seen the day the two of you didn't vie one with the other. If he fancied aught—"

Leo shook his head. "Nonsense. That was but the nature of young boys. This—"

"Part and parcel of the same." Aelfred spoke firmly. "And for that matter, if the lady fancies him, what will you do? Steal her away, again?"

Resignedly, Leo guided his horses out of the traffic and into a wooded lane. "I am strongly considering it. She seems to have liked me better the last time I did so."

Miss Hathersage blushed and murmured a demur.

"Hallo there! Miss Hathersage, delighted to see you again. Servant, Leo." While Leo had wasted time in argumentation, his cousin had kept his eye to his goal. Rob pulled up beside them, and Leo reined in his blacks.

"Your servant, Rob. I see that you remember Miss Hathersage." Leo's lip curled in a wry smile.

"I could hardly forget. How do you fare, Aelfred?" Rob swung down from his horse and handed the reins to Leo's henchman. "May I come up?"

Leo grunted an ungracious acquiescence, and without waiting for it, his cousin climbed up to the curricle bench, obliging Miss Hathersage to slide over to make room. This arrangement placed her womanly curves snugly against Leo.

A circumstance with which he could hardly find fault.

Except that they were equally snug against Rob on the other side. Damnation! What difference did it make to him if Rob was eyeing her?

While all this rearrangement was under way, Leo had allowed his attention momentarily to drift away from his horses. They had sidled farther from the crowded drive of the promenade. He took a firmer grasp on the reins, but for some reason they seemed to be on the fret and fought the bits. Suddenly they shied, and the curricle swerved.

At that precise second, he heard the shot.

And the unmistakable whistle of the ball.

Chapter Ten

The horses tried to bolt, plunging and rearing.

Hades fought to control them.

His cousin pushed Phona unceremoniously to the floor of the carriage.

Panic broke out on the promenade. Coachmen abandoned the drive and whipped their teams across the grass. Gentlemen escorting ladies followed suit, racing them out of harm's way. About half of the mounted men did likewise, but the rest charged into the trees, shouting. A small cloud of pitch-black smoke rose slowly from the woods, dissipating into the cloudless sky.

"There!" Rob pointed and leaped off the curricle, reaching for his mount.

It was not there.

Neither was Aelfred.

He turned in a rapid circle. "Aelfred! Man, where the devil did you…?"

"Do you see him?" Having brought his horses to a stand, Hades twisted in his seat, looking behind him. Phona tried to get back to her place on the seat, but he put his hand on her head and firmly held her below the level of the dashboard.

Phona threw up a hand. "For heaven's sake, my lord! Be there never so many assassins amongst those trees, they are certainly, by now, in full flight."

He glanced down at her. "And be you never so brave, Miss Hathersage, you will stay where you are." His hand did not budge. If anything, he leaned harder.

"Leo, Leo, over here!" Rob's voice carried to them over the tumult.

Hades cast a look over his shoulder. "My God! Aelfred!"

He released his pressure, and Phona rose to her knees. Peeping around the side of the carriage, she saw Rob kneeling beside Aelfred, who was trying to sit up. Hades made as if to jump down, bethought himself of his horses and hesitated.

"Give me the reins, my lord. I shall hold them." She lifted herself to the bench and held out a hand.

After a moment Hades gave her the reins and swung down, already running as his feet touched the ground. Sensing a lighter hand, the horses considered another break for freedom from the tumult. Phona put a firm stop to that and brought them about so that she could see what had transpired.

Clearly, Aelfred had taken the ball. Rob DeBolsover held his handkerchief hard against the groom's shoulder while Hades dashed across the grass. Phona pulled the curricle nearer.

"He's bleeding badly." Mr. DeBolsover lifted his head to glance at Hades, who fell to his knees beside them. "He needs a doctor."

"Get him into the carriage." Hades put his arm around his henchman's waist and lifted. His cousin draped the man's arm over his own shoulders, and, trying awkwardly to keep pressure on the wound, the two DeBolsovers hurried him toward the curricle. Phona steadied the pair, but the men stopped beside her, their expressions perplexed.

"How the devil are we to do this?" Mr. DeBolsover gazed up at the narrow bench. "Miss Hathersage can hardly hold his weight, and you cannot drive and…"

Before she could protest, Hades said, "*She* must drive. You will hold him, and I shall ride up behind and reach over to stanch the wound."

Phona thought a bitter tone tinged his voice. "At least I have enough hands for that."

Leo was once again humiliated when he had Miss Hathersage halt the carriage so that he could send a street lad for his doctor. He could not hold his handkerchief against Aelfred's shoulder with his right hand and reach into his pocket for a coin with his left.

He had no left hand.

Only a useless device designed for driving. The contraptions he had devised to act in place of his hand in various situations served well enough for some things, but they could never replace the clever work of fingers.

Rob settled the difficulty by hastily producing a coin of his own, but the inability galled Leo. However, today he could only set his pride aside and do what he must.

Miss Hathersage brought the pair up smartly before the Pointeforte town house. As he sprung down from his perch, he had just time for a moment of appreciation. His blacks were not an easy team to manage, yet she had driven them through the teeming streets of London with skill and precision.

Pluck to the backbone!

Leo again took one side of Aelfred while Rob steadied the other as they walked his henchman up the front steps. He could tell that his old friend was beginning to flag. In a few more minutes, he would collapse completely from loss of blood.

He heard the patter of his lady's feet coming up the stairs

and past them. She preceded them through the door held open by his butler. "In here."

Leo turned to see that she had flung open the door of a small parlor and was directing them into the room with an authoritative finger. He almost chuckled. She had said she was accustomed to managing her parents' household.

She turned to the young footman hovering helplessly in the doorway. "Go fetch the housekeeper and tell her what is afoot. She will know what to bring. Where is the doctor?"

"He should be here soon, if the rascal I sent for him hasn't taken our coin to the nearest tavern instead." Leo eased Aelfred down onto the sofa.

Rob swung the man's feet up. "I promised him another when the sawbones arrives—and a hiding if he doesn't."

"Not that you will find him. However, the *sawbones* has arrived at his behest."

All four of them looked at the door. A tall, gray-haired gentleman was striding through it.

"Ah! Dr. Thomasson." Leo quickly extended his hand. "Thank you for coming so quickly."

Having the grace to look a bit sheepish, Rob headed toward the foyer. "Your most obedient servant, Doctor. Er…my apologies for… Well, you know. I'll go pay off the lad."

The doctor knelt beside the sufferer. "So, Aelfred, you are taking the shots for your master now, are you?"

"Aye, sir. Seems that I am."

The weakness of his voice gave Leo a twinge of anxiety, but he set himself to assist the resourceful lady who had produced a small pair of scissors from her reticule and was busying herself in cutting away Aelfred's coat.

"Thank you, miss." Thomasson grasped the shirt and ripped.

Leo belatedly remembered his manners. "Uh…Miss Hathersage, may I present Dr. Thomasson."

"My pleasure, miss." The doctor did not look up. "Yes, a nasty wound. Where is—ah!" He glanced at the plump housekeeper who came bustling into the room. "Good afternoon, Mrs. Wheelwright. Now…I want the balance of you out of here. Mrs. Wheelwright knows how to assist me."

Miss Hathersage stood reluctantly. "I can also help."

Dr. Thomasson unfastened his bag. "Out."

Leo took her arm and steered her to the door where Rob now leaned. He nodded at his cousin. "Out."

"Right. Out." Rob stepped back and followed them across the hall to the library.

Miss Hathersage had her knuckles pressed to her lips, tears trickling down her cheeks. She sniffed. "Oh, my. I do hope he will be all right. I…I…"

Leo hastily stepped between her and his cousin, directing a warning glance at her. There should be no reason for her to know Aelfred. She choked off a sob and sank into a chair by the fireplace, wiping at the blood that stained her skirt.

"Allow me to offer you a glass of sherry, Miss Hathersage." He reached for the decanter and a glass. "In fact, I suspect we would all be the better for a glass."

"Lord, yes." Rob snatched up a glass and held it out. Leo filled it and carried it to Miss Hathersage. She sipped it cautiously.

Rob sprawled gracelessly into the chair opposite her. "And now, cos, we have a question to answer."

Leo leaned against his desk, wiping blood from his hands with his handkerchief. "And that is?"

His cousin pushed his finger through a hole in the shoulder of his own coat. "At which of us was the bastard shooting?"

"He would hardly have been shooting at my groom."

Lord Hades—that is, Lord Pointeforte—paced restlessly

around the room. Phona leaned back in her chair and tried not to weep. For the last half hour the discussion had raged fruitlessly. Fruitless, except for one thing. It had come to her attention that her head had been within inches of the rent in Mr. DeBolsover's coat.

Meantime, Lord Pointeforte had sent a footman with a note to her home to inform her parents of her whereabouts and well-being. She expected to see her father arrive within minutes. What an afternoon! Exhausted, covered in blood and, belatedly, frightened.

"I should think we may also be sure that he was not aiming at Miss Hathersage." Mr. DeBolsover refilled his glass.

"Of course not." Pointeforte answer quickly. Just a bit *too* quickly. He cast Phona another of those cautioning glances.

She had been afraid to speak at all for fear of revealing a closer acquaintance with Pointeforte than his cousin knew. But she had to agree. "No, he could certainly not be firing at me. I am hardly known in London at all."

At that moment the door opened, and Dr. Thomasson entered. "Well, gentlemen—and Miss Hathersage—the deed is done. I have removed the ball and sewed him up. His mates are carrying him up to his room. I have instructed Mrs. Wheelwright in his care, but she knows that, in any case. As many times as the two of us have patched up the two of you…"

"Will he recover?" Phona fought to keep her voice from breaking. What, after all, should Pointeforte's groom be to her?

"Oh, I should think so. As long as infection does not set in. Old Aelfred is tough as a boot."

"Thank God for that. I'll call tomorrow to ask after him." Mr. DeBolsover rose and made for the door. "I for one should like to get some of this blood off me. Good evening, Miss Hathersage. Most obedient, gentlemen."

"Well, I'm off, too. Send for me if his fever becomes too high. I'll come round in the morning." Thomasson extended his hand, and Pointeforte shook it warmly.

"Thank you, Doctor, for once again putting our household back together." Hades walked the physician to the door and, a few seconds later, returned to the library, coming to stand before Phona.

She looked up at him, tears once more welling in her eyes. "Oh, my lord! I am so afraid for him."

"Don't cry, Miss Hathersage." He looked down at her kindly. "He will mend."

At the sound of his voice—Hades' voice—tears flowed anew. For a moment it seemed that she did know him. But instead of an ancient fortified lodge, she now stood in a huge, handsomely appointed home.

Without looking, she knew that above her were *two* dazzling blue eyes. This was Lord Pointeforte. She was still experiencing two very different men.

And one of them was about to kiss her.

As he bent forward, his expression slowly changed. His hand came up and lifted her chin. Something glinted in the depths of the blue eyes. Phona shut her eyes as his mouth closed over hers, hot and demanding. His fingers slipped behind her head, laced through her curls, holding her fast.

Sensation rushed up from her legs to the top of her head. Her lips parted, and she could feel his tongue against them. Her knees sagged, and he tightened his arm around her to keep her upright. Oh, dear heaven! This seemed so right. So delicious.

So overwhelming.

She pulled back, trying to catch her breath, and pushed at her disheveled hair. Distracted, she stood and gazed about for her hat. Hades raised one eyebrow and smiled crookedly.

As he knelt and retrieved the chapeau, a discreet knock sounded at the door. Phona hastily stepped back from him and clapped her hat on her head, guiltily trying to push her hair up under it. She gave up and took it off again, turning toward the door as Pointeforte called out, "Enter."

The butler opened the door. "Lord Hathersage."

Papa rushed into the room and put an arm around Phona, leaning down to look into her face. "My dear! Are you all right? I came as soon as I received the note."

He turned to Pointeforte. "Thank you for sending it, my lord. At my club I heard the news of a shooting in the park. Set out for home immediately. I knew Persephone's mama would be frantic if she had word of it. And she was." He lowered his voice. "Confound Alicia Rowsley."

"I am quite unhurt, as you can see, Papa." Phona leaned against his shoulder.

"But you are covered in blood!" Her father glanced down at her dress.

"Yes. I fear this gown is quite past praying for. But I was attempting to aid his lordship's groom." In spite of her determination to remain calm, Phona's fingers plucked anxiously at the ribbons of her hat.

"My man took the bullet. Miss Hathersage acted with commendable resolution. While my cousin and I held him in the carriage, she drove my blacks through the city and brought us safely home. But since the crisis has passed, I fear she is now understandably distressed."

Lord Hathersage looked down at his daughter. Phona did her best to appear *un*distressed, but the effort was doomed to failure. She *was* distressed.

"Now, now." Her father patted her arm. "I shall take you home straightaway." He turned back to Pointeforte, giving him a shrewd glance. "For whom was the bullet intended, my lord?"

"I have no idea. The horses shied and put us in its path."

"Odd happening." Lord Hathersage frowned. "Very odd indeed. Well, let me take my young miss home, before her mother storms your door. Thank you again for letting us know she was safe. Your most obedient servant, Pointeforte." He guided Phona to the door.

"Of course, sire." Pointeforte escorted them out.

As they stood on the threshold, Phona turned to him. "Thank you for an otherwise agreeable drive, my lord."

He let out a bark of surprised laughter. "Indeed. My pleasure, Miss Hathersage. My pleasure indeed."

Leo feared that his very presence had once again drawn danger to Persephone Hathersage. And Rob. And Aelfred. In fact, to anyone unwise enough to associate with him.

But then, the hole had been in Rob's coat, not Leo's. In what dealings nefarious enough to draw a bullet might his cousin have embroiled himself?

Or had Rob, after all, been behind all the attempts to do Leo harm? Had he lured them into that lane? He certainly had the most to gain—the marquessate, an impressive fortune, Darkwood Park. And Celeste had been his cousin's mistress.

A twinge of pain squeezed Leo's heart. He had been fighting this battle by himself for far too long, and he felt very much alone. He could not even discuss his present difficulties with his boyhood companion.

Please, God, let it not be Rob.

And please, let not the target have been the courageous lady who had been sitting between them.

He had never satisfied himself that he had found the leader of the ring of thieves. Leo was convinced that Celeste's brother, Hubert Hardesty, had been only the second in command, but no number of threats had caused him to reveal any other name.

Still, Hardesty had seen Miss Hathersage during her ill-fated stumble into the transfer of the stolen goods to the cache that Leo had so thoughtfully provided the thieves. If Hardesty had revealed her presence to his presumed master, that master might want her silenced. As he wanted Leo himself silenced.

But who would wish to silence Rob? And why?

Those questions being unanswerable at the moment, Leo gave his attention to answering why that lady's father might want to see him. A request that he visit this worthy had arrived the afternoon after the ill-fated jaunt in the park.

Accordingly, Leo found himself in the small but elegant library of the Hathersage home, waiting to see Lord Hathersage. This gentleman came hurrying in, his hand extended in welcome.

"Pointeforte. No, take this chair here. The other one is damned uncomfortable. Demetra's choice, of course. Women just don't understand that men need a bit more room."

"Don't let me take your place, sir. I see that it is your favorite." Leo settled himself into the maligned seat.

Lord Hathersage nodded and sank into the more commodious chair.

"And how does Miss Hathersage fare today? Has she taken any hurt from yesterday's harrowing experience?"

His host rubbed his chin. "Nothing that I can see, save that she seems a bit quiet today. But then, her mama has not given her the opportunity to get a word in edgewise, fussing over her every minute as she has been doing. Would you fancy a drop of brandy? Quite a tolerable vintage."

"Thank you, that sounds very agreeable." Leo watched as his prospective father-in-law got to his feet. "I am sorry to hear that Lady Hathersage is so distressed." He accepted the glass and breathed in the bouquet.

"Demetra is easily distressed. Very delicate sensibilities, you know."

Leo very much feared he *did* know. But enough pleasantries. "You wished to see me, sir?"

Leo did not see the smile he had been expecting. Rather, his host appeared a trifle forbidding. Lord Hathersage set his glass

on the table beside him and reached into his coat. He pulled
out several pieces of paper. On one Leo could see the Pointeforte crest at the top—the note he had written yesterday. The
others—

Lord Hathersage laid the papers on the table, chose one
and handed it to his guest. Leo found himself looking at the
first letter he had written to the Hathersages after absconding with their daughter. His neck suddenly felt hot. Word-
lessly, Hathersage gave him another. Yesterday's missive, the
one with the crest.

Leo was looking at his own bold scrawl on each.

"I thought better of you, Leo. When were you going to
tell me? And how long has this clandestine affair been going
on? Have you been to Gretna Green?"

Leo glanced up at his host. The man regarded him solemnly, a shade of disappointment in his eyes. "No, my lord."
Leo set the letters down firmly. "You do not understand.
Even if I had been so completely lost to a sense of responsibility and honor, your daughter would never have been."

"I am relieved to hear that, of course, but perhaps you had
better explain." Hathersage leaned back in his chair and
picked up his brandy, a frown still creasing his brow.

A moment of relief welled up in Leo. At least this man
was not inviting him to a dawn appointment. He launched
into a full explanation of the circumstances which had
brought him to this point.

Hathersage listened intently. When Leo had finished, he
sighed and said, "That's quite a tale, lad."

"Aye, sir, it is. I realize it stretches credulity, but my associates in the Home Office will vouch for me."

"You know it will inevitably come out."

Leo set his glass aside. "Aye, sir. I fear that it will."

"And in that eventuality, are you prepared to offer for my
daughter?" Lord Hathersage did not look pleased.

Leo looked him resolutely in the eye. "My preference, my

lord, is not to wait for that catastrophe. I would have spoken to you immediately upon my return to society, except—"

"Except what?" There was a shade of menace in the tone.

For answer, Leo simply lifted the arm with its heavy contrivance where his hand should have been.

"Hmm. Have you other disabilities? Something that is, perhaps, unseen?" Hathersage's gaze narrowed and drifted downward.

Leo flushed and jumped to his feet. "Good God, man!" He paced a couple of steps and turned back to his host. "Your pardon, sir. That is a very disquieting thought."

"No doubt. My apologies. So how does your injury affect the thought of marriage?"

Leo gazed at him solemnly. "My lord, can you conceive of a woman who could tolerate half a man in her bed?"

Hathersage shrugged. "If, as you assert, your hand is your only loss, the remaining sum comes to much more than half. Still, I take your meaning. If it were Demetra we are discussing—"

"I would not wish for your daughter that she be revolted by her husband, nor that—"

"Nor what?"

"That we both be trapped in a comfortless marriage."

"I understand your concern, Leo, but I think you wrong Persephone. She is made of sterner stuff than her dam. You might be pleasantly surprised. She is a very sensible young woman."

Lord Hathersage swirled his brandy and studied the amber liquid for a few moments. Leo seated himself again and waited, all the arguments he had had with himself over the last several weeks roiling in his head. From one moment to the next he went from being afraid to touch Phona, to feeling compelled to kiss her, to being horrified by the idea of brushing against her with his false hand.

Or, worse yet, allowing her to see the hideous stump at

the end of his left arm. How could he ask Persephone Hathersage, or any other decent woman, to join him in his bed?

At last, Hathersage looked up and said, "I doubt you will have the luxury of a choice. Lady Hathersage tells me that her alleged friend, Mrs. Rowsley, has been hot on the scent of Phona's whereabouts during her absence. She is bound to have raised questions throughout the *ton*."

Leo sighed. "I feared as much."

"Yet I would not compel you two to marry if you don't fancy one another. I don't—"

"After knowing your daughter for this long there is no question of compulsion on my part, sir. I greatly admire Miss Hathersage."

Hathersage nodded. "As you should. And do you love her?"

Leo considered for a moment. Certainly he desired her—a matter not diplomatically mentioned to her father. From the moment he had tied her to her horse. From the moment she had heroically downed his ale, making a face all the while. From the moment he had carried her into his house, he had desired her.

And he had become annoyingly possessive. But…

"I am very fond of Miss Hathersage, sir."

"Hmm. That will have to do, I suppose." Hathersage nodded. "It makes little difference now, in any event. While I shall accept your assurance that the two of you behaved just as you ought, I believe, unless she strongly objects, you must marry—and at once."

"If she will have me, it will be my privilege to have Miss Hathersage as my wife."

A surge of feeling filled Leo. An odd combination of anxiety and…

Triumph.

Phona marched down the stairs to face the two most important men in her life. She knew that Pointeforte was in the house, closeted with her father. And she knew that this summons could mean only one thing. Pointeforte had not given her time to adjust to the situation into which he had, willy-nilly, cast her.

Just as he had given her no opportunity to decline his offer of hospitality in the first place.

Drat the man! Perhaps Papa would be willing to wait before making a decision. But—Mama was sure to insist on a long engagement so as to have time to plan an expensive wedding.

Whether Phona wanted one or not.

That would give her time to reconcile the two personas of Hades and Pointeforte. She loved one of the men housed in that body. That she knew. But the stranger quartered there with him? Would she love him, as well? Phona sighed. She had a strong notion that she was soon to find out.

"Ah, Phona, my dear. Come in." Papa rose as she entered the room, and Pointeforte followed suit. "I have something which I need to discuss with you."

Phona kept her eyes on her slippers. "Yes, Papa."

Her father cleared his throat. "Lord Pointeforte has made a request of me." He glanced at her uncertainly. "But come, let us all sit down."

Pointeforte pulled forward a third chair, and Phona sank into it, eyes still on her footwear. She could not find the courage to look at either of them.

Before her father could stumble over any more words, Pointeforte spoke. "I have asked your father for your hand in marriage, Miss Hathersage. I hope you will not disappoint me."

Phona's gaze flew to his face. He was watching her steadily. She took a deep breath. "Lord Pointeforte, as we have discussed, I hardly know you now. Perhaps in time—"

"Persephone." Her father's voice broke in. "It is not a matter of time. There can be no time."

She looked at him questioningly.

"I know the whole, Phona."

"You told him!" She glared at Pointeforte. "You promised that you would *never* tell anyone."

Hades returned a steady gaze. "He knew. I was betrayed by the handwriting on the note I sent yesterday. He matched it with that of my earlier letters."

Phona's eyes beseeched her father. "Papa. Oh, Papa! Please believe that I behaved as you would have wished. And Lord Hades—Lord Pointeforte—was never less than a gentleman."

"Hades? What the devil is this *Hades* business all about?"

"I did not know who he was. He would not tell me his name, so—"

Lord Hathersage let out a roar of laughter. "I suppose that comes of your mother's determination to play that damned myth to the hilt." He chuckled, shaking his head. "Of course. Why did we not tumble to that long ago?"

"But you see, Papa, Lord Pointeforte was disguised. You would not have known him yourself, and I had not met him before. Now he seems quite different—a marquess, in fact. I do not know what to say to his proposal."

"There is only one thing to say, Persephone. You must be married immediately. Otherwise—trust me—the story will out eventually and you will be quite ruined."

"In which event I shall marry her anyway." There was no compromise in Hades' face.

"Spoken as you should, Leo. But I will not gamble with my daughter's future." Her father's face took on an unwontedly stern expression. "You will be married inside the week."

"His groom! You shot his groom?"

"The bloody horses shied just as I pulled the trigger." He drew the knife out of his boot and began to sharpen it.

"But the long and the short of it is that you failed."

A dangerous quiet descended on the room as he stroked

the blade. Swish. Swish. Swish. At last he responded. "I need to get closer. I have never favored a gun."

A derisive snort erupted from his companion. "You think you can just waltz up to one of them and cut his throat? In any event, you know the old man favors something more subtle."

"Ha! The old man is just that—old." The man slowed his pace.

Swi-ish. Swi-ish. Swi-ish. A drop of sweat formed on his forehead, and his breathing deepened.

His companion sneered and rose to his feet. "Never mind. I will think of something. Meanwhile, I'll leave you alone with your mistress." He strode out of the room.

Swi-ish. Swi-ish. Swi-ish.

Chapter Eleven

"A week!"

The shriek of distress filled the library. "I cannot possibly plan a wedding in a week." Lady Hathersage flung herself into the chair that Leo had vacated and pointed an accusing finger at him. "This is your fault, my lord. Entirely your fault. First you tell me that you carried my only daughter away for weeks, and now, after that reprehensible admission, you expect to marry her. How could you? And you want to do it within a *week?*"

Lord Hathersage sighed loudly. "Yes, Demetra, they must marry within the week. Today is Saturday. By this coming Friday, they will be married."

Lady Hathersage had to resort to her smelling salts and leaned heavily on the arm of the chair. "No," she moaned. "No. You cannot mean it."

Leo glanced at his prospective bride. She refused to look at him. He turned back to face her mother. "Indeed, I do mean it, my lady. It is my greatest wish to marry your daughter, and to do so immediately."

"Oh!" Suddenly Lady Hathersage sat up and emitted an alarmed cry. "No, oh, nooo! You cannot have... She cannot

be… Phona?" She cast her stricken gaze on her daughter.
"Are you… Surely you cannot be… Oh, Phona. How could
you?"

Horror spread over Miss Hathersage's face. "Mama! No!
I am not… How could you think such a thing of me?" She
drew herself up and glared.

Her mother began to weep loudly. "But, Phona, why then
this unseemly haste?"

"It is Papa who makes that requirement, not I." Angry
tears gathered in the corners of his intended's eyes. "I am not
in the least ready to marry, so please cease insulting me."

Lord Hathersage gave Leo a resigned look. "They are not
taking this well."

A masterpiece of understatement if ever there was one.

Lady Hathersage continued to sob. Her daughter fought
her tears and continued to glare. Leo gazed at his future
father-in-law helplessly. That gentleman rose and took the
glass out of Leo's hand.

"Only one thing to do, lad." He walked to the decanter.
"Have another brandy." He refilled both glasses and returned
Leo's to him.

As Leo, now totally befuddled, took a long pull, his prospective mother-in-law lifted her head, raised her vinaigrette
to her nose and took a delicate sniff.

She glared balefully at Leo. "It is your doing, of course.
Yours. You forced her, just as you did that other poor girl.
My Phona would never have…"

Leo drew himself up to his full height and took a step
toward her, the blood beating in his ears. Lady Hathersage
cringed dramatically. A red haze of anger clouded his vision.
Leo halted and took control of himself. He closed his eyes
and reached inside himself for calm.

Taking a long breath, he stepped back, his jaw still tight.
With punctiliously cold courtesy he said, "Allow me to
assure you, my lady, that I do not rape virgins." When she

continued to huddle in the chair, he turned away adding, "Nor do I strike women."

Lord Hathersage materialized at Leo's elbow and placed a hand on his shoulder, but directed his gaze at his wife. "Come now, Demetra, give over. You owe Lord Pointeforte an apology."

His wife fumbled for her salts and again fortified herself.

"I... Very well." She gave Leo a cautious glance. "I trust I am mistaken, my lord."

Not much of an apology, Leo mused. But more than he expected to get. Had a man spoken those words to him, blood might well have flowed. His alliance with the Hathersage tribe bid fair to prove a trifle...stimulating.

He crossed to where Miss Hathersage sat, her face a stone mask. Going down to one knee, he took her tiny hand in his good one. "Miss Hathersage, will you marry me—within the week?"

"I...I suppose..." She took a breath and gave her mother one last angry glance. "Yes. Yes, my lord. I will marry you this week."

Leo stood. "So it is settled."

"Not this weeek!" Lady Hathersage again fell back in her chair. "It cannot be done."

A frown puckered her lord's brow. "My decision is made, Demetra. I do not need to explain to you the hazards of delay. You are better versed in them than I."

"Well, yes, George." Lady Hathersage lifted her gaze to him. "Of course they must marry. But *not* this week."

Her husband's scowl increased. "Yes, my lady, *this* week. Let us have no more argle-bargle."

"But, George..."

Egad! This might continue all night. Leo had had enough.

"My lady, I understand your reluctance to relinquish your daughter so precipitously. Nonetheless, the marriage must take place without further postponement."

"But, my lord…"

"Enough, Lady Hathersage." Leo started toward the door. "On Friday, six days from today—" he turned back to look directly at her "—I am coming for my bride."

What a debacle! Had a proposal of marriage ever gone so awry? A single candle casting a pool of dim light and a compress of lavender water on her aching head, Phona lay on her bed and stared at the ceiling.

Hades had stalked out of the house in something perilously akin to a temper. Phona had fled to her room. The voices of her parents, raised in disharmony, followed her up the stairs.

She *hated* turmoil.

Shortly after Phona had cried herself out, Mama knocked on the door. She slipped into the room and came to sit on the edge of the bed. Taking Phona's cold hand into hers, she stared into the middle distance for a space, then at last, cleared her throat.

"I am sorry to have distressed you so, my dearest. I know that you would never behave dishonorably. But you were in *such* a situation…" She patted Phona's hand. "If he… If there is any chance that you are… We must care for you. Please tell me. I vow I will not reproach you."

Phona opened burning eyes. Would Mama never believe her? "As I told you, Mama, there is no chance that I am with child. None at all. You wrong Lord Pointeforte." After a moment she gazed into her mother's eyes and added, "And you wrong me."

"Oh, Phona." Mama reached down and pulled Phona into her embrace. "Forgive me. I did not wish to hurt you. I…I sometimes become a bit overwrought."

Phona could not help but smile.

Mama began to rock her gently. "Can you bear it, Phona? Can you accept him as a husband after he carried you away in such a manner? And with such a mutilation? If you cannot, I vow…" Her voice became more determined. "I shall spirit you away and hide you and he will never—"

"Mama." Phona disentangled herself and sat up straighter. "Thank you, Mama, but there is no need for such extreme measures. I am sure that Lord Pointeforte saved my life. I heard the other man…" Phona shuddered at the memory, and her mother again clasped her in her arms. "They would have killed me, Mama."

"Oh, my poor love." Her mothers arm's tightened around her. "You have been very brave."

Phona took a breath. "And, truly, Lord Pointeforte was very kind to me. And even though I did not know who he was, I…I rather liked him."

"Ah." Her mother gave her a shrewd glance. "I thought perhaps— So you can tolerate marriage to him, knowing he is…injured?"

"I believe so, if I can but become accustomed to the notion of being a marchioness."

"So, then." Mama stood and patted Phona on the shoulder. "I will send his lordship a lovely note and invite him to a nice dinner tomorrow evening and all will be well. But how your father expects me to give you a proper wedding… I must send immediately to Madame LeBlanc. You must have traveling clothes. And—oh, dear heavens!—a wedding gown. And I must go."

Moments later, she bustled out of the room.

So Mama would invite his lordship to a nice dinner and all would be well, would it? Phona sighed and lay back down. What a tangle! In less than a week she would be forced into marriage to the man she loved.

And his alter ego would be forced into marriage with her.

Hades and Pointeforte. The outlaw and the nobleman. Her beloved and a stranger. And who would *she* be? Lady Hades? Or the Marchioness of Pointeforte?

* * *

Phona arrived at the church in solitary splendor.

The arrangement proved necessary because she and the train of her gown had required the whole interior of the carriage.

"You cannot arrive at the church in a crushed dress, dearest." Mama had plucked and tucked at her until Phona was ready to scream.

How in the world had Madame LeBlanc managed to create such an elaborate gown in the time before they left London to return to the Hathersage estate? Most likely it had been intended for a more foresightful bride. Just her luck to be married in someone else's gown.

Mama would have had the ceremony in London, but Phona had wanted to be married out of the home in which she had grown up, where she was comfortable. The idea pleased Papa, and she had him to thank for convincing Mama to give up trumpeting her *coup*—actually snaring a marquess for her inept daughter—to the *ton*.

Besides, Mama well knew what the *ton* had to say about hasty marriages.

Papa had ridden to the church beside her coach, Mama following in another, bolstered by Mrs. Rowsley and Suzette, whose fiancé rode escort to them.

Again, Phona had stood her ground against Mama's advance, insisting on wearing her hair as she thought Hades would like it. If *he* thought her beautiful, whom else should she seek to please? She hoped Lord Pointeforte would agree with Lord Hades.

Now she stood with Papa and Margarite in the vestibule of the church, nervously biting her lip. She had not seen Hades since Mama's "nice dinner" the evening after the ill-fated proposal. On that occasion he had behaved with quite alarming courtesy, while Mama played her usual coquette as though there had never been words between them.

Phona and his lordship had only a few minutes to speak with one another privately as she took her leave of him. For the first time since she had known him, he seemed uncertain. They stood, awkwardly gazing at one another.

At last he said, "Miss Hathersage, there is something I must ask you."

She looked up uncertainly. "Yes?"

"Since you have honored me by agreeing to be my wife, I must know—" He hesitated a moment, then lifted his left arm. "Can you bear me as a husband, knowing that this will part of our marital life?"

Phona was taken completely off guard. "You are concerned about that?"

"Yes, Miss Hathersage, I am greatly concerned about that." He watched her gravely. "If you cannot, I will, of course, respect your wishes. I will not force my attentions on you."

She took a moment to give the question the consideration it deserved. She had never actually seen the awful amputation. Would she be repulsed? There was certainly nothing to find fault with in the rest of his person. In fact, she had wanted to be kissed, held close by him for months.

But could she admit that to him?

Finally she said, "At the lodge I became quite accustomed to seeing you with only your shirt covering your wrist. I did not find that distressing."

"But can you tolerate my touch as a husband? I will certainly keep my injury away from your person."

"I accepted your touch readily enough when I needed it, even when you needed both arms. I have felt the touch of your injury."

Phona reached out and took his right hand. When she would have taken the left, he jerked it away. She stood looking into his half-familiar face. After a space she said, "I have no problem touching you, my lord."

He brought her fingers to his lips, his hand shaking. "Thank you, Miss Hathersage."

Her bridegroom quickly turned and walked away.

There was no mention of love.

The next day he had repaired to Darkwood Park, apparently to brace himself for his nuptials.

As the organ music swelled, Phona did her best to peek into the church. Hades must have come into the nave.

Suddenly Phona felt frightened. She was dreaming. She would soon awake. Both Hades and Pointeforte would fade into the morning light, and she would once again be the awkward Miss Hathersage, rapidly approaching the Shelf.

Surely she could not be marrying a man who had tied her to her horse? And how could she be poised on the verge of marriage to a marquess? Perhaps she had been spirited away to the realm of faeries one night. At any moment the dawn would break, and she would be deposited abruptly in bed.

Papa nudged her toward the door, and Phona blinked herself back to the present and clutched her father's arm. He patted her hand absently. All at once he exclaimed, "Why, the rogue!"

"What, Papa?" Phona tried to see into the darkness of the church. "Is he there?"

"He's here right enough. The rascal has not shaved. His face has a week's beard."

Phona burst into laughter. She could now hear the titillated murmur from the guests. Covering her chuckles with her bouquet, she whispered, "It is quite all right, Papa. I imagine that he is putting me at my ease."

"By failing to shave?" Her father scowled.

"Just so, Papa. Is he wearing an eye patch?"

Papa thundered, "Eye patch!" and Phona hastily shushed him.

"Come, we must go. Everyone is waiting." She took a step and Papa followed.

Halfway down the aisle he muttered, "Cursed rascal. I'll put a bug in *his* ear." Phona pinched his hand. She hoped her posy covered not only her blushes, but her laughter.

Against all odds, they arrived in good order at the chancel. Her father glared at Hades, and her bridegroom grinned audaciously back at him. Phona gazed up into his face, and surely enough, she beheld not only six days' worth of black beard, but a black silk eye patch.

But wasn't it on the wrong eye? Surely it had covered the right eye before. Now it was on the left. She hardly heard the vicar as he asked who bestowed the bride in marriage. A loud "harumph" alerted her to the fact that her father had just given her away.

She turned her eyes to him, to find him looking at her, a tear coursing down his perfectly shaven cheek. Phona lifted a gloved finger and brushed it away. Another followed it. "Oh, Papa." Her tears sprang to her own eyes. She leaned against his chest and sniffed. "I love you."

Another "harumph" and she felt her hand being carefully placed into that of Hades. His closed greedily around hers. Phona looked up at the twinkling blue eye and smiled. Hades drew her closer with an arm around her waist and gazed into her face.

Phona now saw nothing but the man she had come to love.

Suddenly he pulled his gaze away and nodded in the direction of the vicar, who had quit speaking. That worthy was looking at them expectantly, bushy gray eyebrows arching toward his high forehead. Oh, dear. What had he just said?

Phona glanced at her groom. He shrugged. One of the guests snickered. She sighed and waited, blushing furiously. At last the vicar repeated, "Do you, Leopold DeBolsover, take this woman to be your lawfully wedded wife?"

Hades' "I do," boomed to the rafters of the nave.

Phona followed him through the rest of the vows, looking

the while into the face that had at last become familiar. For the first time in days she did not feel disoriented.

After all, this was Hades.

When Phona had come through the door on her father's arm, Leo thought for a moment that his heart had stopped. He took a step forward before he heard Rob, at his back, whisper, "Steady."

The girl he had carried, exhausted and bedraggled, into his home had become a spirit of the air, a queen of Faerie draped in silk gauze, silver beads and seed pearls. Leo could hardly see her face, for she had lifted her bouquet of delicate white flowers to shield the lower portion, but above the posy he could see a pair of brown eyes sparkling with laughter.

A cluster of curls at the crown of her head glowed, catching warm sparks of candlelight in the mahogany depths of her hair. Behind it a veil of lace worked in silver streamed down her back. Several errant curling tendrils trailed against her cheeks.

He had thought her beautiful at his lodge, with her curls untamed. Now she took his breath away. His body tightened and filled in response.

Leo could not wait to take her in his arms. He had an arm around her waist long before the vicar invited him to salute his bride. The kiss he bestowed on her had, in all likelihood, given the onlookers something to gossip about for months to come.

Nor had he released her throughout the wedding breakfast, at the end relinquishing his newly acquired wife only long enough for her mother to throw her arms around her neck, sobbing out a dramatic farewell.

Leo had anticipated further difficulty with the fair Hathersage, but none had so far materialized. Now he wondered if she had merely been lying in wait. When after several minutes her weeping showed no sign of abating, he placed his hand gently on her shoulder. "Lady Hathersage, it is time for us to depart."

"Oh, my lord, grant me but a few moments more with my precious child."

"Now, Mama…" Her precious child made an effort to disengage herself. "It is not as if I were going to the moon. I shall be living at Darkwood Park. We shall be neighbors."

"But you are going away!" Lady Hathersage tightened her coils.

Leo's hackles began to rise. "Please, my lady. You must let us be on our way."

"Not yet. Not just yet." A new onslaught of tears assailed them, and Leo's jaw clenched.

Once again, Leo had had more than enough. By God, he had abducted this lady once, and he could damn well do it again. He pried his mother-in-law's arms away and shoved her unceremoniously into her husband's embrace.

Leo then scooped his bride into his arms and fled with her out of the house and down the steps to his carriage. Rob would just have to fend off pursuit in the old way.

Phona tumbled into the coach, clutching the long train of her gown to her breast. Her bridegroom followed her and, in one deft motion, set her on the seat, relieved her of the train and tossed it onto the floor. As the carriage jolted away, he pulled her across his lap and kissed her fiercely.

When they were obliged to breathe, he gazed at her and sighed. "Are you sure you are comfortable with my ardor, my lady?"

Phona could only nod breathlessly.

"Thank God. I have thought of nothing this interminable week save the image of you in my bed. I feared we would never win free."

Phona laughed and tucked her feet up onto the seat. "I see that you have already learned how to deal with Mama better than I have. Argument is useless. I don't know why I persist in attempting reason."

"Because you are a reasonable person. However, something tells me it is a fatal policy. She wields tears like a sword."

"Yes, exactly. But she does love me, you know."

"I suppose." He settled her more comfortably against him. "But I am unwilling to spend even another minute wasting time on her vapors." His mouth again covered Phona's, this time softly. He slowly slid his tongue across her lips.

Sensation shot through her, and she gasped. Her own mouth opened slightly. He groaned and allowed his tongue to move deeper, stroking it over the sensitive inner surface of her lips. He had never kissed her quite that way before. Phona felt herself melting.

Cautiously, she let her own tongue reach out and touch his mouth, feeling the prickles of his beard on its tip. He pulled her closer and now his tongue touched hers. Phona sighed and her mouth opened wider. Hades made a sound deep in his throat.

Phona closed her eyes and let her head fall back over his arm, and suddenly her mouth was free, damp and cool. He was now placing hot, wet kisses on her throat. Feelings she had never before felt raced through her, starting at the juncture of her legs and flowing upward.

"Ah, sweet lady. How I have longed to do this." He fumbled behind her and unfastened the first few hooks of her dress. Then he carefully teased one breast out over the curved neckline.

"And this." He touched his tongue to the top of her breast. Phona's whole body clenched, and a little shriek escaped her. Hades laughed softly. "Ah, so you liked that. Then let us try this." He trailed the tongue slowly downward toward her taut nipple. Phona's breathing grew faster. "Ah, yes, and this."

His mouth closed over the straining bud, and Phona arched upward, her cry rising above the rattle of the coach. Hades quickly abandoned her breast to cover her mouth with his, muffling the sound.

"Oh, my lord." He released her, and she gazed up at him. "Is this what it means to make love?"

"Only a small part of it, my lady. Only a very small part." He tugged her dress back over her breast. "But I have no intention of introducing you to more in a bounding carriage. You deserve four safe walls and a soft bed. It is not far to Darkwood Park. I can contain myself that long." Grinning, he turned her to sit beside him on the seat. "And so must you."

"Certainly I shall try." Phona smiled shyly. "I must confess, my lord, that I have been a teeny bit anxious about making love. Our kisses at the lodge were very enjoyable, but the rest of it…"

Hades leaned across and placed a kiss on her nose. "Do not concern yourself, Lady Pointeforte, I can see that the marriage bed will pose no difficulty for you."

A twinge of embarrassment shot through Phona. "Oh, my! Am I too brazen, my lord?"

"You are every bridegroom's dream, my lady." He slipped an arm around her shoulders and turned her head toward him with his fingertips. "Both modest and passionate. No man could ask for more."

"I thought perhaps I was not quite…not quite ladylike."

"Aha! I believe I hear the echo of Mama's voice."

"Very likely. But if you do not mind…"

His laughter reverberated through the coach. "Hardly, my lady!"

Silence settled over the carriage. His bride leaned in the shelter of his arm, her head against his shoulder, her eyes closed. Leo leaned his head back against the squabs and also attempted to rest from the rigors of the day.

But he could not relax. Mixed with the images of her
delicate nude body stretched across his bed were others that
persisted in intruding, no matter how he sought to banish
them. Leo fought them as long as he could, but at last he was
forced to surrender to the truth of it.

He was terrified.

As his carriage approached his ancestral home and this
long-desired culmination, he could now think of nothing but
his fear that she would draw back from him in revulsion at
the sight of his ghastly stump.

Images of his shirt accidently dropping to the floor
assailed him. Of her recoiling from him, of even her great
courage failing in the face of such deformity.

Oh, God. Let it not happen that way.

He would not *allow* it to happen that way. All the weeks
at his lodge, he had been careful never to let her see it,
always wearing the shirts designed to cover it.

Even the awful night she had helped Aelfred cut his
britches off, he had determinedly contrived to keep his naked
wrist out of sight, crammed under a pillow. Better she see
his male member than that grisly mutilation.

As they reached the approach to Darkwood Park, Leo
made up his mind. She would not see it tonight, either. She
might view the balance of his naked body, but not that. He
would plan carefully. His shirt would never fall. His amputation would stay concealed.

He would spare her that horror.

They swept up the drive and pulled up smartly to the
main doors of the imposing mansion. Footmen wearing the
livery of the Marquess of Pointeforte came running down the
wide stairs. They assisted Leo out of the carriage, and he
turned and lifted down the new marchioness, briefly placing
his left arm under her right to balance her.

Leo *hated* touching her with his dead left glove. It served
well enough to hold champagne, but not for his lady. Yet at

the church he had been forced to rest her hand on it as he slipped the ring on her dainty finger.

Leo had been in terror of that process, too. What if he had not been steady enough to succeed? He had visions of the ring escaping his grasp, bouncing down the chancel steps and rolling away down the aisle with Rob and him in hot pursuit.

Throughout the ritual, he had felt his cousin hovering behind him, at the ready to avert just such a disaster.

Be damned to him.

He could, by God, place a wedding ring on his wife's hand.

Chapter Twelve

Mₒre footmen lined the stairs as Leo led his marchioness into her new home. He nodded to them as he passed. At the great double doorway Leo stopped and turned to her. "Is this where I should lift you over the threshold?"

She gazed back at him, her head tilted thoughtfully to one side. "I have no idea, my lord. I should think so."

Leo just wanted to arrive at his bedchamber with all the confounded ceremony behind them, but women found ritual important, didn't they? He would not let his new lady down.

He gathered her up into his arms and carefully carried her through the door. A burst of applause greeted them. He set her on her feet, grinning in spite of himself, and looked down at her.

"You are blushing, Lady Pointeforte." She looked adorable. Leo's body began to swell. He had best get them to a bed, and quickly.

The footmen followed the bridal couple into the grand entry hall, lining up on one side of the entry. The maids stood in a row opposite them. Between the two rows a tall, dignified man and a plump woman, both of them gray-haired, marched toward them.

The man stepped forward and bowed deeply to his new mistress. "Welcome to your home, my lady. I am Eggars, your butler. We all hope that you will be very happy here."

His lady smiled nervously. "Thank you, Eggars. I am sure that I shall be."

"And this is Mrs. Oglethorpe." Leo indicated the woman. "Your housekeeper."

The woman's face lit in a warm smile. "So happy we are to have a bride at Darkwood Park, my lady. Allow me to introduce you to your staff."

And she and Eggars proceeded to do so—at tedious length. His lady had a smile and a word for each of them. Leo's patience barely saw him through yet another ceremony.

When finally they had done, Mrs. Oglethorpe asked, "My lord, at what time should we serve dinner?"

Leo groaned. Must he also endure a ceremonial dinner? "Have you gone to great trouble for it, Mrs. Oglethorpe?"

He detected a knowing twinkle in her eye. "Well, my lord, not above the usual. Eggars and I thought you and Lady Pointeforte might be rather tired after the wedding and the drive here. Cook has prepared some dainties for you, but has saved the welcome dinner until tomorrow when your family will be here to meet your bride."

Leo smiled with relief. "Very thoughtful of the three of you. You may send a light repast to my private sitting room at seven o'clock."

She curtseyed. "As you wish, my lord. Shall I show Lady Pointeforte to her rooms?"

"No, thank you." Leo bestowed a dismissing nod on the crowd. "I shall myself conduct Lady Pointeforte upstairs." As the staff lingered curiously, he glanced sternly around and added, "By myself."

Suddenly everyone seemed to decide that he had urgent duties elsewhere.

* * *

But Phona did not see her own suite of rooms at all that day. In all likelihood Lily had laid out her elegant bedclothes, but they had never graced Phona's body.

Hades, tugging her hand, had led her up two pair of stairs and down a very long hall—almost at a run. At the end of the corridor he flung open a door and ushered her into a sitting room done in dark wood, wine-colored upholstery and rich Oriental rugs.

"Welcome to my private domain, my lady." Before Phona could catch her breath, he pulled her to him and kissed her hard. "I believe there is another threshold we must cross."

He picked her up and carried her across the rugs to another door. As soon as they had cleared it, he kicked it shut and turned the key. With long strides he crossed to a huge bed hung in wine velvet and graced with carvings of nymphs and fauns. How curious.

But Hades gave her no time for a careful appraisal of the activities of the woodland spirits. The covers had been thoughtfully turned down. He laid her on the sheets, wedding gown and all.

"Ah." He came down beside her, one arm and one leg thrown over her. "If one more person had insisted on one more delay, I would not have been held responsible for my actions."

Phona chuckled. "It did seem a rather lengthy process, my lord."

But now that she was here, in her husband's bed, another distraction might prove welcome. Kisses were all very well, wherever he placed them, but the actual consummation might be…

Hades seemed to sense her sudden apprehension. "Do not be anxious, my lady. It is only I, Lord Hades, and we are yet a long way from mating." He touched his lips to her forehead. "A very slow…" they touched her eyelids "…long…" her nose,"…way." His mouth found hers, covering it in a leisurely, warm kiss.

When he finally raised his head and gazed down at her, Phona lifted a hand and gently touched his beard. "Did you grow it back just because I missed it?"

"I did."

"And this?" She touched the eye patch.

"And that. I want you to look into the face you know, when I take you in my arms. Don't move." He placed a detaining hand on her shoulder and got up from the bed.

Hades stepped out of sight behind a fold of the bed curtain, and Phona heard the rustle of clothing, a thump as something landed on the floor. Now what was that? She turned toward the sound just in time for him to reappear, buttoning the sleeve of his shirt over his left wrist. His coat, waistcoat and cravat were nowhere to be seen.

Nor was his left hand.

Or rather the glove that passed for it. She had not seen him without it since they'd left the gorge. And then he had been wearing his hook. Phona had not considered what she would see in the marriage bed.

Certainly not the hook.

But apparently, while his unbuttoned shirt lay open against his bare chest, he was not going to doff it. He sat on the edge of the bed and pulled at a shoe. "Cursed fashionable footwear." He grinned cheerfully at her. "Hard as the devil to get them on or off."

Phona started to sit up. "Should I help, my lord?"

"No. Thank you." He pushed her back down. "I have them." He tossed them toward the middle of the room and rolled onto the bed, lying propped on his left elbow beside her. "Now that I am comfortable, let us attend to you."

Something in Phona shrank back. "Uhhh… Of…of course."

"No fears, my brave lady." He dropped a light kiss on her nose. "No fears today. Only desire and joy."

Desire and joy. Could she truly bring that to him? She, the awkward Miss Hathersage. He, Lord Hades, god of the Underworld. Leopold DeBolsover, Marquess of Pointeforte.

"I think we shall begin at the top." Phona felt his hands tugging at her veil. A moment later he pulled it free and tossed it aside.

He twisted a curl around his finger. "Your hair is beautiful. Dark, but with a warm fire." He kissed the tendril and released it, his hand sliding down her neck, brushing her breast. Phona shivered slightly.

"But I think we now need to attend to the other extremity."

Something had completely deprived Phona of speech. She could only lie, trembling slightly, as his hand drifted down her body, over her bodice, across her skirt, until it reached her feet. He tugged one slipper off and then the other, tossing them over his shoulder.

"What tiny feet." He lifted one and kissed the instep, his mouth warm through her stocking. The warmth coursed up Phona's leg until it reached the joining, where it created a delicious tightness. When he kissed the other foot, her hips lifted off the bed.

She heard a satisfied chuckle. "Ah, yes. But we cannot have these concealing stockings."

His hand slid up the silk, pausing, descending and again ascending toward her garter. Phona's trembling increased until it seemed it must shake the bed. She was hardly aware that his arm gathered her skirts upward.

He deftly untied the garter and drew the stocking down, trailing kisses down her leg, his beard tickling her skin. He moved upward again to run his tongue slowly up and down her inner thigh.

The warmth between her legs grew to a fire, tightening Phona's whole body. By the time he had removed the second stocking, she was arching her back, losing contact with the real world. His hand rested between her legs, pressing on some hidden place, circling.

Pressing. Circling. Pressing. Circling.

Suddenly the world around Phona disintegrated. She heard her own scream as sensation poured through her, flooding her, overwhelming her. The colors of the room wheeled around her, the shapes broken, as stronger feelings that she had ever imagined raced through her helpless body. She clutched at Hades' shoulders, gasping.

Then all at once she fell back against the bed, limp.

His beard tickled her ear as he whispered, "An excellent first lesson."

"More?" The room was still swimming around her.

His voice was warm. "Oh, yes, my lady. Much more."

He let her rest while he calmed her, stroking her arms and face until she once more lay relaxed against him. It was the hardest damn thing he had ever done. He so wanted her. Wanted her right *now*. Wanted to taste her breasts. Wanted to bury himself to the hilt. Wanted to—

Leo sat and lifted her, reaching around her to the fastenings of her wedding gown. Years of practice had taught him to do things with only one hand. In a matter of minutes he had undone the dress and pulled it and her shift over her head.

She clutched at it for a moment as she realized her armor was disappearing. He waited, and she released it, hiding her face against his shoulder. He held her close and stroked her back until the tension went out of her. Then he laid her back against the bed and leaned over her.

"Now, sweet lady…" He covered her mouth with his for a heartbeat before continuing. "Now we shall explore the possibilities of *more*."

Leo let his mouth move down her throat, pausing to leave

damp spots as he went. Her dainty breasts were open to him now. He lifted one and kissed a circle around it. She began to stir against him again. Damnation! He was full to bursting.

He closed his mouth around the nipple, and she moaned. Leo could not stand this much longer. He rolled up to his knees. "Help me with the buttons."

She gazed at him for a moment, puzzled, and then he saw understanding dawn on her face. He started undoing the buttons on one side of the flap of his britches, and she quickly began to unfasten the other. Then the flap dropped free, and his straining shaft sprang out. Leo heard her gasp.

"Touch me." He could hardly speak.

Slowly, timidly, she reached forward and ran her fingers along him. He groaned and quickly leaned over her, moving her hand away. Much of that and he would be finished. He slid his body down between her legs until his mouth was over her breasts.

Leo began to feast on them, moving his mouth from one to the other, holding one in his hand, teasing with tongue and fingers until she was writhing beneath him. He pressed his body against hers, and with a shriek, she exploded in his arms.

He could not wait any longer. Leo moved forward and joined his body with hers. She cried out, but as he thrust faster and faster, she moved against him, striving for more. And then he heard his own shout. Felt the molten sensation pour through him. Felt every nerve in his body vibrate. Felt the triumph of a god.

Hades, Lord of the Underworld, had claimed Persephone.

How absolutely astonishing. Phona lay beside him, utterly spent. Who would have thought the simple act of coupling would be so exquisite, so all-consuming?

She lay wrapped in Hades' arms, almost asleep, her head on his shoulder, the crisp hair on his chest teasing her nose.

In fact, she was about to sneeze. Drawing back a bit, Phona freed an arm and rubbed her nose.

Hades roused from his doze and rose up on one elbow, smiling down at her. "Now, Lady Pointeforte, we are truly and thoroughly wedded and bedded. Are you happy with the results?"

Phona stroked his beard. "Very happy, my lord Hades." She giggled. "But your patch has abandoned your eye for your forehead."

"I should not be surprised." He pulled the errant scrap of silk back into place.

"No." Phona pushed it back up. "I think I prefer you with two eyes, my lord."

"That's a relief." Hades drew the patch off and threw it in the general direction of the growing pile of garments on the floor. "The cursed thing itches."

Phona sighed. "Your eyes are so lovely. It will not do to keep one covered."

"I am encouraged. Perhaps you will soon be able to tolerate me as a marquess rather than an outlaw." He lifted his head. "But, hark. I believe I hear the sounds of our 'dainties' arriving in my parlor. Perhaps we should go and investigate."

"But, my lord, I am completely naked! I cannot go anywhere."

"I would not object, but I see a perfectly fine wedding gown." He stood and pulled it from the pile on the floor. "Ugh. It scratches."

Phona sat up on the side of the bed. "Indeed, it does. So many beads. But I can wear it—"

"No." Hades tucked in the tails of his open shirt without buttoning it and fastened his britches. Crossing the room, he knelt to rummage in a large chest. "Here you are." He returned carrying a large linen nightshirt. "These served us well enough when first we met. This one can do so again."

"But the servants—"

He raised one eyebrow and smiled wryly. "After they bring our meal, there had best be no servants—not anywhere in sight, in any event." He pulled her toward him on the bed, stepping between her legs. "And I believe we might give them another few minutes."

Phona reached up for the kiss, her arms circling his waist. How could she already feel more stirrings of desire? She was utterly exhausted. Nonetheless, her breath began to come short.

But alas—she was getting a crick in her neck.

Just as she felt forced to move, Hades straightened, rubbing his back. Phona chuckled and rubbed her neck. "Perhaps we should prepare for our dinner."

"Just so." He laughed and pulled the nightshirt over her head. Phona struggled with the engulfing fabric to find the neck and arm holes, at last emerging into the light. He regarded her thoughtfully. "That has about finished your coiffure."

He pulled the last few pins out of her hair and ran his fingers through it. It fluffed out in its usual cloud, and he buried his face in it. "I like it this way. So soft and free, just like the rest of you. But come. I am damned sharp set."

Phona stood, holding the long garment off the floor with both hands. "I'm ready, my lord."

Hades gazed at her thoughtfully. "No. Something else is needed for a bridal dinner. Ah!" He found her bridal veil tangled in the sheets and retrieved a few hairpins from the pillow. Holding the veil at the crown of her head with his forearm, he carefully pinned it in place and stepped back to admire his work. "There. My beautiful bride—just as I prefer her."

Phona laughed. "In a man's nightshirt and a bridal veil, my lord?"

"Even so." Hades bussed her soundly one more time and led the way to the door. He opened it a crack and peered out. "The coast is clear, my lady. Come, dinner awaits us."

* * *

Phona could only marvel at what the Pointeforte establishment considered "a light repast." A long table had been arrayed as a buffet laid with a dazzling choice of foods—chicken in aspic, buttered lobster with asparagus, fruit compotes, a chantilly crème, tidbits of roast beef in its own juice, prawns broiled in bacon.

Antique silver and delicate china sparkled, and buckets of iced champagne stood at either side of a smaller table set for dining.

"Well! It seems as if Cook has outdone herself." Hades sampled a fingerful of sauce.

"If I so much as taste even a third of this, I shall be stuffed like a goose." Phona strolled along the table, devising a battle plan, but before she could implement it he drew her to her chair and helped her to sit.

"I suspect you will find lovemaking to be hungry work." He picked up her plate. "I shall serve you. Tell me what you fancy."

In the end he heaped her plate so high Phona was sure she must leave most of it untouched, but his prediction proved correct. She was starving. As the food steadily disappeared, she noticed that nothing on the table required a knife to cut it. Everything could be eaten with only a fork or spoon.

Apparently Lord Pointeforte's household made certain accommodations to his needs, very likely without consulting him in the matter. He certainly would not have allowed it had they asked. She had never seen him ask any concessions for himself, but he evidently chose silently to accept their consideration.

A strange, proud man she had married.

She must never forget that.

When the last sweet that she could possibly consume had passed her lips, Hades' intense blue gaze met hers across the debris. "Come, my lady. We need to be more comfortable."

Leo rose and helped her up, then, taking her arm, he guided her to his favorite chair. "Let us indulge your unlady-like taste for port."

She laughed. "*My* taste for port! Indeed, my lord, you wrong me."

"Very likely." He sat and pulled her into his lap. "But now we are free to indulge ourselves as we wish." He poured a glass and held it to her lips.

She took a long sip. "I fear with the port and the champagne, I shall become quite tipsy, my lord."

"Aha! My plan exactly. I shall have my wicked way with you." He grinned and offered her another sip.

"I may be mistaken, but I believe you have already done that." She snuggled her head against his shoulder.

"I have only begun."

"Heaven help me! I may not survive." She cast him a serious glance. "Are you satisfied, then, with this marriage? You did not feel an obligation—"

"Obligation be damned!" He sat up a bit straighter and looked at her severely. "I have wanted you since I tied you to that horse. I very nearly set my scruples aside and had my wicked way with you long ago. Had I not feared…"

"For my reputation?" She gazed into his face.

"Nay, though I should have. But I could have corrected that problem. I feared I might not return to you one night."

"You…you mean you feared for your life."

"Yes."

"And now?"

"Now…? I still fear for it. And for yours." Instinctively he tightened his arms protectively around her. "At whom was that bullet in the park aimed, my lady? It might have struck any of the three of us."

"And, thus, any of the three of us might have been the intended victim."

"Logically, yes, although I believe it was myself. Nonetheless…" He set down the glass. "I do not wish to frighten you, but you must be on your guard. You must not trust strangers, or—"

"Or?" She gazed steadily at him.

Leo saw not a trace of fear. "Or anyone of whose friendship you are not absolutely sure."

"I see." She grew very still in his arms.

"But you need not be afraid here, my lady. Every door to these rooms has been guarded since we closed them. By men I know well."

"But who, my lord? Who might wish to shoot any of us? It clearly has something to do with the marquessate. You are the marquess. Rob is your heir, is he not? And I might be suspected of carrying the next one." A delicious blush started above the overlarge neckline of the nightshirt and suffused her dainty face. "Or at least, *now* I might. But no one could know whether we had… I mean, on some other occasion… I mean…"

She stumbled to a halt, and Leo laughed aloud. "I hope no one knows how much opportunity we had. But yes, I agree. It is clearly the marquessate, and therefore—"

"And therefore the foremost suspect must be Rob."

"Yes." Damnation, it hurt to say it. Pain welled up inside him at hearing the words spoken aloud. "Rob is the obvious suspect. And yet…I cannot bring myself to believe it. I do not believe it."

She straightened herself in his lap. "Then let us consider alternatives. Who is next in the succession after Rob?"

The pain in Leo retreated a bit and gave way to a heartening warmth. "You will never know, my lady, what a relief it is to have someone with whom to discuss the situation. It is times like this I most miss my brother—" A different pain intruded, and Leo was forced to break off and clear his throat.

She touched his beard gently, and suddenly the back of his

eyelids prickled. Devil take it. He had not wept for Percy in three years, and he did not intend to do it on his wedding night. Leo drew a deep breath and closed his hand around hers.

He pressed his lips to her fingers. "He and Rob and I grew up together, my closest friends. We talked about everything. Now Percy is gone, and I obviously cannot discuss this with Rob." He sighed. "In fact, I believe I have so feared finding Rob at the bottom of all the various attempts to forbid my succession, that I have not wanted to address it with anyone."

"Quite understandable. But we must find the answer, or none of us will be safe." Her deep brown eyes gazed up at him.

He kissed her forehead. "There is someone else behind this. I am sure of it. Someone connected with the thieves, most likely their true leader."

"Why do you believe that?"

"Because Celeste Hardesty, who accused me of rape and tried to have me hung, was later arrested wearing some of the stolen jewelry."

His wife frowned. "Being hung would certainly have kept you from the title. I have never understood the little I know about the situation with Miss Hardesty."

Leo grinned. "And I am not going to explain it to you on our wedding night."

"Hmm." She settled for giving him a narrow-eyed glance. "Very well. This hypothetical person follows Rob in the succession?"

He gave the question some thought. "Most likely."

"And who is that?"

"I do not know. Until recently our family has had very few male offspring. I had but one brother, and my father had but one. Beyond that, for at least two generations, I believe there was only one surviving male offspring. I suspect we might be required to look to my great-great-grandfather to find the next branch of the DeBolsover tree."

"And you have no knowledge of those— What? Third or fourth cousins?"

"None. I know of no other DeBolsovers in the country, in spite of having several agents looking for them."

"Yet there must be some." She sat up taller and looked at him. "We must ask Mama. She knows every detail of every member of every family in England. And the others who will be here tomorrow evening may know something. All of our families will be here."

"I fear they will." Leo sighed. "And we will be back to polite behavior. However—" He began to unbutton the night-shirt she wore. "We still have tonight."

Chapter Thirteen

Hades opened the neck of the nightshirt and pushed it off one of her shoulders, placing a kiss on the tip of it. She leaned her head against him as he moved his lips to her collarbone, slowly and gradually working his way to her throat. A new tension enveloped Phona. Her whole body came alive, every inch of skin longing for a like caress.

When he reached her throat, she thought he would end at her mouth. Phona let her head fall back over his arm and allowed her mouth to open a bit, ready for him. But he did not kiss her lips. Instead, he tugged the nightshirt farther down and proceeded in the direction of her breasts.

Heat blossomed between her legs as the warmth of his mouth traveled slowly over the top of her breast. Another tug, and the oversize garment allowed her nipple to emerge. Hades covered it with his lips, doing something quite amazing with his tongue. Phona moaned and arched her back.

He shifted her in his lap, relieving the weight on the shirt. "I believe, my lady, that if we try, this will come down over both sides." He pulled, working the nightshirt down her arms, trapping them against her sides. "No, matter. I think this will be satisfactory."

Slipping his arm under her back, he lifted her until he could reach either breast with his mouth. What he did exactly, Phona could not tell, but whatever it was, it was driving her mad. She could not stay still.

Her body moved of its own accord, arching, relaxing, arching again, growing tenser and tenser. She could hear her own voice whimpering. She wanted to reach for him, to pull him to her, to hold his head against her, but her arms could not get free of the shirt. All she could do was lie in his arms and let him have his way. His incredibly devastating way.

Phona could feel his shaft growing under her hips. Suddenly he groaned and lifted his head. He set her on her feet between his legs, locked his arms around her, and slid forward until his shaft pressed hard against her.

He continued his attention to her nipples until, had he not held her upright, her knees would have dropped her to the floor. She pressed against him shamelessly, uttering small cries.

Suddenly he exclaimed, "Enough of this."

Before she knew what he was about, Hades seized the linen binding her arms and ripped it apart. The nightshirt fell to the floor, and he followed it, kneeling before her, kissing her breasts and her belly and her thighs and—

He turned and lay back on the floor, lowering her with him. Somehow he had opened his britches. His fingers pressed against her inner thigh, opening her until she sat straddling him. He slid his hand under her bottom and lifted her. What did he want her to do?

Phona came to her knees, and he guided her above his shaft. Did he want…? He must want her to…?

He growled deep in his throat. "Lower yourself."

He *did* want her to. She carefully eased down. The tip pressed against her opening. A little more. Slowly and carefully. A little more…

He surged upward, and suddenly he was completely inside her.

"Aah! Dear lady." He pulled her down until her breasts were directly over his face, her bridal veil falling around them both. "Do what you must."

At first Phona could not move. Dared not. And then his hand and mouth advanced on her nipples again, tasting, touching, intoxicating. And then she could not stay still.

In the sheltered tent of the veil, she began to move, lifting and lowering, circling, pressing. The tension between her legs increased past bearing. Arching her back, she pressed harder. Harder. And then his hand was helping her, pressing in exactly the proper place.

This time Phona came apart, screaming in spite of herself. But if the guards outside the door heard, they did not come to investigate. Hades moved faster, and she writhed against him, all sense of herself lost in him, her cries lost in his as he pumped his seed into her innermost self.

When at last she fell limply across his chest, he fastened his arms around her and held her to him as though he would never let go.

"Phona dearest, you simply cannot!"

"Cannot what, Mama?" Phona sighed and turned on the dressing stool as her mother bustled into the room. She knew very well what her mother meant, of course.

"Your hair, dearest. That style is much too…too young. You simply must wear it done up. You are no longer a young girl. You are a *marchioness*."

And about to preside at her first formal dinner as such. Phona shuddered. All of tonight's guests, including Mama and Papa, had arrived at Darkwood Park during the afternoon and were expected to stay the night. Both hers and Hades' families were to be in attendance.

She would have the dubious pleasure of meeting a large

number of women who had presided over Darkwood Park before her. Hades' sister-in-law. His mother, Lady Aldborough. His grandmother DeBolsover.

She kept telling herself it was *only* family.

Only the DeBolsover clan there to examine her. *Only* assessing her every flaw. *Only* determining her worth as a marchioness.

Perhaps Mama had the right of it. Everyone knew Lady Hathersage to be a paragon of fashion. As always, she looked splendid tonight, gowned in pale blue satin, with her smooth gold hair coiled on her head. Sapphires and diamonds sparkled at her throat.

Phona peered into the dressing mirror and tugged at a curl. She did look very young. Not surprising. She *was* young. Very young and very…curly. But Hades liked her curls.

The recollection of her new husband pulled her thoughts away from her twittering parent and back to last night. And this morning. And this afternoon. Delicious thoughts. His hand. His mouth. His scent. Phona felt the flush start at her breasts and flood upward.

"Phona dearest? Are you all right? You look very pink and with that gown…" Mama unfurled her fan and anxiously stirred the air around her daughter's face.

Phona blushed hotter. Did Mama know what she was thinking? With what patience she could muster, Phona gently pushed the fan aside and returned to the present difficulty. "I am fine, Mama, but you know what will happen if Lily dresses my hair up in a knot. Besides, Lord Pointeforte likes my hair—"

"Oh, Phona dear." Mama waved a dismissing hand and uttered a delicate little laugh. "Men know *nothing* about such matters. But I have brought Halby to you." She turned toward the door. "Halby, do come in and assist us." The older maid entered the room and came to stand behind Phona.

"What do you think of the dress, Halby? I suppose it will do, but perhaps…" Mama placed a finger over her lips and struck a thoughtful pose.

"I think Lady Pointeforte looks charming in that gown, my lady. That soft rose is quite becoming to her coloring. And the ivory lace is very fine. It complements the pearls."

Phona sent the dresser a silent blessing. The dress might almost have been a copy of the one Hades had brought to the gorge for her, although—as it had been purchased under Mama's critical supervision—the neckline dropped not nearly so low.

Phona gazed at Halby in the mirror. "Do you think we might braid—"

"Oh no, dearest. Braids are so…so frumpy."

Phona sighed and closed her eyes. But Halby stepped into the breach. "Not when properly used, my lady." Her practiced fingers separated out a few strands. "I think we may contrive to…"

In the end Phona rose to greet her first guests in her new home adorned by a gravity-defying arrangement of braids anchoring a profusion of curls. She managed to prevent the addition of a large plume, and Mama tut-tutted worriedly that she was not formally enough attired.

Phona worried that, in the middle of dinner, her hair would fall into her plate. She stepped into her first appearance as Lord Pointeforte's lady with all the confidence of a mouse in a room full of cats.

Dinner had been prepared in one of the smaller formal dining rooms. Phona muddled through the introductions and greetings in the drawing room none too badly, although she had an anxious moment when Hades' great-aunt Mandeville leveled her lorgnette in her direction and asked in the loud voice of the extremely deaf, "So *this* is the chit?"

The elderly lady had been quickly shushed by her

younger sister, Hades' octogenarian grandmother. But all in all, Phona thought, no one had actually sneered at her. No one asked her age. No one pointed slyly to the tangle of curls.

But what were they thinking about her?

Phona took her place at the foot of the table with a sigh of relief. Arrayed before her were the combined strengths of both the DeBolsover and the Hathersage tribes, including several maternal uncles.

At the far end of the long table, clad in black and wearing his deceptive left glove he used for eating, sat Hades. He seemed so far away. Not only in space, but in aspect. Although he had doffed the eye patch, he still had not shaved.

While his dark hair had not grown out enough to tie at the neck, he had combed it straight back, giving him much the same appearance. The severe style and the dark shadow across his lower face brought vivid memories of the time she had first seen him. A time when she had feared him.

Feared him? Phona could hardly reconcile the notion with the playful friend, the gentle lover he had since become. But this evening the Marquess of Pointeforte evoked shades of DeBolsovers past, conquering marcher lords holding their demesnes, not only at the pleasure of the king, but by the strength of their arm. By their cleverness and guile.

By their diplomacy.

Phona chuckled behind a forkful of creamed lobster. Poor dear. Sitting as he was between Mama and his mother, Lady Aldborough, Hades needed all the skills of a veteran diplomat. Or perhaps a modicum of cleverness and guile. And if the expression on Mama's face was any indication, he might soon need the strength of his arm to keep the peace.

She had the easy task with Papa and Lord Aldborough flanking her. The two gentlemen talked of gentlemanly things. Politics, about which Phona knew very little. Pugilism, about which she knew nothing. Horses, about which she knew a great deal. But all she really had to do was listen attentively and nod intelligently at what she hoped were the proper times.

Next to Lord Aldborough sat the unwitting donor of the two gowns Hades had purloined from the cache of stolen goods, the Dowager Marchioness of Pointeforte. What a strange title for someone so young and beautiful. One thought of a dowager as bent and silver-haired, walking with an ebony cane as Hades' grandmother did.

On the contrary, Lisette DeBolsover had yet to see her thirtieth birthday. Attired in lavender, Percy's widow was graced by soft, light-brown tresses, suitably and attractively twisted into a sleek knot at the back of her head.

A shiver ran down Phona's spine. Was that a hairpin that had just slid down the back of her gown? She gave her head a tiny experimental shake. Yes, Halby's creation was loosening. She resisted the impulse to touch it, Mama's words echoing in her head.

Poking at one's hair is a very unattractive habit, Phona dearest, one I do hope you will strive to correct.

How many little habits had Phona striven to correct at Mama's behest? There seemed to be no end of ways in which a young lady might make herself unattractive. No doubt a marchioness might have the same shortcomings.

The absence of one expected DeBolsover continued to be evidenced by an unoccupied chair. Phona had seen Hades scowl at Rob's empty place several times. It did not seem in character for his cousin to fail them on such an auspicious occasion, but truly, Phona did not know him that well. Perhaps the only known Pointeforte heir was wont to disappear at inconvenient times.

When Lisette glanced in her direction, Phona ventured a tentative smile. "Has there been no word from Rob?"

Lisette frowned, shaking her head. "No, none."

"Now what has become of the rascal?" Lord Aldborough

joined the discussion. "Has he forgotten all his manners since he took up residence by himself at Maplewood?"

"Maplewood?" Phona had heard the name before, but did not really know what it was.

"It is the estate their grandfather set aside for his younger son, Rob's father. Now it is Rob's." Lisette daintily applied her napkin to perfect lips. "It is not far from here."

"I see." Phona was glad to know that the DeBolsovers cared for all their offspring, that Rob had a place of his own. Too often younger sons were left with nothing. "Are both his parents dead, then?"

"Aye." Lord Aldborough laid down his fork. "His father has been dead these many years. Mrs. DeBolsover died…" He cast a glance at his wife, but as etiquette forbade addressing those at a distance down the board, he was denied the benefit of her memory. "Hmm…"

"When Rob was young." Lisette came to his aid. "That is why he grew up in Lady Aldborough's care, with Percy and Leo."

The young dowager returned her attention to her dinner partner, Hades' maternal uncle. For all her smiling beauty, Phona thought the young widow carried a sadness in her eyes. How could she not, losing her husband after so few years?

They had not even had a child together. Tears threatened to gather behind Phona's eyelids. She could not bear even the thought of losing Hades. Especially now, after learning the joys of his bed. She gazed down the table at him, and felt the color rising into her face again as she recollected those joys.

He looked ready to bolt, even though Mama had turned the full effect of her charm on him. Or perhaps *because* Mama had turned the full effect of her charm on him. And Phona thought *his* mother looked disapproving.

Alas, unfortunate lad. Caught betwixt and between.

Perhaps she could give him something to look forward to. She caught his eye for a moment and smiled as provocatively as she knew how. An answering smile lit his face, and for just a second he let his tongue stroke his lower lip. Blushing furiously, Phona quickly ducked her chin.

And suddenly detected an ominous wobble atop her head. Oh, dear heaven! Halby's masterpiece was collapsing. Something slid from the top of her head toward her ear. Horrified, she threw up a hand to halt the disaster. Hades burst into laughter.

Which called Mama's attention first to him, then to her. Her mother bowed her head and covered her eyes with one hand. Lady Aldborough glanced first at Mama, then at Phona, paused, and hastily hid a smile behind her napkin. Aunt Mandeville aimed her lorgnette. Hairpins rained to the floor.

Tears sprang to Phona's eyes. Why had she allowed herself to be persuaded? Why hadn't she just left the dratted stuff loose?

Just as she was about to excuse herself and retire in disgrace, Eggars hurried into the room and went straight to Hades' chair. Hades looked up at him inquiringly. Eggars's agitated voice carried clearly to all corners of the room.

"It is Mr. Rob, my lord. He has been hurt and—"

A commotion at the door caught everyone's attention. With two footmen doing their best to detain him, Rob stumbled into the room, dripping blood.

"Oh, I am sorry, my lord." Eggars abandoned Leo and started for Rob. "I did not want to distress the ladies."

"Nonsense." Hades' grandmother, her chair crashing to the floor as she jumped to her feet, made for her injured grandson. She stumbled in her haste, losing her grip on her cane. Lord Hathersage leaped to her aid. Leo's mother ran past them.

But Leo outdistanced them all. He slid an arm around his cousin's waist and maneuvered him out of the doorway into the corridor, followed by his mother, his grandmother's voice and his disheveled wife.

"Rob! What the devil happened?" He turned to the nearest footman. "Send a rider for Dr. Haverstance. Go, man!"

"Ambush." Rob coughed, and a small amount of bloody froth came to his lips. Another gush welled out of his upper chest.

"Oh, dear heaven." Leo's mother grasped her foster son's opposite arm. "It has struck a lung. Get him to a bed."

Signaling a footman to help, Leo thrust a shoulder under one of Rob's and grasped that leg. The footman took the other side, and together they carried him up the stairs, his head lolling.

"I believe he has lost consciousness." His mother leaned close to her nephew's face. "But he is breathing. Get his coat off, Leo."

Somewhat to Lady Aldborough's startlement, Leo slipped a knife out of his sleeve and went to work on the coat. He had it off and was just starting on the shirt when his wife and his sister-in-law burst into the room, arms full of bandages and towels. Not far behind came a brigade of footmen bearing hot water.

Leo almost smiled. The DeBolsover women were nothing if not efficient. He grabbed a folded towel and pressed it to the wound. "It looks like a knife wound. Thank God. A pistol would have caused much more damage. And luckily it is high. Still…" He shook his head. "If it has nicked his lung…"

At that moment their patient moaned. "Ar-Arthur."

"Who?" Leo glanced inquiringly around the room, but everyone just shook their heads, puzzled.

Suddenly his cousin tried to sit, and Leo was obliged to rest his weight on him. "Don't move, Rob. You will increase the bleeding."

Rob continued to struggle. "Arthur. Must bring…"

Leo pushed harder. "Be still, old man. We will find Arthur in good time."

But his cousin grasped Leo fiercely by the lapel, dragging himself up. "Go! Go…bring Arthur…"

Exhausted and struggling for breath, he fell back on the bed and his assembled relatives looked at one another in bewilderment.

"Who is Arthur, dear?" Lady Aldborough leaned nearer her nephew's lips.

"It doesn't matter." Leo continued the pressure on Rob's chest. "We must concern ourselves now with Rob."

"No! No, damn you." The words were broken by more coughing. "Go. Go…"

Leo glanced up as Phona stepped up to the other side of the bed. She placed a gentle hand on Rob's forehead. "*Where* is Arthur, Rob?"

That was the question they should be asking, of course. Leo could barely hear the answer.

"Maple…wood." Rob's eyes closed, and Leo feared he was dead, but a moment later another whisper emerged. "Go…"

"Good enough. Someone will go. Rest now."

"*You… You* go. Now!"

"All right, cos. I will go. Now save your strength." Rob subsided, and Leo lifted his head. "Where is that damned doctor?"

It had seemed an eternity until Dr. Haverstance arrived at Darkwood Park. Rob had lapsed into unconsciousness, and Leo had been loathe to leave him until the doctor came. However, he had been infected by the urgency of his cousin's demand. Someone—someone named Arthur—needed him at Maplewood.

So now, with a party of outriders, he rode through a chilly

night. The night immediately following his wedding night. A night for which he had far more pleasant plans. He had kissed his new wife as thoroughly as he could with their combined families watching and left her bidding him good hunting.

A strong lady. One worthy to be a DeBolsover.

"Here, me lord!" At a shout from his scout, Leo spurred forward and dismounted. "This would be the place they done it."

Holding a lantern aloft, his man knelt beside something dark lying on the ground. "This'd be Mr. Rob's groom, I'll warrant."

Sitting on his heels, Leo peered at the man. Dead. No doubt about it. He let his gaze roam over the ground. "There." He pointed with his riding crop. "That must be his pistol."

"Aye." The scout picked it up, held it to his nose, and sniffed. "Both barrels been fired. He put up a fight."

"As I'm sure Rob did also. We'll find his pistol in the morning, I don't doubt." Leo looked around at the gathered men. "Does anyone know—was Mr. DeBolsover's groom named Arthur?"

"Nay, me lord." One of his riders spoke up. "It'd be Jeb, I'm thinking."

"Then who the devil is Arthur?" Leo was not expecting an answer and did not get one. "Very well. Let us continue to Maplewood. Perhaps the answer is there."

"We gonna just leave him here, me lord? Don't seem right to let the dead lie alone."

Leo considered for a moment. "No, it does not seem right. But he cannot be harmed further. I do not wish to leave a lone, living man to keep vigil with deadly mischief afoot."

A hasty murmur of agreement met this opinion. They all remounted, and Leo led them out at a gallop for Maplewood. Whoever Arthur was, he might be in grave peril.

As they rode up the drive, not a light showed. The rambling house, old but well-kept, was completely dark. The cavalcade drew rein at the front steps, and Leo's men fanned out as he climbed to the front door and gave the knocker a vigorous rapping. And they waited.

And waited longer.

Enough of that. Leo slammed the knocker again and pounded on the door with his crop for good measure. At last he was rewarded by a voice, distant but approaching, bidding him to hold his damned horses.

"Who's there?" came a muffled shout from behind the door.

"It is I, Pointeforte. Let us in, man."

"Pointeforte you say?"

"Yes, damn it! The Marquess of Pointeforte. Leo De-Bolsover. Open the cursed door."

"How do I know you are who you say you are?"

How indeed? Since Rob had made Maplewood his residence, Leo had been too occupied with his own recovery and with fending off his enemy—who, he feared, might be Rob himself—to visit him.

"Let us just say that if you do not open to us at once, the Marquess of Pointeforte will be the man who kicks the door into your face." Leo gave it a boot to reinforce his threat.

A key turned in the lock and the creak of hinges was heard. Leo stepped closer.

And found himself staring down the barrel of a pistol.

The door had been suddenly flung open, and a determined-looking man clad in a nightshirt and frock coat barred his way. "Now who do you say you are?"

Hastily moving back a step, Leo asked, "Are you Arthur?"

"I?" The man looked puzzled. "I am Hartvard, Mr. De-Bolsover's butler."

"Is Arthur here?" If he could only determine who the hell Arthur was…

The gun never wavered. "I shall inquire."

And the door slammed in Leo's face. His lunge proved just too slow to stop the rattle of the key. Damnation! He had never anticipated resistance. He gave the door another resounding kick.

Fortunately, he was forced to endure little delay this time. After only a few seconds during which Leo could hear the murmur of a hasty conference, the door opened again, and the pistol reappeared.

Correction. *Another* pistol appeared. The first one was still held by the butler. A tall, thin woman with an iron-gray braid wielded the second. She looked as though she knew how to use it.

She looked Leo up and down. "Yes, I believe he may be Pointeforte. He has the look of a DeBolsover."

"I *am* a DeBolsover! Pointeforte! May I now please speak with Arthur, whoever the devil that may be?"

"Mr. DeBolsover is sleeping."

Mr. DeBolsover?

"Then wake him. I have had enough of this obfuscation."

She gave him a look that might have stricken him to the ground where he stood and covered him in frost. "Yes, my lord."

This time Leo was quick enough to push inside the door before it closed on him. He stood in the entry hall, the butler still training his weapon on him. The large, shadowy form of a footman loomed behind him. They had not asked him to sit.

Mr. DeBolsover? Where the hell had an unknown De-Bolsover sprung from? Could this be his elusive enemy? Had Rob allied himself with some undiscovered cousin?

When the answer was made evident, Leo could only stare with his jaw slack. The gray-haired woman came walking carefully down the stairs. In her arms a…a…

A very small boy clad in a nightshirt.

Four or five years old. Who in the world…?

The butler nodded. "Lord Pointeforte, may I present Master Arthur DeBolsover."

Chapter Fourteen

The nurse set the child on his bare feet at the bottom of the stair. "Master Arthur, please speak politely to Lord Pointe-forte."

To the lad's credit, though obviously fuddled with sleep he did not cling to his nurse's skirt. He delivered his greeting forthrightly. "Your most 'bedient servant, sir."

Leo gathered his scattered wits and stepped closer to the boy. He went down on one knee, bringing his face to the boy's level. "Well said. Your name is Arthur?"

"Yes, sir." At the questioning, the child edged closer to his nurse. She put a protective hand on his shoulder.

"Can you tell me your father's name, Arthur?"

"Mr. DeBolsover."

Leo rubbed his forehead in frustration and looked at the butler.

"That would be Mr. Robert DeBolsover, my lord."

Leo sprang to his feet. "You mean my cousin?"

"Yes, my lord."

Good God! Rob had a son that no one knew about? "Where may I find Master Arthur's mother?"

"For her, my lord, you must look to the churchyard."

"My mother lives in heaven with the angels. That's 'cause she is dead."

At this unexpected announcement Leo turned his attention back to his newfound first cousin once removed. In the boy's presence, how might he inquire as to his legitimacy?

But as if reading his thoughts, Hartvard said defensively, if obscurely, "Banns, my lord."

Banns. "Then they were wed?"

"Aye, my lord. These five years ago and more." Obviously the butler had been loyal to his mistress.

Five years! Had he so lost contact with his boyhood companion that he did not know that? Did *none* of his family know it, not even his mother? Of course, she had wed Lord Aldborough ten years ago and moved away. She might not have known.

But a son four years old? A legitimate son.

Another Pointeforte heir standing in someone's way.

Phona sipped from her cup of tea and regarded her new sister-in-law. Lisette sat across the bed from her, also recruiting her strength with the tea Eggars had just brought them. A third cup sat on the tray, but Dr. Haverstance had left the room on some errand of his own.

In the bed Rob lay, propped against several pillows to ease his breathing. His eyes were closed, and Phona doubted that he was conscious. She found herself glancing every few seconds to reassure herself that his chest still rose and fell, no matter how slightly.

Lisette sighed and set her cup on the tray. Phona thought she detected the sheen of tears in her sister-in-law's eyes. She was wondering whether she should address this observation when Lisette spoke.

"It is very difficult, you know."

Not knowing exactly *what* was so difficult, Phona did not

know quite how to respond. She decided on being direct. Gently she asked, "What is, dear?"

"He looks very much like Percy."

Phona's heart clenched. She had never seen the elder De-Bolsover brother, but she had noticed a resemblance between Hades and his cousin. She said as much. "I can seen how distressing that might be for you. It is very disturbing to think—"

"I sat by his bed then, much as we are now." The tears began to drip down the young dowager's face. "He just quietly left me. Without even a word."

"Oh, Lisette!" Phona jumped up and went around the bed to her. She knelt and clasped her sister-in-law's hands. "I am so, so sorry. How did it occur? Did he fall ill?"

"No. He always drove too fast. A wheel came loose from the curricle, and he was thrown into the ditch. He lived a few hours, but his neck—" Lisette dropped her face into her hands.

Tears sprang to Phona's eyes in response. "Oh, my dear."

At that moment Dr. Haverstance came back into the room. "Come now, ladies. Don't go measuring this one—" he nodded at the bed "—for grave clothes yet. He has too much reason to stay alive."

The doctor lifted Rob's wrist and counted for a moment, then returned his gaze to them. "Four generations of bad luck. Well, I can't speak for the eldest Lady Pointeforte's husband. Before my time. But I know myself of two accidental deaths. The carriage mishap the two of you were discussing and the lord before that, your father-in-law. Shooting accident. And now this latest generation seems rather prone to calamity, also."

Phona bristled. How could he speak so before Lisette? Or herself, for that matter. She rose to her feet. "Dr. Haverstance, your words do not convey comfort. In fact, they are rather frightening. Lady Pointeforte—" she indicated Lisette "—is already distr—"

The doctor turned to her, all contrition. "Forgive me, my lady. Just thinking aloud. Bad habit of mine."

Lisette reached for Phona's hand. "Do not fret on my account, Phona. I am an old friend of Dr. Haverstance."

He patted her shoulder. "Yes, indeed, my lady."

Before Phona could respond, she detected the rattle of carriage wheels and the stamp of horses. She ran to the window and looked down into the drive. She peered into the darkness at the riders, her heart beating hard in her chest. There he was! Safe.

"It is Lord Pointeforte." She spun around and ran toward the door before she bethought herself of her companions. She jerked to a halt and turned to Lisette. "Forgive me—"

Lisette waved her on. "Do not concern yourself with me. Go to him."

He had the very devil of a time persuading young Arthur's legion of defenders to allow him to bring the boy. Rob had effectively inculcated in them his fears for his son. Fears with apparently all too much foundation. Clearly Rob had as much to fear as Leo himself.

At long last, Leo bundled them all into Rob's coach. He had sent out scouts while the prolonged process of gathering up a small boy's necessities had taken place. Now he rode alongside the coach with the balance of his outriders.

Hartvard had insisted on coming, riding inside with Arthur and his nurse, pistol at the ready. Leo suspected the nurse still carried her piece as did he and his men. All in all, they were a rather warlike group.

They came thundering up the drive to Darkwood Park just as the sun cleared the treetops, painting the sky with delicate pink and gold. Weary to the bone, Leo dismounted and opened the carriage door.

Arthur sat up from where he had been dozing with his head in his nurse's lap. "Are we there?"

Leo reached out, and the boy came willingly into his arms, trailing a blanket. He gazed into his newfound relative's face. "You look like my papa."

"Yes, your papa and I are cousins. Cousins often resemble one another."

"Is this a house?" Arthur gazed up at the intimidating pile before him.

"Yes." Leo laughed for the first time since Rob had staggered into his dining room. "It is my house. Welcome to my home."

Arthur looked it over critically. "*My* house has a name."

"Perhaps I should have said, 'Welcome to Darkwood Park.'"

"That's all right." The tiny hand patted his broad shoulder. "We all make mistakes."

"Indeed we do." Now who had told the lad that? Leo chuckled as he tucked the blanket around the child and started up the wide stairs. Apparently Rob had made a mistake of colossal proportions. Otherwise, they would all have known about Arthur.

He opened the door.

And stepped straight into the arms of his wife.

She flung her arms around them both. "Oh, my lord. I was so worried. But…? Who might this be?"

"This would be Arthur." He leaned over and embraced as much of her as he could reach, kissing her briefly. "I believe that he is Rob's son."

"Dear heaven!" She gazed at the boy. "And you had no knowledge of him?"

"None at all. I don't think any of the family did. How is— I mean, is Rob—?"

"He is holding his own."

Thank God. Leo sighed with relief.

Arthur gazed curiously at Phona. "Who is this lady? Why did you kiss her?"

"I kissed her because she is my wife." Leo smiled. He could see that having young Arthur about might prove a challenge.

By this time the nurse had caught up to them. "Master Arthur, it is not polite to ask so many questions. Here, my lord, I will take him."

She reached out, but Leo found he did not want to relinquish the boy yet. "That is quite all right, Mrs...?"

"Trammell."

"Thank you, Mrs. Trammell. I find Arthur's questions to be very natural under the circumstances." He turned back to his lady. "Where is Eggars—ah! Here you are. Would you please ask Mrs. Oglethorpe to have the nursery suite made ready? I'm sure Mrs. Trammell will wish to stay there with Master Arthur, but Hartvard will need rooms."

"I shall stay in the nursery suite also, my lord, if you do not object."

Startled at this request, Leo gazed at Hartvard with puckered brow. Surely those quarters were beneath the dignity of a butler. "Are you certain, Hartvard?"

"I gave my word to Mr. DeBolsover, my lord, to watch over his son."

"Very well." Leo shrugged and nodded to Eggars, and the butler went off to execute his orders.

For the first time Arthur's lip threatened to tremble. "Where is my papa? You said you would take me to my papa."

"And so I shall." Leo turned to Phona inquiringly.

She shook her head doubtfully. "He was not coherent when I left the room. Dr. Haverstance and Lisette are with him. Your mother has gone to rest. But we need to explain…" She moved closer and took the child's hand. "Arthur, your papa has been hurt, but the doctor is helping him. We will take you to him for a moment, if you promise not to disturb him. Can you be quiet as a mouse?"

Arthur put one finger to his lips. "Shh."

"That is correct. Shh." Phona chuckled. "Come. He is upstairs."

Leo took a few steps, then, realizing that he had an entourage, halted. "Yes? Hartvard? Mrs. Trammell?"

The butler spoke for them. "We would also like to see Mr. DeBolsover."

Apparently Rob's staff did not much trust his family. Leo sighed. "Very well."

He marched them all up the stairs. As soon as they entered the room, his cousin's eyes sprang open. His hand reached toward them, and a whisper emerged from his dry lips.

"Arthur."

"Yes." Leo set the boy on the floor beside the bed. "And you, my dear cos, have some explanations to make."

It was not truly the longest night that Leo could remember, but at the moment it seemed to be. As soon as Rob's household had been assured that he still lived, and that neither he nor his heir was in any danger from the Marquess of Pointeforte, Leo had sent them all away and swept his bride out of the room.

During his absence she had managed to dismantle the tumbling arrangement of her hair and tie it back with a ribbon. He did not like the dark smudges he saw under her eyes. Apparently she had kept vigil with Rob all night.

He led her up to his rooms, steering her toward his own bedchamber when she hesitated uncertainly at the door of her own. He ushered her through the door, closed and locked it.

"Ah." He wrapped his arms around her and crushed her to him. "What a coil this is." He dipped his head and covered her mouth with his. She tasted of tea and smelled of roses and delicious woman. He might have stood thus forever, save that his aching neck rebelled.

He released her and tugged her toward the bed. Sitting on the edge of it, he spread his legs and pulled her to him. He rested his head against her breasts, breathing in her scent, reveling in her softness. This, this was homecoming.

Not only his lifelong home. Not only his own bed.

Her.

"Are you very weary, my lord? You have been on a horse most of the night." She smoothed his hair back from his forehead.

"That and laying siege to my own cousin's home." He looked up at her and laughed. "I would like to think that *my* household would be so well defended." Sobering, he began to unfasten her gown, reaching around her to find the hooks. "Apparently Rob fears not only for himself, but for the boy."

"With good reason." She let the dress slide down her arms, then laid her hands on his shoulders and gazed down at him. "As have you."

"I fear you are correct. Someone seems determined to eliminate the whole DeBolsover clan." He pulled the straps of her shift off her shoulders. "Mmm, you smell luscious." The shift joined the dress on the floor.

"Not the whole clan, my lord. Oh!"

She gasped as Leo closed his mouth over one nipple, nibbling gently. He felt her knees go slack, and his body grew hard in spite of his fatigue. "No. You are correct. Somewhere there must be an unknown descendent, attacking from the dark."

"Ahh." She collapsed toward him as he shifted to the other nipple. "Is Arthur—" She uttered a little sigh.

"Apparently legitimate." He drew her across him and rolled her onto the bed. He was about to throw his leg across her when it came to the attention of his tired brain that he was still in his boots. And coat. And the damn false glove. The straps that held it in place still lapped around his shoulders and chest.

Leo groaned. He could divest himself of the coat, but the confounded boots required help. They were too tight to pull off with one hand, and his valet absolutely forbade a bootjack in his dressing room. It damaged the leather.

And then, there was the glove. The goddamned glove. He could unfasten the straps himself and remove it, but the shirt he wore tonight was not designed to cover his bare wrist.

She would see it.

She would see his hideous deformity.

As he hesitated, she said, "My lord?"

He rubbed the back of his neck in exasperation and stood. "Forgive me, my lady. I must ring for Jemsford to help me with my boots and change my shirt."

"I should be happy to help you, my lord." She sat and moved toward the edge of the bed.

"No!"

She paused and gazed at him in confusion. "But I..."

"Thank you, but I do not relish the image of you naked, on your knees at my feet."

She giggled. "That does sound rather decadent, but I do not mind." Standing, she grasped his collar. "Here, let me help you with your coat."

She tugged it down over his shoulders a bit and reached for the left cuff, preparing to pull it off over the glove.

"Don't!" He jerked away from her. "Don't touch it."

She stopped and sat back down on the bed, gazing up at him with huge, hurt eyes. "I don't understand, my lord."

Leo scrubbed at his face. Damnation. He was the greatest brute in nature. A cad. A blackguard. He went to his knees before her. "I...I'm sorry." He gathered both her hands in his one good one. "I do not want you to touch—to *be* touched—by my infirmity. It is gross and ugly..." He bowed his head against their clasped hands.

"Oh, Hades." She rested her cheek on his hair. "How can

you say that? I see *nothing* about you that is gross or ugly. I do not mind touching any part of you."

He released her hands and wrapped his arms around her waist, laying his face against her bosom. "Ah, my courageous lady. I have no doubt you mean what you say, but I could not bear it. I want to keep that affliction from you."

"But at the moment it is keeping *you* from me."

Leo could not refute the accuracy of that statement, but while his aching body protested the delay, he could not bring himself to bare his amputation. Not yet.

Perhaps not ever.

There had been nothing for it. Hades had been determined to go to his dressing room and call for his valet. Before he left, he had insisted that Phona lie down again in the bed and had carefully tucked the bedclothes around her nakedness.

She lay alone, on her back, tears trailing from her eyes into her hair. She felt that she had failed him. Try as she might, Phona could think of no argument that would make him feel differently about his injury, so she had simply let him go.

But perhaps that is exactly what she should have done. Perhaps, in time, when he was more comfortable with her, with the marriage, he would change. Perhaps he would come to trust her.

Perhaps even to love her.

But thinking of his fear, his revulsion toward his own body, Phona could only weep.

She had been nine parts asleep when he returned to the bed. He slipped in beside her and pulled her against him. Phona tried to rouse, but could only murmur groggily.

"Never mind." He kissed her forehead. "We both need to sleep."

She rested her head on his shoulder, and by the time she

saw the light of day again, it was after noon. Something was tickling the nape of her neck. And something was stroking her breast. Phona opened one eye. She found herself lying on her side with her back to Hades. He was nuzzling under her ear now.

As she lay, enjoying this lovely mode of awakening, his hand left her breast and began to smooth the skin of her stomach. She wiggled closer, and he groaned. He pushed his hips against her, his shaft hard against her bottom. She essayed another wiggle.

This time the groan was louder. When his hand slipped lower, she sighed in delight and wiggled her bottom again.

"Ah, sweet lady." Hades turned her toward him. He kissed her lips, his tongue making tantalizing forays into her mouth. His hand never left that special spot as he moved the kisses lower, stopping at first one nipple and then the other.

Phona again lost all capability of speech. She closed her eyes and floated in space, uttering tiny moans. All at once he was above her, spreading her legs with his muscular thighs. The tip of his shaft pressed against her, then began to slowly slide into her.

She cried out and lifted to him. He gradually withdrew. Phona tried to follow, but could not bring her hips high enough. But then, again, he was thrusting into her. In and out. Slowly. Carefully. In and out.

She heard her own voice whimpering. Her body desired, craved, strove. In and out. She pressed against him once more, and the space she was in began to whirl. Faster now. Faster. And faster.

Phona shrieked. All around her lights flickered, blue and white. Her skin tightened, tingling, from her legs to the crown of her head. Her face. Her breasts. Her belly. She heard his voice mingled with hers.

And then, bit by bit, the universe righted itself. Came back together. Her skin shivered back to normal. Her body crumpled, warm, relaxed, breathless. Hades lay propped on his forearms, his forehead resting against her, his deep breathing melding with hers.

He wore nothing but a shirt.

One with a cuff that buttoned firmly over his wrist.

"Great God in Heaven! Now he has announced his marriage to the Hathersage chit. I should have put a ball in her legs when I had the chance."

"Or a knife." Swish. Swish. "No doubt the lusty bastard will waste no time getting himself an heir. Yet another heir of which we must rid ourselves."

"Indeed. She may even now be carrying one." His companion threw himself impatiently into a chair.

He squinted down the edge of the blade, and the corners of his lips turned up in something that could hardly be called a smile. He drew the knife across the top of the table, adding several shallow cuts to the scarred wood. "Never mind. I shall personally rid us of her."

Chapter Fifteen

This was a council of war.

Leo saw it as soon as he came into the room.

And, from all appearances, an interrogation. It had all started innocently enough. A request from his grandmother that he meet her in the gold drawing room for "a little chat." He should have known. He had encountered her "little chats" before.

As he came through the door, six pairs of eyes fixed on him. All female. Four of them present or former Marchionesses of Pointeforte. And, of course, the only unoccupied chair was the one directly within the sights of the eldest of them.

Not an auspicious state of affairs.

Leo had been the recipient of that gaze on numerous boyhood occasions. After a cautious pause, he crossed to her and kissed her cheek. "Good afternoon, Grandmama." He indicated the circle of women with a sweep of his hand. "Our 'little chat' seems to have grown."

"Do not be impertinent, Leopold. Sit down."

Leo sat.

Futilely doing his best to appear in control of the situation, he assumed a casual pose and glanced at his wife. She shrugged, but her eyes twinkled. Leo turned to his black-clad grandparent. "Here I am, Grandmama, at your behest. May I know what has brought us all together?"

She regarded him without benefit of optics, her clear, blue eyes easily piercing any facade he might present. "I have spoken with Robert this morning."

Ah. Very good. Perhaps this meeting might be deflected from his own shortcomings—whatever they might be on this occasion—to Rob's. He had spoken with Rob himself, but nonetheless asked, "And how does my cousin fare this morning?"

"Improving—as you know."

Hmm. Not a successful ploy. Perhaps he should make another attempt. "What did you discuss that has required this assembly? The advent of Arthur?"

His grandmother's expression became, if possible, more disapproving. "Among other things. Apparently, Robert legally married the daughter of one of his tenants. A tenant! What could he have been thinking? Little wonder he kept it secret."

Just as Leo was framing his next move, his mother spoke up. "Very unwise, of course. But just as I regard Rob as my son, I shall regard Arthur as my grandson." She cast Leo a significant glance. "Although I, at last, have hope…"

Leo looked at Phona, who was blushing furiously. He smiled. "Enough, Mama. But, yes." He directed a stern look in his grandmother's direction. "Arthur is Rob's child, whoever his mother may have been, and he will be treated as such."

His grandparent glared at him. "Do not be absurd, Leopold. Arthur is a DeBolsover. Certainly he will be treated accordingly. That, however, is not what I wish to discuss."

As he had feared. Leo flinched inwardly. Outwardly he gazed expectantly and politely at his grandparent.

"I believe, *Lord Pointeforte,* that you have failed to keep the rest of us informed. Apparently, the very determined ill-wisher by whom you have been beset in recent years is still at work."

Oh, no. He had gone from being *Leopold* to *Lord Pointeforte.* Not a good sign. And it seemed that the troublesome events he had been trying to keep from the women who cared for him were about to be revealed to them. "And what makes you believe that, Grandmama?"

She sniffed. "My little chat with Robert, of course."

Another "little chat." With Rob full of laudanum. "What did my helpful cousin tell you?"

The elderly lady ticked off the accusations on her bent fingers. "That he has been attacked before. *And* that someone shot at the two—no, the three—of you in the park. *And...*" She paused portentously. "Mrs. Wheelwright told Mrs. Oglethorpe—"

Leo covered his face with his hand. When the housekeepers came into it, he was doomed.

"—that someone sent you poisoned sweets in London. That when Mrs. Wheelwright's mouser got into the box of sweetmeats that was delivered unexpectedly to the house, it died a terrible death. And that they smelled strongly of almonds. She said she set them out for the mice and they died, too." She finished her recitation and leaned back in her chair, arms folded, gaze riveted expectantly on Leo's face.

"Grandmama..." He had worked very hard to keep these difficulties from the ladies of the family. He should have known better. "Yes, Mrs. Wheelwright says that. I, myself, could not smell the almonds, but the animals did die." He turned to his mother. Her face had gone white. "I did not wish to worry any of you."

His grandmother's gaze again went through to his bones. "*And...*I believe, Leopold, in addition to the assaults about which we are now informed, you have kept yet another to yourself. You are limping, Leopold. When a bridegroom is limping after his—"

"Grandmama!" Face flaming, Leo sprang to his feet, winced and sat again. She was correct, of course. The bullet wound in his thigh had never completely quit aching, and the activities of the last two days had seriously aggravated it.

Not that he wanted that fact pointed out to all his female relatives.

"Oh, do sit down, Leopold. So what have you been doing to apprehend this rascal? You cannot have been ignoring the threats."

Suddenly his mother-in-law spoke from her seat beside Phona. "I know what he has been doing."

All eyes swiveled in her direction. Leo frantically shook his head at her. His wife reached out and clasped Phona's mother's wrist warningly.

Ye gods! The woman was going blurt out the whole tale.

Lady Hathersage moved her daughter's hand and gave Leo a reproving glance. But to his surprise and infinite relief she did not expose his masquerade as a bandit to the rest of them. She said, simply and discreetly, "He has been pursuing matters singlehandedly."

"Exactly." It was his grandmother who spoke, but all the women nodded gravely. "Obviously a mistake. You need our help, Leopold."

Leo smiled. He had never considered the distaff side of the family as help. Rather, he saw his responsibility to protect them as part of his problem. "I appreciate the sentiment, Grandmama. If you were men—"

"There *are* no DeBolsover men, save you and Robert— and now young Arthur, of course. But Robert is injured, very likely by the same miscreant who has attacked you on numerous occasions, and Arthur is too young. We must protect them, too."

A spark of irritation flared in Leo. He drew his eyebrows together. "I am doing my best to do just that, Grandmama."

"What we must do," his wife intervened, "is to determine who is behind these dastardly incidents. Obviously, they are attempting to clear a path to the marquessate."

"That does seem to be the case." Leo's mother reached over and patted her daughter-in-law's hand. "I believe that both Lisette and I may also have been the victims of this scoundrel. He may have widowed us both."

"Yes," Lisette agreed, squeezing her hand in return. "Last night Dr. Haverstance called their deaths bad luck, but I agree with Lady Aldborough. Accidents such as those which killed our loved ones could easily be arranged. And now both Rob and Leo have been assaulted, evidently more than once. And poor Aelfred wounded— We must get to the bottom of it."

"Indeed." Leo made a wry face. He had been unavailingly attempting to root out their enemy for three years.

"My daughter and I have been discussing this problem." Lady Hathersage posed prettily as she spoke, finger touching chin. "This must be laid at the door of the next heir. Of course, the rest of you should know better than we who that might be, but…" She gave them time to feel their lack of perception. "But I definitely recall *my* mother mentioning a gentleman who *her* mother told her came courting *her* mother. Her family was not at all pleased, you know, because of his wild ways, but—"

"Good heavens, Demetra. Come to the point." Grandmama turned her gimlet gaze away from Leo to his mother-in-law. "Are you talking about your great-grandmother?"

"Of course." Lady Hathersage pouted. "Did I not say so?"

An unladylike snort erupted from the eldest Lady Pointeforte. "Well, what is the balance of it? Who was this long-forgotten wild gentleman caller?"

"A DeBolsover." Demetra delivered her coup d'etat with chin triumphantly in the air. "A younger son."

Suddenly Aunt Mandeville, who had been dozing in a corner with a lace handkerchief over her eyes, coughed and blurted something that sounded like, "Pollipup."

Leo's mother turned to her. "Yes, Auntie?"

But Lady Mandeville once more subsided into slumber, snoring softly.

"Ah." Leo looked at his mother-in-law. "The younger son of my great-great-grandfather?"

"I suppose he would be." Lady Hathersage nodded thoughtfully.

"Blollipber." His great-aunt mumbled again, and her sister shushed her.

"Does anyone know what happened to this young man, Mama?" Phona turned to her mother.

"Well, *I* do not. Surely Lady Pointeforte does. It is her family, after all." She nodded at Leo's grandmother and narrowly avoided adding a disdainful sniff.

Grandmama's eyes narrowed dangerously. "In this, Lady Hathersage, you seem to have the advantage of me."

Aunt Mandeville issued something between a comment and snore. "Bulliber."

"What are you trying to say, Amelia?" Grandmama turned to her older sister and scowled. "If you have something to add, do wake up and tell us what it is."

Lady Mandeville roused herself, carefully folded the handkerchief and tucked it into her pocket. She sat up and said, "Named Bolliver."

"Bolliver DeBolsover?" Leo's raised an eyebrow. "Surely not."

"No, no, no. Do not be silly, Leopold." His great-aunt lifted her lorgnette and scowled at him. "He was disowned. Became Bolliver."

"Indeed? How do you know this, Amelia? You were never a DeBolsover." His grandmother sounded more than a little doubtful.

"Courted our grandmama, too. Don't you remember, Cecilia?" She turned to the rest of the group. "She doesn't believe I know anything, anymore. But I very clearly remember Mama telling us about him. He came into the garden after everyone had gone to bed and called out under the window and tried to entice Grandmama to come out. The grooms heard him and chased him through grounds." She turned to her sister. "You should remember the story, Cecilia. Her papa was furious."

"Humph. I never heard that young rascal was a De-Bolsover."

"Oh, yes. Mama told me, when they were discussing marriage to Pointeforte for you. She wasn't certain that the blood was good. After all, to do such an outrageous thing—"

"Nothing wrong with DeBolsover blood." Grandmama drew herself up haughtily. "Just because you married that scamp, Mandeville—"

Leo covered a grin. "Uh...ladies?"

Two pairs of eyes rounded on him. "What?"

Hazardous territory here. Thank the gods men dueled only with pistols. Leo sidestepped. "Aunt Mandeville, when you said this rowdy gentleman became Bolliver, did you mean—"

"Changed his name, of course. Said DeBolsover was too hard to pronounce and as they no longer wanted him—" His aunt Mandeville cast a speaking glance at her sister. "Young people are so slow nowadays."

Leo ignored that bit of bait. "So while we cannot discover any DeBolsovers not of our immediate family, there may be DeBolsover descendants going by the name of Bolliver living in England?"

"Slow." His great-aunt shook her head sadly. "Did I not just say that?"

"Yes, Aunt Mandeville, you did." Leo got to his feet. "And I thank you very much."

* * *

"Ambushed, by Jove!"

"You certainly were." Phona burst into giggles as, a quarter of an hour later, Hades collapsed into a chair in their private sitting room and drew her into his lap. "I feared your Grandmama would send you to bed without your dinner for keeping secrets."

"So did I." He grinned at her. "Clearly there is only one thing to be done."

"What is that?" Snuggling comfortably, Phona put her head on his shoulder.

"Flee! Pack our bags and abscond to the lodge in the gorge. I am outnumbered, outsailed and outgunned." He started untying the ribbon in her hair.

"Maybe they will all go home soon."

"Ha!" Hades jerked the ribbon out of her hair. "Never a chance. Grandmama smells blood. She won't be satisfied until the villain has been tracked to his lair. Besides, Grandmama's and Aunt Mandeville's home is in the dowerhouse, not a mile away. They all have rooms in this house, too. How Lisette tolerates them both every day…"

"I think they are rather dear."

"Huh." He ran his fingers through her hair, fluffing it into a wild halo, then relented. "Yes, I am actually quite fond of both of them, even though Grandmama can reduce me to a small boy with one glance."

"And Lisette—" Phona tugged at the knot of his cravat. "Also a dear."

"Indeed she is. She and Percy were very much in love. But my mama is not going away until Rob is better, and she has the opportunity to get to know a new grandson. And *your* mother…" He groaned. "I suspect she will not budge as long as she suspects that there is any danger to you."

"Oh, no! Not she. Nor will Papa."

"So we are surrounded. It is time to retreat." He planted a kiss on her throat.

Phona laughed. "But if we are surrounded, to where may we retreat?"

"To the bedchamber. We shall barricade the door and make a stand." He kissed her briefly, then sobered. "But in truth, as much as I would like to spirit you away to the lodge, I do not think I should leave Darkwood Park now. Rob and Arthur are vulnerable. I shall send word to my agents to search for Bollivers rather than DeBolsovers. If they find them, we will decide what to do next."

"And now?"

"And now to the bedchamber."

He let her slide off his lap and stood, only to sit again suddenly and pull her back. "Damnation. I am in my boots again, and wearing my false glove. I must go in search of Jemsford."

"Truly, my lord, I don't mind helping you with your boots and—"

"But I told you I don't want you dealing with my injury. And even though I must do so occasionally, I don't like touching you with this glove, especially when making love. It seems like sacrilege."

"Oh, Hades. How can you think such a thing? I am no goddess to be revered, only a woman, flesh and blood, and if this continues, we shall be interrupted every time we wish to—uh…retreat."

He laughed ruefully. "That certainly appears to be true."

"If you hate the glove so, why do you wear it every day? You did not do so when we were at the lodge."

"Because it is grotesque to see the coat sleeve end…empty. And I am afraid it will overset my mother to see it. I did not have the glove at the lodge, or I would have worn it in your presence. There I was expecting only…rough work."

He sat silent for a few moments, staring into the middle distance, and Phona decided wisdom lay in holding her tongue.

At last he said, "I have always had a horror of mutilation. As much as I admired Lord Nelson, it was very difficult for me to look at him." He turn his gaze back to her. "He had lost most of his arm, you know, and had truly lost an eye. I took him as a model for my disguise as a brigand. That sort of thing happens to men of violence."

"You chose someone who repulsed you."

"Yes. Yes, I did." Hades thought for a moment. "As I have come to repulse myself."

Phona's heart broke at those words. She leaned back and favored him with a severe look. "Well, my lord, *I* am not repulsed by you. And I will happily deal with any of your accoutrements. But I will not insist on it."

"Ah, sweet lady." He pulled her closer and buried his face in the side of her neck. "I am fortunate to have found a woman with your courage. I could hardly face life of celibacy."

His arms tightened, pulling her higher. His mouth skimmed the top of her neckline. Phona could feel his shaft under her bottom stirring, getting firmer.

"Are you willing to make love with a fully dressed man?" His tongue left warm, damp spots on her skin, and his hand cupped her bottom, sliding over the silk, the sensation taking her breath.

Phona gasped. "I believe that may prove to be a stimulating experience, my lord."

"Then, my lady, I shall do my very best to be stimulating."

Leo let her slide down into his lap again, so that he could kiss her lips. He eased his hand across her soft bottom, letting his fingers find the indentation between the halves.

How he longed for two good hands!

One for each side of her derriere. One for her bottom and one for her breast. To hold both breasts as he devoured them. To hold her face between them as he kissed her.

She sighed and moved against his hand and, his limitations suddenly forgotten, his shaft filled, grew harder, pulsed. The sound of his own breath began to echo in his ears. He cupped her, his hand gradually moving forward until it was underneath her thigh.

She shifted restlessly, and he began to throb, his breathing becoming harsh and ragged. Lifting slightly, he parted her legs enough to slide his hand against their joining.

He stroked her through the fabric of her skirts until she was moaning softly into his mouth. Longing for the union his lower body demanded, he plunged his tongue into her mouth, thrusting and withdrawing, echoing the unconscious motion of his hips under hers.

Suddenly, feeling confined by the chair, Leo lowered her gently and followed her to the floor. Desperate now to be nearer to her, he pushed her gown up to her waist and bent to kiss her inner thighs.

As she lifted her hips, he caught her hand and laid it against the buttons of his britches. He whispered roughly, "Now. Now, my lady, now I want your help. Unfasten them."

She began fumbling with them, and Leo returned to stroking her, opening her and letting his fingers slip inside her. She moaned and made a mull of his buttons, but at last he felt himself spring free.

He rolled onto her and entered in a single thrust. Her hips rose to meet him, writhing against him. He could hardly contain himself until he heard her cry out, felt her tightening around him until he could contain himself no longer.

His cry joined hers, shouting triumph as he pumped his seed into her. Claimed her in the manner of men and women since the beginning of time.

Once again, made her only his.

* * *

Swish. Swish. *"Now is the time to act. They are all together at Darkwood Park."*

"And how do you propose to enter? Just drive up to the door and announce yourself?"

"Why not? We have as much right to be there as they do." Swish. Swish.

"Were that the case, we would not have a problem."

"I lose patience with this problem." He held the steel up to the light. *"One way or the other, I will soon pay my respects to the new Lady Pointeforte."*

Chapter Sixteen

"Aha!" Hades burst into the morning room with a letter in his hand. "We have them."

Phona's heart leaped up in her chest, as it did every time she saw him. She had almost come to accept him as Pointe-forte. Could she truly be married to this man she loved so deeply? To whom she would willingly open her soul? To whom she gave her body with a whole heart?

Who would not allow her to see all of his.

They had been married for two weeks now, and in that time Phona had spent not a single night in the tall, curtained bed in her own bedchamber. Every evening after dinner Hades insisted they retire early to their private sitting room, there to sip port, leaving the assembled family to their own devices.

As predicted, they were all still there—Mama and Papa; Lord and Lady Aldborough; the dowagers, determined to protect the DeBolsover heirs from their enemies; Rob, slowly mending; and Arthur, thrilled to be the center of so much attention.

Had ever a pair of newlyweds been so beset by kith and kin?

Yet so far not even Grandmama had dared interfere with

the hasty departure of the newlyweds. They made love in his bed, in the big chair in the sitting room and on the floor. Phona had never dreamed there might be so many ways of pleasuring another person. That *the marriage bed* was merely a figure of speech.

Hades had ceased wearing the false glove, and thus there had been no further hindrance in divesting him of his evening clothes. In the afternoons, when he had enticed her upstairs, he had finally allowed her to help him pull off his riding boots, but he still would not remove his shirt with the concealing sleeve buttoned over the wrist.

He would not allow her to touch it.

The thought pained Phona. How could he believe she would ever turn away from him? She found every inch of him strong and beautiful. Masculine. Desirable. Just seeing his face caused her to tighten with need.

But this morning he seemed fairly bursting with another sort of excitement. Phona put down the needlework she had been using to pass the time as all the women in the room looked up at her husband.

"You have found them?" Phona stood and crossed the room to him. "Your men have found the Bollivers?"

He slipped an arm around her waist. "Aye. They are living no farther away than Sheffield."

A fierce gleam came into Grandmama's eye. She struck the tip of her cane against the floor. "The scoundrels! Set the law on them immediately."

Hades held up a hand. "Not so fast, Grandmama. We have not even seen these people. There is no proof at all of any wrongdoing on their part."

"But this proves that they exist." Phona peered at the letter in his hand.

"Yes. And I shall certainly investigate these people immediately. Mr. and Mrs. Bolliver are Lionel and Adelaide.

They have an adult son, Maximilian, living with them. Has anyone ever heard of them?"

A general shaking of heads ensued.

Lady Hathersage ventured, "I would think that they are not received in society. *I* have never encountered them."

"Bring 'em here." Aunt Mandeville roused unexpectedly from her chair in the corner.

"An excellent idea, Amelia." Grandmama nodded. "Give us an opportunity to look them over. Besides, if they are connections of ours, it's high time we all got to know them."

Hades rubbed his beard thoughtfully. "Perhaps. That would give me more control of the situation than if I went to them. But I hesitate to expose the rest of you to any danger they might represent."

"There are only three of them," Phona pointed out, "and only two of them men. Lord Aldborough and Papa would help you watch them. But I cannot imagine their attacking us here. They must immediately be suspected, if they did so."

"The girl has some sense about her." Grandmama nodded. "Invite them, Leopold."

"I shall consider it." He took Phona's arm. "Now, if you ladies will excuse us, I need to speak with Lady Pointeforte privately."

As he guided her out of the room, Phona did her best to ignore the knowing looks that followed them.

"You deceive no one, you know." Phona allowed him to tug her into their sitting room.

Hades grinned. "No. Most likely not. But they daren't challenge me. It would be altogether improper to mention such a thing."

"I doubt your Grandmama would be deterred for a moment by propriety. She is simply delighted at the prospect of yet another DeBolsover heir."

He shrugged out of his coat. "And we certainly do not want to disappoint Grandmama."

"Oh, certainly not!" Phona knelt and began pulling off the tall boots. "I am sure your only thought is to please her."

"Have you not noticed, my lady, that I most often please myself?" He worked at the knot of his cravat.

Phona sighed. "I wish I had your ability to do so. I still find myself trying to please Mama. Even when it means that my hair falls into my plate at my first dinner party as Marchioness of Pointeforte."

"It did not fall into your plate." Still grinning, he lifted her and coaxed her onto his knee. "Although it was a near-run thing."

"Ha! Had Rob not rescued me with his dramatic entrance, bleeding all over the dining room, it would have. Why do I never learn?" She rubbed her cheek against his wide shoulder.

He drew her up into a long, deep kiss. "And you would still have outshone every woman in the room."

She dropped her head back and let herself sink into the kiss. In his arms she felt herself the equal of the most renowned beauties of all time,

He broke the kiss and gazed down into her eyes. "One day, when this present danger is behind us, I shall take you to London and proudly parade you before all the *ton*."

"Oh, Hades." She smiled into his eyes, then began unbuttoning his shirt. When she had it open, she pushed it aside and pressed her lips to his chest, relishing the sensation of the hard muscle beneath the skin.

She stroked her hand across him and, inside the shirt, up over his shoulder. "I love the way you feel." She slid the hand down his upper arm, testing the strength under her fingers. "You are beautiful, too, in a different way. Strong and smooth. I could never think of you as any other way."

"Lovemaking words, my lady. Not reality." He speared his

fingers through her hair and held her head still, his mouth inches from his. "Please do not try that love too far. I could not bear for you to discover the reality."

"Oh, Hades." She thrust her hand into his hair, mirroring his gesture. "Please. Do not doubt me."

"I don't doubt you, my lady. It is just that—"

"Yes, you do." Phona pushed back from him a trifle. "I know you believe that no woman could accept your condition, but you should know me better by now. I accepted you with an eye patch and a hook—" She broke off, a large lump forming in her throat. "And…smelly clothes and—"

"Don't cry. Please." He pulled her close. "Give me time. Perhaps in time I will become accustomed."

"If that is what you want. What you need." She sniffed. "I would readily give you anything you need."

"I know. And what I need now, my brave sweet lady, is more of you. Much more." In one smooth motion he rested her against the arm of the chair and flipped her skirt up over her head. His hand found the joining of her legs.

"Oh! Hades—"

Leo lay on the floor of the nursery, stretched out on his side with his head propped on his false glove so that his working hand might deploy his share of the toy soldiers.

When Leo had gone to look in on him, Arthur had complained of boredom. "Papa is sick, and he can't play soldiers. Mrs. Trammell won't play. She is too old to sit on the floor."

So Leo had stepped into the breach. He could not, however, claim that his mind was on his military strategy. He must soon decide how to handle the matter of the Bollivers. Were he and his family safer with them nearby or at a distance? The question rolled about in his head to the exclusion of all else.

A fact of which his young cousin did not hesitate to remind him. "Cousin Leo, you are not paying 'tention."

Arthur gave him a reproachful glance. "*You* are the British. *I* am Napolin. You moved Napolin's army."

"Napol*eon*." Leo hastily begged pardon and replaced the offending pieces. "But you'd best beware, Napoleon. The British horse are threatening your flank."

"My cannon will stop them. Boom! Boom!" He flung a miniature cannon into his enemy's cavalry, scattering the little horses left and right.

"That stopped them, all right." Grinning, Leo gathered up his defeated army. "But that isn't exactly the manner in which a cannon is used."

"Why not?" The boy cocked his head, interested.

"It is used to shoot various missiles—" Suddenly, Leo's throat closed. He could not get out a single word. *Various missiles—ball, chain, grapeshot... Grapeshot... Blood... Pain...*

He stood abruptly, carelessly scattering the bravely painted soldiers. "Come. I do not wish to play at war anymore."

"All right." Arthur got up from the floor, too, and gave him a cautious perusal. "Your hand is crooked."

Leo glanced at his left arm. Sure enough, the wired fingers were distorted from his having leaned on them. They stuck out in several directions. He bent them back into normal position.

Arthur stepped closer and peered at them more closely. "Is your hand broken?"

"No— Well, yes, in a manner of speaking."

Arthur drew away suddenly. Reached out. Snatched his hand back. Gazed at Leo with some trepidation.

What should he tell the lad? He didn't wish to frighten him. That was why Leo had donned the glove to visit him in the first place. But weirdly broken fingers...? It would probably be better for the boy to understand the truth.

He sat in the nursery rocker. "War is not truly a game, Arthur." Leo lifted the child into his lap. "A charge from a real cannon took away my whole hand. This—" he held up the device "—is only a padded glove with wires inside it."

The boy looked at it, curious, but still uncertain. "May I touch it?"

Leo hesitated. He did not want *anyone* to touch it. Still... The fears one could see and touch were far less terrifying than those one could only imagine. He did not want Arthur to be afraid of him.... Or of his hand.

Or his lack of a hand.

"Very well." He held the glove out.

Arthur gently ran one small finger across it. "It just feels like a glove."

"Yes. That is what it is."

"But you don't have a hand inside?"

"No. As I told you."

Arthur patted the glove very carefully. "Does it hurt?"

"Not anymore. You may touch it without hurting me." That was not quite true. At times phantom pain made it seem as if the hand were still there. Still being shredded by the grapeshot.

The boy closed his tiny hand around two fingers, snatching it back when the wires changed shape.

Leo took one of the fingers and bent it into an odd position. "See, it doesn't hurt. Now you put it back as it should be."

Arthur gingerly bent the wires, looking up at Leo inquiringly when he had finished.

"Very good, Arthur." Leo deformed two more fingers and held them out.

The child giggled and quickly moved them back into place. "I can do it."

"Yes. You did well. Now—" He set the boy on the floor. "Let us play hide-and-seek. I know a multitude of hiding places in this great house."

"Oh, good! I'm a good hider." Arthur darted toward the

door. "But let's go to the kitchen first. Mrs. Oglethorpe gives me cakes."

As Leo followed the small figure, he pondered fears that one could see and touch as opposed to those that remained hidden.

"Oh, Phona, dearest, no! Not *lavender.* It is so…so funereal."

Phona sighed. Again. As always when Mama entered her dressing room. She turned from the mirror to look at her mother, resplendent in a peacock-blue gown and plumes.

"Good evening, Mama. You are looking very handsome this evening."

"Do you think so, my dearest?" Mama pirouetted gracefully. "Halby and I were not quite certain that this arrangement of the chignon was perfectly done, but I believe it will serve." She gave her hair a tiny pat.

"It serves very attractively. You are quite perfect."

"Thank you, my dear. I always insist on perfection. But come— You are not really going to wear that dismal gown to dinner, are you? This is an important occasion, meeting the Bollivers for the first time."

Phona felt herself bristle, recognized the beginning of the old anger. She liked her gown. Besides, it perfectly matched the necklace of amethyst and diamonds Hades had given her just last night. Her jaw tightened. "Lavender does not necessarily indicate mourning, Mama, and I believe it suits my complexion quite well."

"But it is cut so low. Halby, do you think—"

Could she never leave Halby out of it? "It is quite suitable for evening, Mama. Your own gown is just as—"

Suddenly Phona broke off the thought and stood.

She was done with argumentation. She was done with anger. Surely by now she should know that she could not reason with her mother. Demetra Hathersage would *never* be logical. She would *never* allow that her daughter could make good decisions about her clothes and hair and—

No, not even the man she loved.

Nor would her mother *ever* express approval of her. Phona was not perfect. She never would be. After more than twenty years of trying to achieve Mama's image of perfection, Phona had given up. She would not allow Mama's drive to produce a perfect daughter to continue to control her.

If the love of her life approved of her…and if *she* approved of herself—

Who else mattered?

In a tone she had never used before, she calmly said, "Mama, I am going to wear this gown tonight."

For a heartbeat her mother's dainty mouth hung open, sensing a change in her daughter, not sure exactly what it was. At last, she spoke rather cautiously. "Very well, Phona."

She gave her offspring a narrow-eyed glance. "But do let Halby see what she can do with your hair. It is rather—"

"Thank you very kindly, Mama. Halby is so talented. I appreciate your offer to share her services." She smiled at the maid hovering near the door. "But Lily and I have a style we are planning to try." She leaned over and kissed her mother on the cheek. Then, linking their arms, Phona walked Mama to the door. "I shall see you in the drawing room shortly."

Mama gazed into Phona's face for a long moment, her eyes big. Were those tears? Yes, very likely. But Phona refused to be moved. She had weathered countless bouts of her mother's tears. Phona smiled steadily.

Mama lifted her chin. "Very well. I shall see you at dinner."

She tossed her head and marched out of the room.

Not a strand of her hair budged.

Phona sighed and sank down onto the dressing stool. She

should have felt, perhaps, victorious. But she did not. She felt... How did she feel? Satisfied? Yes, to some degree. But her true feeling... How could she express it? Ah!

She felt like Phona.

His newly discovered cousins had yet to put in an appearance. Time to do the pretty. Leo accepted a glass of sherry from a footman, nodded his thanks to the man and set out to make his rounds of the dowagers.

Grandmama and Aunt Mandeville sat near the fire. He bussed them each on a cheek and moved on to his mother and Lisette. They stood by the windows, gazing out over the park. He saluted each of them in like manner and shook the hands of his stepfather and father-in-law.

That completed Leo's duties to the immediate family, with the exception of his mother-in-law, who had not yet graced them with her presence. Even as he thought of her, she came through the door, a lovely pout on her face. Hmm. Now what had put her in a pucker?

Just as he began to wonder where his own wife was, she came in. Leo's breath stopped, as it did every time she walked into a room. She was so desirable. So luscious in lavender silk with his amethysts gracing her throat, the upper curve of her breasts tantalizing him.

Leo smothered a grin. For this occasion she did not wear her hair atop her head. Rather, the amethyst tiara held her curls back from her piquant face, allowing only a few to gather around the edges, the balance fluffing out behind in a warm, glowing cloud. No wonder his mother-in-law was pouting. She and her dresser had apparently been overruled.

In recent weeks he had noticed that his lady carried herself with increasing confidence, but tonight she seemed to have even more poise. She sailed regally into the drawing room, every bit the marchioness she now was.

He started toward her, but no sooner had she passed

through the door than Eggars stepped into it and cleared his throat portentously. "Mr. and Mrs. Lionel Bolliver and Mr. Maximilian Bolliver."

Leo came to full alert. Striding forward to greet his guests, he tried quickly to take their measure. The elders appeared middle-aged, perhaps fifty years old. They seemed very much a couple, the gentleman round-faced and white-haired, his florid cheeks suggesting a lifetime of good living.

Mrs. Bolliver sailed in like a ship of the line. Tall and big-bodied, a touch of color also gracing her round cheeks. Yet while her mate seemed to be the stylish bon vivant, she looked stern and matronly, dressed in an out-of-date fawn gown that did not flatter her steel-gray hair.

The fashionably dressed younger man behind them, however, was an entirely different matter. Tall and dark, his DeBolsover blood manifested itself in his countenance, while his lean, muscular body clearly belonged to a predator at rest.

Or could it be said that he *was* at rest?

Maximilian Bolliver gazed around the drawing room, his eyes resting briefly on each of the men, evaluating, analyzing, much as Leo himself was doing. Suddenly Leo became uncomfortably aware that the room contained primarily women.

He had never wished for Percy and Rob more. But Rob lay upstairs, convalescing and weak, and Percy— Had Percy already fallen victim to these people? Had Rob? Leo thought for a moment of Arthur and had to restrain himself from bolting upstairs to the nursery.

But Arthur and Rob had guardians of their own. Mrs. Trammell would not let the boy out of her sight, and Hartvard was sitting outside Rob's door.

Leo's marchioness halted and turned back to her guests. He came up beside her, and as she extended a welcoming hand to Mrs. Bolliver, Leo bowed to that lady's husband. "I am Pointeforte, at your service, sir. Welcome to Darkwood Park."

Bolliver returned the bow. "Your most obedient servant, my lord." He indicated the tall man, now standing beside him. "My son, Maximilian."

The younger Bolliver stepped politely forward and bowed. Leo held out his hand. "Welcome. I am happy that you could join us."

"Thank you, my lord."

Did Leo detect just a hint of mockery in the inoffensive words? A trace of resentment in the voice? Maximilian's smile seemed to differ from a sneer only in the slightest degree.

All the more reason to keep an eye on him.

Leo's eyes narrowed as his wife placed her tiny hand into Maximilian Bolliver's large one. The man's gaze roamed over every inch of her—her face, her gown, her jewels. And damn him! Her breasts. When he had examined her thoroughly, Bolliver's regard returned to Leo.

He smirked.

Leo had just been insulted in his own home.

Holding the other man's stare, Leo drew in a long breath. At the end of the breath, he turned, giving Maximilian his shoulder, and bowed to the man's mother.

Apparently oblivious to her son's conduct, she beamed at Leo. "Lord Pointeforte! How kind of you to invite us to your home. Who would have thought that you would find us after all these years? Such distant cousins. But of course, we knew of the connection. Mr. Bolliver had the story from his papa, don't you know? He told him—"

"Now, Adelaide, don't run on so." Mr. Bolliver patted his wife's arm. "Lord Pointeforte doesn't want to hear the story again. Apparently, he already knows it."

"I must confess I did not until recently. My aunt—" Leo nodded toward Aunt Mandeville "—had the tale from her mother. But come. Let me make you acquainted with the rest of the family."

He steered the trio around the room, making introductions and watching Maximilian Bolliver. That gentleman behaved properly until they came to Lisette. Then he gave her the same perusal he had given Persephone.

And gave Leo the same direct sneer.

What the devil was the man doing? Why was he casting down the gauntlet?

And exactly what gauntlet was he casting?

Chapter Seventeen

The dinner could hardly be called a dazzling social success. In the first place, Phona could not possibly arrange the seating at the table to alternate ladies and gentlemen. Hers and Hades' maternal uncles having returned to their homes, there were simply more women than men.

Thinking that Maximilian would prefer conversation with younger ladies, she had been obliged to place poor Papa between Grandmama and Aunt Mandeville. He had gamely struggled to make conversation with two rather deaf old ladies, while across the table Mama, as was her wont, flirted with Lord Aldborough, who showed her flattering, but quite proper attention.

The attention shown by Maximilian to Lisette, his dinner partner, had been anything but proper, and his manner was not flattering. Every time Phona glanced their way, he was touching her. Lisette seemed not to know where to look, embarrassment staining her usually serene face. Phona did not at all care for Maximilian Bolliver.

Meanwhile, she and Hades had to listen to Mr. and Mrs. Bolliver, seated beside them respectively as guests of honor, ramble on—he about his complicated business affairs and she about the family connection and how pleased she was actually to be within the revered portals of Darkwood Park at last.

At least Phona's hair had not fallen into her plate.

After port had been passed and tea had been tippled, she felt more than happy to return with her husband to the privacy of their suite and collapse into her favorite chair.

Hades likewise sprawled in his, tugging his neckcloth loose. "Ye gods! What an evening."

Phona sighed. "It was a bit of an ordeal, was it not? What did you think of the Bollivers?"

"I think they are up to no good." He stood to shrug out of his coat and hang it on the back of the chair. "At least, Maximilian is not. Had any other man behaved as he did tonight, he would have felt my fives in his face."

"And you would have been facing a dawn appointment in the morning." Phona smiled. "I appreciate your restraint."

Hades grimaced. "He was inches from crossing the line— was certainly putting me on notice as to something. I'm not quite sure what."

"That he intends to kill you and take your place perhaps?" Phona's heart sank.

"That is my first thought, of course, considering recent history. To take my title, my fortune." He scowled. "My women. The way he looked at you and pawed Lisette— He is fortunate to still be breathing. He knew very well that as his host, I would be obliged to tolerate him...up to a point. He judged that point to a nicety."

Phona shuddered. "I must admit he frightened me a bit. What else could he be doing, beside provoking you? Perhaps he would welcome a duel."

"As a way to kill me?" Hades leaned back in his chair and glared at the ceiling.

"Possibly. Do you think his parents are in it with him?"

"That is something else I do not know. I found Bolliver

rather scaly, and she is very encroaching, of course. I do not find myself inclined to trust any of them."

"Another thing upon which we agree. What will you do?"

"For tonight, with them staying in the house, I intend to keep watch." Suddenly he sat up straight. "Damnation. This whole matter has addled my wits. Since I do not plan to disrobe, I told Jemsford that he might retire. He was not feeling well. But for this duty I want my hook. I must ring for him, after all."

They both stood at once. Phona stepped forward and placed a hand on his chest. "One moment, my lord. There is no need to roust out poor Jemsford. I am not afraid of your hook. I can help you."

"But in order to don it, I must take off my shirt and—"

"And you do not wish for me to see your injury. I know." She gazed up into his face. "But the man is ill. He does not need to be dragged out of bed, to be required to dress, to walk downstairs through no end of drafty corridors—"

Hades stared down at her, his expression fraught with pain.

Phona stroked his beard, never taking her eyes from his. "It is a matter of trust, my lord. I want you to trust me, and—"

She dared not say she wanted him to love her.

He drew in a long breath. "My lady, I trust you with my life. My honor. My... But this... This terrifies me."

"I know."

A long pause ensued. At last he said, "I let Arthur touch the glove. I did not want him to be afraid of it."

"I am not afraid of it."

"I did not let him see—"

Phona waited. This was a decision she could not force on him, as much as she wanted his full faith. She had said enough. More than enough.

After what seemed an eternity, he sighed. "Let us go to the dressing room."

* * *

Leo's heart beat as it had before every naval battle in which he had taken part. It thundered in his ears. His gut clenched and his breathing rasped so that he barely heard her soft words.

"Tell me what I should do."

He shook his head and brought himself back to the present. "Help me unbutton my shirt." That much was easy enough. She had seen his chest and the straps crisscrossing it before. Her small hands started at the top, and his big one started at the bottom. All too soon they met, and the shirt was open.

She touched one of the straps, her brow puckered. "I have always wondered how these work."

Leo smiled slightly. "Curious, as always."

"Indeed, my lord." An answering smile played around her lips. "That is how we met in the first place. Now what?"

He took another fortifying breath. "Help me off with my shirt."

She pulled his right sleeve off, and, closing his eyes, Leo slipped off the left. He could not bear to look at her face. To see her expression when she saw the contraption supporting his false left hand.

She touched the straps around his arm. "Hmm. This is rather an ingenious arrangement. It should support quite a bit of weight. Did you devise it yourself?"

Leo opened his eyes to see her gazing at him expectantly. "Aelfred and I did it together. God, I wish he were here."

"So do I. I miss him. Do you think he will be with us again soon?" Her voice betrayed not a hint of loathing.

"I think so. I had word from him yesterday. He is mending." Small talk. Ordinary conversation. An emotional cushion.

"I am glad to hear that. Now... How should I proceed?"

Leo gathered his courage once again. This was the worst

part of all. "We must—" He cleared his throat. "Please, unfasten the straps."

Her clever fingers made short work of that. As the straps fell away, he clutched the glove, not willing yet to completely bare his wrist. Finally he forced himself to remove the leather cuff to which the glove was attached. For a moment the silk tube which prevented chafing stayed in place.

Then it hung on a buckle and was dragged to the floor.

His breath stopped. Leo looked at her, searching her face for repugnance. He found none.

She lifted both his forearms and brought them together, studying them. Then she kissed the back of his right hand— his left forearm just above the wrist.

She gazed up at him with tears in her eyes. "Your hand is so beautiful, my lord. I am so sad that you no longer have both of them." A tear trailed down her cheek.

"Oh God." He threw his arms around her and clutched her to him. "I do not want to lose you."

They had completed the task silently and returned to the sitting room, Phona to give half-hearted attention to her needlework, Hades to pace the floor. He had urged her to go to bed, but she demurred.

She hardly wished to be asleep if danger in the form of the Bollivers—individually or in concert—invaded their rooms. The pistol he had given her lay on a table near to hand.

And she had much to think about. He'd said he did not want to lose her. Surely that was a hopeful sign. Could he actually be beginning to love her, aging, awkward spinster that she was? Or did he simply desire her passion in the face of his amputation?

Hades had made the rounds of the various doors to the suite, assuring himself that they were all locked. He had also mounted several expeditions, his own pistol in his hand, into the corridors onto which the family's bedchambers opened. He returned each time to report that he found all quiet.

He had just completed what seemed to Phona to be his one-hundred-forty-fifth circuit of the sitting room—give or take a few tours—when a sharp knock sounded on their door.

An imperious, if breathless, voice whispered loudly, "Leopold! Leopold…open the door…at once."

"Grandmama!" Hades bolted for the door.

He hastily turned the key and opened to her. The old lady all but fell into the room, gasping for breath.

"Lady Pointeforte!" Phona tossed her embroidery aside and raced to her, placing an arm around her for support. "Whatever is the matter? Here, take this chair."

"Robert… Robert…"

Hades knelt by his grandmother and took her hands. "What? Has something befallen Rob?"

She vigorously shook a finger at him, gulping in air. He and Phona both leaned in close to her. "You… You must…go."

Hades nodded. "Yes, I am going. But—quickly—tell me what will I find?"

"A…a man," she gasped out. "He was bending…over Robert… Holding a pillow. I hit him with my stick." The dowager weakly brandished her cane and slumped back in the chair.

"Damnation!" Hades jumped to his feet. "Stay with her." He was running. "Lock the door."

Phona dashed to secure the lock, then returned to the dowager. "Are you all right, Lady Pointeforte? Perhaps a cup of tea or a bit of sherry—?"

The old lady shook her head and stated emphatically, "Brandy!"

Phona had her doubts as to the wisdom of this libation, but decided not to engage in an argument she would likely lose. She poured a small portion of the liquor into a goblet and put it into the trembling, veined hand.

She knelt. "Now tell me exactly what happened."

"Couldn't sleep." Grandmama took a large gulp of the brandy, swallowed, gasped and coughed. "I heard a footstep in the corridor." She knocked back the brandy and held out the glass. As Phona hesitated, Grandmama glared at her and pointed an autocratic finger. "More."

Phona sighed and poured another dollop. "You saw someone?"

"Followed him. Just thought I would see what was what."

"Maximilian?"

"No. None of those Bolliver upstarts. Fair-haired." She took a long swig. "He went into Robert's bedchamber. The butler was nowhere to be seen."

"Oh, my. And then what?"

"What I said. I looked in, and the scoundrel had the pillow over my grandson's face." Grandmama sat up indignantly. "So I slipped up behind him—" She mimed lifting her cane. *"Whack!"*

A thread of unease had begun to wind itself through Phona. "Is he still there?"

"I should think so. The misbegotten cur started to turn on me, but Robert roused and seized him. *Whack!* Hit him again." The old lady sank back in her chair, exhausted, and closed her eyes.

Whack. Phona tried to picture that frail old woman delivering a disabling blow. The image refused to form.

"Lady Pointeforte, do think you might be able to turn the lock behind me?"

Bleary old eyes opened and regarded her with annoyance. "Yesh, of coursh."

Not a good sign. But Hades might need help.

"Very well. I must go and find Hades—" Bother! She *must* learn not to call him that. "That is, Leo." Phona picked up the pistol and, with the other hand, tugged Grandmama out of her chair.

As Phona moved toward the door, the old lady wobbled along beside her. Phona readied her weapon and opened the door a crack. Peering into the corridor, she saw no one. She turned back to Grandmama.

"Shh." The swaying dowager placed a finger against her lips.

In spite of her tension Phona smiled. She closed the door and waited until she heard the lock click. And suddenly realized—

She had cut off her own retreat.

Leo pounded down the hallway, skidding around the many bends in the corridors, and flew into Rob's bedchamber. In the dim pool of light from the night candle, he discerned a crumpled shape lying by the bed. Good for Grandmama! She had sent the bastard to grass.

He knelt by the figure on the floor, about to use his hook to turn him, when the figure rolled over and muttered, "Leo."

"Rob!" Jerking the hook away, Leo slipped a gentle arm under his cousin's shoulders and helped him to sit. "Are you all right?"

"Well enough." Startled, Rob suddenly drew back from the hook. "Good God, what is that on your arm?"

"A very handy plaything." Leo had forgotten that his family had never seen it.

"If you say so." Rob coughed. "The blackguard tried to smother me. If it hadn't been for Grandmama—"

"Game old bird, Grandmama," Leo agreed. He helped Rob back into the bed. "But where the devil did the scoundrel get to?"

"Stumbled out of the room holding his head. I tried to stop

him." He coughed again. "That's how I came to be on the floor. Grabbed him, and he pulled me off the bed."

"Maximilian?"

Rob shook his head. "Hubert."

"Hubert? Who the devil—?"

"Hubert Hardesty."

"Celeste's brother?" Leo could not believe his ears. "He should be halfway to New South Wales by now."

"He's not. Somehow he has got loose."

"Damnation. Then if *he* has not been transported, where is Celeste?"

"I am here, my lord."

Leo whirled. Just stepping through the door he perceived the slender, golden-haired girl who had been both Rob's mistress and Leo's accuser. The woman who had betrayed them both. In her dainty hand a large pistol.

Pointed at him.

He cursed himself for a fool. Why had he not locked the damn door? He took a step toward her.

The pistol came up, aimed straight for Leo's chest. "No, no, my lord. Stay where you are."

Leo stopped in his tracks. The hand holding the pistol looked remarkably steady. But he already knew, this was not a woman to be trifled with. He could hardly prevent himself from sneering. "Well, is *this* not an interesting reunion—the three of us together in one place? Where is your brother?"

A sly smile curved her mouth. "You are quite mistaken, Lord Pointeforte. I have no brother. If you please, very carefully lay your weapon on the floor and kick it in this direction."

"No brother?" Leo eased his pistol out of his belt. Would he have time to fire before she did? Looking at the resolution in her face, he felt inclined to doubt it—and she had already taken aim.

He carefully placed the pistol at his feet and gave it a

cautious shove toward her. After all, it was hardly his only weapon. "Then who is Hardesty?"

"My husband." She took a few steps into the room, her wary gaze never leaving Leo.

"Husband!" Rob raised himself on his elbow, staring.

"Husband!" Leo took a step nearer the pistol. If he could just get his hook on her... Perhaps when she stooped to pick up the weapon.

"Do not come closer, my lord." She reached out with a foot and raked the pistol toward her. It disappeared under her skirt. "Yes, I have been married to Hubert for several years."

Rob lay back on the pillow. "Damned generous husband."

She cocked her pretty head. "Tolerant, at least. But for a very good cause."

Damn the wench, she was enjoying this. Leo backed toward the bed, putting himself between her weapon and Rob. "I suppose that Hardesty is in league with the Bollivers?"

Celeste kept backing toward the door, dragging the gun with her. "Not at all, my lord. He *is* a Bolliver."

"But how—?"

She wrinkled her pert nose. "The younger son. At least, for the present. Mrs. Bolliver was a Hardesty. It is his second name."

"Ah, all becomes clear. Where is this paragon of husbandly tolerance?" Leo leaned against the bed and folded his arms.

A small pucker formed between her eyebrows. "That is what I am presently attempting to determine."

"So you have lost him? How careless of you." Leo's mind raced. He must find a way to disarm her.

Without being shot.

"Do not expect your taunts to disturb me, my lord." Her weapon remained leveled at his heart.

"So, now that you cannot find him, what will you do? Shoot us yourself?"

"Oh dear, no, my lord. We cannot do that. You and your wife—and the boy, of course—are going to accompany us on a certain to be ill-fated carriage drive later tonight. Mr. Bolliver and Max are readying the horses."

She smirked. "And in the wreck, I believe *dear* Lady Pointeforte will be found to have fallen into a great deal of broken glass. What a pity. She had such a lovely face."

Rob lunged forward and almost fell out of the bed again. Leo caught him and steadied him, his own muscles tense. "You so much as touch my son, and I shall hunt you down and—"

Her pretty face distorted in a sneer. "I very much doubt it, Mr. DeBolsover. *You* are going to die in your sleep. We cannot have murdered bodies littering this fine establishment, now can we?"

She kicked Leo's pistol into the hall. He launched himself at the door, but quick as a cat, she slammed it and locked it.

He failed by a mere second to shove his hook into it.

A second realization followed hard on the heels of the first one.

Arthur!

Phona's original intention had been to go to Hades' aid, and her heart still tugged her powerfully in that direction. But she knew Hades to be well able to defend himself. Arthur was not. And Mrs. Trammell alone could hardly be expected to overcome Mr. Bolliver or Maximilian.

She set off in the opposite direction down the corridor toward the nursery apartment, slipping along the walls as silently as she could. Dark shadows lay between the wall sconces, which had burned low. She darted from shadow to shadow, keeping the pistol in front of her.

Now and then, a floorboard creaked, and Phona froze, listening. She heard soft rustling in the walls, but naught else. How many generations of mice had made their home in the centuries-old house? How many sets of enemies had stalked one another through its halls and chambers?

As someone now stalked her?

A thrill of fear shot through Phona. Her mouth went dry and her breathing was labored. She had never before engaged in such a conflict. The only physical altercation she had ever experienced had been when Hades kidnapped her.

She realized now that he had been careful not to hurt her. She doubted that she could expect the same consideration from the Bolliver men.

Phona did not feel at all equal to this challenge. She wanted nothing more than to run back to her sitting room and demand entrance from Grandmama.

But could she live with such cowardice? Live knowing she had sought safety while a helpless child was carried away? Or murdered? The thought stiffened her spine. Hades called her courageous, and by heaven, she would act courageously.

Whether she felt it or not.

As she approached the door of the playroom, Phona heard a muffled report, then voices raised in protestation and the sounds of scuffling, bumping and wailing. Abandoning caution she dashed the rest of the way and plunged through the door.

And stopped in her tracks.

Not Maximilian, not Mr. Bolliver, but *Mrs.* Bolliver stood in the middle of the room, one arm holding Arthur sideways on her hip, and the other brandishing a knife. Mrs. Trammell, her empty pistol at her feet, clung to the arm clutching the boy, in spite of the fact that blood dripped from her shoulder onto the floor.

"Let go, you old cat, or I'll cut you again." Mrs. Bolliver slashed at the nurse, who dodged back only long enough to avoid the stroke, then grabbed for the other woman again.

"Demon! You spawn of the devil! Let go of him. Let go,

I say!" The nurse's breath hissed through her teeth as she struggled to keep her grip. She wore only her nightgown, her gray braid swinging behind her.

"Stop it! You are hurting Trammie." Arthur pounded with all his might on the intruder's ample stomach. His legs flailed and kicked, but his captress only grunted and thrust with her blade, connecting again with Mrs. Trammell's arm before she could move out of range. The nurse gasped, but hung on.

Phona hesitated. She was shaking like a blancmange. Even though she knew how to fire the pistol in her hand, she had no illusion that if she did so, her aim would be true enough to avoid hitting Arthur or Mrs. Trammell.

Mrs. Bolliver's attention was directed fully at the nurse, who refused to relinquish her hold, even though blood now poured to the floor. Phona crept into the playroom, glancing left and right for some more reliable weapon. Perhaps if she just came a bit closer—

At that moment her gaze fell on the old stick-horse. *Whack!* If a fragile old woman like Grandmama could do it, Phona decided, *she* could. She laid the pistol on the first flat surface she encountered and seized the stick-horse.

Running full tilt into the fray, she swung the wooden head of the horse with all her strength. At that moment, however, Mrs. Bolliver sensed her approach and half turned toward her. Though Phona had aimed at her head, the horse struck the larger women on the shoulder.

It was not the blow Phona had desired, but nonetheless, the kidnapper stumbled, and her hold on Arthur loosened. His nurse gave one last tug on the arm of her enemy, and he fell to the floor, landing on hands and knees.

"Run, Arthur!" Phona made ready to strike again. "Hide!"

Wasting no time, the boy scrambled to his feet and fled as if the hounds of hell were at his heels. Which, Phona thought, they seemed to be. Mrs. Trammell moaned and sank weakly to the floor.

Mrs. Bolliver turned on Phona, blade in hand. Phona stepped back toward her pistol. With Arthur and Mrs. Trammell out of the way, her chances of hitting her intended target had vastly improved.

But, grinning the most evil grin that Phona had ever seen, the other woman charged, knife held out before her. Phona had no time to reach the pistol. She lifted the stick-horse.

Whack!

The wooden head of the horse connected with Mrs. Bolliver's with a satisfying sound. The big woman staggered. Dropped the knife. Went to her knees. Phona hit her again. And again.

The intruder fell to the floor and rolled onto her back.

Whack.

Chapter Eighteen

Damnation! He must get out of here. These people meant harm to his Persephone.

Leo and Rob looked at one another, and several seconds of colorful and enthusiastic swearing ensued, the subject of which was deceitful women in general and Celeste Bolliver in particular.

As soon as he had vented his spleen, Leo began to consider means of escape. This room had no connecting parlor, and unless his ancestors had been sufficiently provident as to build in a secret door, there was no egress into the building.

Leo knew of no such secret portal.

"It will have to be the window." He strode to the glass and looked out.

"Are you daft, cos? We are sixty feet above the ground." Rob rolled up onto an elbow to gaze at the window.

"No sailor worth his grog is afraid of heights. I cannot stay here and leave our crafty cousins to do their work." Leo waved the hook at him. "I told you this was a useful toy. If only I had a rope—"

"Allow me to point out that you have none. Damn it all!

And I lie here of no help whatsoever. A liability, in fact." Rob fell back against the pillow.

"Cannot be helped, Rob. But I should leave a weapon with you."

"You will need all you have on you." Rob pointed at a pile of his clothes. "But there should be a blade in my boot. I don't think I had time to draw it when they attacked me."

Leo rummaged in the pile. "Aha! We are in luck." He pulled the knife from its scabbard and handed it to his cousin, who slipped it under the bedclothes.

Leo opened the casement and, leaning out, gazed down. "I do not require a rope. I have trained at climbing walls without one. These old stones are rough and pitted, and the ivy is thick a little farther down."

Rob leaned toward him again. "Do you think it will support your weight?"

"Well... Some of it will." Leo swung his legs over the sill and eased himself down.

"Damn it all, Leo..." Rob tried to sit. "I still say you are touched in your upper works, but there is much at stake. Go and God speed. Take care of my son."

"You take care of yourself. I shall go to Arthur." And to Persephone. Leo found a purchase for his hook and, feeling about with his hand and feet, started down the wall.

Dear heaven! Had she killed her? Phona approached cautiously and could hear the Bolliver woman's heavy breathing. Thank God. She did not want to kill anyone. Not even someone as wicked as Adelaide Bolliver. She knelt beside Mrs. Trammell and helped her to sit.

"Arthur...?" The whisper was so weak Phona could hardly hear it. "Where is Arthur?"

"I believe Arthur is safe for the moment." Phona prayed that she spoke the truth. The boy loved to hide. Surely he could avoid capture until she could stop Mrs. Trammell's bleeding and immobilize Mrs. Bolliver. "Here— Press hard on this wound. I believe it is the worst."

Hoping that the woman would last a few minutes before she fainted, Phona looked Mrs. Bolliver over. Was she feigning unconsciousness? Phona retrieved the pistol and poked her in the ribs. No response. She put both the pistol and the knife in the nurse's lap. "If I cannot control her, do not let her reach these. Shoot her if you must."

"Very happily." Mrs. Trammell nodded grimly. "I have no idea how she gained entrance. I am quite sure I locked the doors."

"She must have stolen a key to one of the connecting rooms." Phona grasped both the big woman's wrists and strained to pull her into the adjoining school room. The woman showed no signs of reviving.

Making sure all the doors to that chamber were locked and the keys removed, Phona proceeded to secure the rest of the suite. She then returned to Mrs. Trammell and examined her wounds. "Let us bind these quickly. I must go in search of Arthur."

"Never mind me. Just go."

It was a heart-wrenching decision. But Phona could not let the loyal woman bleed to death. She shook her head. "It will take only a minute."

Phona quickly ripped a sheet into bandages and bound the nurse's wounds as tightly as she could. "I believe that will do until I can summon help."

"I am keeping you from Arthur. Go. I shall pray for you."

"Thank you." Phona patted the older woman on the shoulder.

She was very much afraid that tonight she would need every prayer.

Finding the holds he sought, Leo looked down for a moment. It was, indeed, a very long way to the earth. But there was a window directly below him, and another directly below that. At least he would not have to take the height in one long, grueling descent.

Feeling alternately for fingerholds, toeholds and hook-holds, Leo made his way almost to the first window. Suddenly, the stone under his right boot crumbled. His weight came down all on the left, and that foothold also flaked away, leaving him hanging from only his fingertips and his hook.

When his heart had ceased thundering in his ears, Leo cautiously tried several new supports for his feet. None of them held. He was traversing an area of softer stone. Every promising projection proved rotten, turning to crumbs beneath his boot.

Very well, the devil with it! He could go down to the window using only his arms. It wasn't far. Muscles straining, he gained a few inches at a time, moving first one side and then the other.

And then the crack supporting his fingers gave way.

Leo's fall stopped hard against the straps holding the hook to his body. Thank God the hook was firmly planted between the stones! As he tried to find another purchase for his fingers, he realized that the slack in the straps allowed his right foot to touch the stone lintel above the window. At last! A bit of solid footing.

With a sigh of relief, he was able to take his full weight off his arms. Leo found enough new holds to work his way down until he could drop his feet to the windowsill. Panting, he crouched there for a few seconds to recover his breath. Perhaps he could enter the house from this window.

But no.

The confounded shutter was tightly closed and latched from the inside. Leo indulged himself in a bit more swearing. Well, then. Nothing for it but to continue. He had no time to rest.

His wife might need him. Might be in grave danger. But she and Grandmama were safely locked in their suite. He need not worry about them at present.

Surely?

If anything happened to her— But that would not occur. It could not occur. It *must* not occur.

He could not bear it.

He had survived the loss of his hand.

He would not survive the loss of his Persephone.

Pistol in one hand and stick-horse in the other, Phona slipped quietly out of the playroom and peered both ways down the hall. She could see no sign of movement. Listening, she heard only the sounds of the old house.

"Arthur?" she murmured cautiously. No reply.

She began to move up the corridor, peeking into alcoves and behind tapestries. No little face peeked back at her. After several minutes of searching and whispered calls, Phona began to feel panicky. If one of their scoundrelly cousins came across him, they might kill him out of hand.

At last Phona admitted defeat. She could not search the whole huge house alone. She must seek help. But who? Who else but those upon whom she had depended all her life? Phona made her way to her parents' bedchamber.

"Mama. Papa." Phona tapped lightly on their door.

Hearing thumps and mutters from within, she did not risk another sound. She had no idea who might be just around the corner of the hallway, or in an adjacent room, just awaiting the opportunity to seize her.

"Phona? What the devil—?" The door opened, and her father's welcome face showed in the space. Seeing her armed to the teeth, he grasped her arm and pulled her inside. "What's toward?"

"Phona, dearest, are you well? Pointeforte has not—?"

"I am fine, Mama, but I fear Pointeforte is in danger."

"Danger?" Papa locked the door hastily. "Tell me."

Phona threw herself into his arms and told him all of it, struggling to keep back sobs. "We must help him, Papa. But first we must find Arthur."

"This is no job for you, minx." Papa reached for his britches, pulling them on over his nightshirt and stuffing it in. "You are to stay here with your mother. I shall find the lad and go to Pointeforte's assistance. Which I doubt he needs. Here—give me the pistol. Mine is not primed." With these words he took the gun out of Phona's hand and slipped cautiously out the door.

Mama, hands over her mouth, cried, "Oh, Phona! What shall we do? How did something this terrible come about at Darkwood Park? It is one of the most respected estates in—"

Ignoring the rest of it, Phona opened the door a crack and listened. Her father's footsteps had disappeared around the turn in the corridor. She turned back to her mother. "I am going to find Arthur. And then Pointeforte. Papa might not find them."

"But, Phona, dearest! Papa distinctly told you to remain here." Mama threw back the bedclothes and bounded out of bed.

Phona opened the door a bit wider. "Where is Papa's pistol?"

Mama seized her flowing lace peignoir. "I'm sure I have not the least idea. Oh, Phona! Must you?"

"Yes, Mama, I must." Phona clutched the stick-horse. "I will come back as soon as I can. Lock the door behind me."

"Nonsense," announced her mother, shoving her feet into her marabou-trimmed slippers. "I am coming with you."

Leo tried to put his fears for his wife firmly out of his mind and concentrate on his descent. She was safe, he kept telling himself. She was safe.

About halfway to the second window, he encountered the ivy he had seen from above. It grew thick with the tenancy of centuries. Leo knew from boyhood ventures that the lower stems were as strong as small tree limbs. They had been more than enough to hold the weight of a youngster.

But he was hardly a youngster now. DeBolsover blood made for big frames—handy in a fight, chancy in a climb. His strength was an advantage, but his weight? Well, nothing for it—

Still relying on the stones, Leo cautiously made his way through the upper branches and thick leaves, until it became increasingly difficult to work his hand and feet through to the building. Time to try his luck.

Leo seized a strong-looking stem. Tentatively tried it. It seemed to hold. He swung down a little farther and looped his hook around it. Carefully letting go with his hand, he put his weight on the hook.

But the hook slipped along the stem, refusing to catch. Leo made a grab with his hand and stopped the downward flight. He peered over his shoulder at the ground. Hmm. Perhaps another twenty feet.

He braced his feet and let himself down with his hand. Now he needed two good hands. He tried thrusting the hook into the stone and grasping with his hand. Ah. That seemed to work.

About fifteen feet from the earth, the tendrils holding the ivy to the building gave way, sending Leo down another fast five feet. He caught another branch and stopped himself once more, but not before he had banged his chin against the house. Blood began to trickle down his neck.

The devil with it! He would either make it, or he would not. Arthur needed him. His wife needed him. Leo increased his pace. For a moment all was well.

Then the ivy came loose again.

Dropping rapidly, he grasped another branch. It also came

loose. He got his hook into a crack. It immediately pulled out. He grabbed desperately at the ivy. It came away from the house in his hand.

Leo was going down.

And in no small hurry.

Once again armed with her faithful steed, Phona moved along one side of the corridor while Mama, dripping lace and ribbon, slipped along the other. They peeked behind every object they encountered—statues, potted palms, wall hangings, unlocked doors.

They found no sign of Arthur in the nursery wing, but took a moment to look in on Mrs. Trammell. They found her frighteningly pale, but still alert. When Phona turned back the covers to check the bandages, her mother went almost as white as her patient.

"Phona, dearest," she gasped, averting her gaze. "How can you?" She swayed a little in her tracks.

"Mama!" Phona glanced over her shoulder. *"Do not dare faint!"*

"My vinaigrette…Oh, my, I do not have it… Oh, my…"

"Mama, if you faint, I will leave you here on the floor."

Her mother gasped again. "Phona! Dearest, you wouldn't!"

Phona was too occupied to answer. "Find another blanket."

She tied off a fresh bandage, and her mother rummaged in a blanket chest, murmuring, "You really would not. I know you would not."

Phona pulled up the bedclothes, and with Mrs. Trammell's bloody bandages out of sight, Mama became braver again. She helped Phona spread the blanket, and even tenderly tucked it under the nurse's chin.

"There, my dear Mrs. Trammell. Have courage. We will soon bring someone to aid you." She patted the woman's gray hair. "And please do not bleed any more."

"I shall do my best not to do so, my lady." The nurse smiled wryly.

"Come, Mama." Phona picked up her stick-horse and started for the door. "Unless, of course, you wish to remain with Mrs. Trammell. I am sure she would appreciate your company."

Mama drew herself up haughtily. "If my daughter is going into danger, *I* am not the mother to stay safely behind."

"Hmm. Then let us—" A loud thump from the school-room interrupted her. The door handle rattled.

Mrs. Bolliver's voice shouted, "Open the bloody door!"

Phona turned in that direction and glared. "Not bloody likely, madam!"

Mama turned pale again. "Persephone Proserpina! Phona! Dearest! Such language—"

"Not now, Mama. Come. We have a boy to find, and we had best do it *bloody* damn fast."

If there was one thing Leo possessed in plenty, it was weapons. He knew the hiding places of more pistols in the old mansion than he cared to think about. He only hoped that his so-called guests did not.

The ivy had slowed his descent, dumping him with great suddenness, if a minimum of dignity, at the base of the building. The shrubbery had broken his fall, so he had survived the tumble from the wall with naught but a few bumps and scratches.

Now he was reaching into the drawer of his library desk for the firearm he knew to be there. Finding it, he wasted no more time getting upstairs. First, he must take the key out of Rob's door so that his enemies could not enter.

If they had not already done so. The thought spurred Leo into a run. He raced up the stairs, taking them two at a time, and ran down the corridor to Rob's bedchamber. Leo came to a screeching halt. The key was not in the door.

"Damnation!" He knocked softly on the panel. "Rob? Rob, are you all right?"

A soft reply. "Aye. No one has returned."

"She must have taken the key. I am going to secure Arthur."

And my wife.

Without waiting for a rejoinder, he sprinted toward the nursery. Surely Rob would be safe. He and his knife should provide a sufficiently unwelcome surprise to the next intruder bent on smothering him. And on the way past his own rooms, he would look in on Persephone and Grandmama.

He came around the last bend in the hallway at a fast jog and came to a scrambling stop. Kneeling on one knee before the door leading into Leo's sitting room, absorbed in an attempt to pick the lock, was Hubert Hardesty Bolliver.

Leo's heart almost rose in his throat. His wife. Only by the exercise of the utmost discipline did he stop himself from charging down the corridor and throwing himself at the black-guard. And most likely stopping another ball.

Moving stealthily, Leo covered about half the distance to the intruder before the man heard him. Hubert Hardesty Bolliver jumped to his feet, spinning to face Leo, at the same time fumbling at his belt for his pistol.

Before he could draw it, Leo spoke grimly. "If you wish to die here and now, Bolliver, continue to draw that weapon."

Hubert froze, then slowly moved his arms out to his sides, palms turned up.

"Very good." Leo took a step nearer. "Now please raise your right hand above your head. Yes, thank you. And now use your left to very carefully place the pistol on the floor."

The man did as instructed, then straightened. "Very well, Pointeforte, you bloody traitor. When you betrayed us, I was arrested and obliged to stay out there in the Thames for a stinking month before Papa could bribe the guards. Do you know what it is like in those hulks?"

"Very unpleasant, I hope. As I recall, you tried to have me killed. At least I am not a bloody murderer."

"Well, now what?" A smirk twisted Hubert's face. "Will you call the watch? You would have to call very loudly from here."

Leo smiled. "No, I shall shoot you myself. You are an escaped felon." He had the pleasure of seeing the other man blanch. "But not immediately." He gestured back the way he had come. "Step over the pistol and walk past me to the last door on your left."

If truth be told, Leo would have liked nothing more than to lodge a ball in the man. Hubert Bolliver was deceitful, violent, cruel… But Leo had yet to acquire the callousness required to shoot a human in cold blood.

He knew that Bolliver would do it in the blink of an eye. Had seen him do it. He would have killed Persephone out of hand had Leo not been able to deceive him. If she had not kept her head and lain still.

Leo watched his prisoner like a hawk until he was opposite the door of the hall linen closet. He had noticed earlier that a key was in the keyhole. Where had it come from? It should be on Mrs. Oglethorpe's key ring.

A chill swept over him. Had they harmed his housekeeper? If they had, he would no longer have any compunction about shooting them. He glared at Bolliver. "Unlock that door."

Very slowly, the man did as he was bid.

"Now open it."

The smirk returned to Bolliver's face. Suddenly he jerked the door open.

And Hartvard, bound and gagged, fell out of the closet.

Leo resisted the impulse to look at Rob's butler, choosing instead to keep his gaze firmly riveted to his enemy. The man made as if to run, but Leo raised his pistol a mere inch, and Bolliver subsided.

"Into the closet." Leo gestured with his weapon. "Now!"

Bolliver complied, and Leo slammed the door and turned the key. With that threat removed, he knelt and removed the gag from the butler's mouth. "Are you hurt?"

Hartvard shook his head as Leo sliced his bonds. "Nay, my lord. I was on duty by Mr. DeBolsover's door when this young lady came up to me. Said she needed help with her key—just down the hall. I thought she must be a guest, so I went to help her." The butler flushed. "I never should have, I know now, but she was so little and lovely—"

"That you never suspected her." Leo yanked off the last rope. "Do not feel alone, Hartvard. Welcome to a growing group."

They had returned to the pistol lying on the floor. Leo scooped it up and handed it to Hartvard. "Take this and go back to Rob's door."

"Aye, my lord." Hartvard trotted off down the hall.

Leo turned to the door to his own rooms and tapped softly. No answer. He rapped more firmly. Still no answer. Leo knocked loudly. "Persephone!"

He was just about to try his own hand at picking the lock when a querulous voice from within said, "Hold your horshes. I am coming."

Leo sighed with relief. Grandmama. And three sheets to the wind by the sound of it. He grinned. Who knew the old lady had a taste for the bottle? The key scraped in the lock and the door opened a crack.

Leo pushed it open and was obliged to grab his grandmother's arm to keep her from falling. "Grandmama! Where is Persephone?"

"Left." She allowed him to guide her to a chair. An empty glass sat on the adjacent table. Grandmama gestured at the goblet. "Never could hold my brandy."

"Never mind. Where is Phona?"

"I told you. She went to help you."

Good God. A lump of ice settled into Leo's stomach. "She is abroad in the house? How long ago?"

"Don't know. Been asleep." The old lady's eyelids drooped. "Thought she said something about the boy."

Leo ran for the door. He locked it from the outside and put the key in his pocket. He needed more help. Someone must look in on Mrs. Oglethorpe, and quickly. And help patrol the halls.

Aldborough. The man who had helped his mother rear him. The only father he had.

Why had he not called on him before?

Phona seized the stick-horse and bolted for the door. Her mother followed, clucking in agitation. Phona led the way around the first bend in the corridor, and they once more began the process of searching the new area.

Still no success. A terrible fear that Arthur had been taken by the Bollivers began to wind itself around Phona's throat. Her mother followed cooing, "Arthur, dearest, *do* come out. Come to Phona and Lady Demetra."

Suddenly, from around a corner, Phona heard the rasp of boot leather on the wooden floor. She froze, listening. Then turned to her mother. "Quickly, Mama. Hide."

"Ohnohnohno…" Mama gazed about in panic.

Phona clutched her arm. The footsteps were getting closer. "Here!"

She dragged her mother into a shallow alcove behind a tapestry. The space was small and dusty. As they backed into it, Phona glanced at her mother, and even in the dim light realized that the tapestry was being held outward by Mama's voluptuous bosom.

"Oh, Mama. You must turn around. Now."

"But—"

"Do it, Mama." The footfalls had turned the corner. "Just do it. And press hard against the wall."

Her mother turned reluctantly, whispering, "But, Phona dearest— I am sure there are spiders."

"Shh." Phona pressed herself tightly into the space. The steps continued in their direction. She held her breath. Beside her, she could feel Mama trembling.

In fact, the tapestry was trembling. Oh, no! Closer observation revealed that Mama's equally voluptuous backside now elevated the tapestry. Phona put her hand in the small of her mother's back and pushed. Mama gasped.

And the footsteps stopped.

Phona looked down to see the toes of a pair of brown boots, just visible at the bottom edge of the tapestry. They were not Hades'. His were black. Her father's were—no, he had on his bedroom slippers.

Suddenly, the tapestry jerked and fell to the floor.

Phona looked up into the sneering face of Maximilian Bolliver. He carried a large knife.

Having sent his stepfather to make sure of the housekeeper's safety, Leo set off in the direction of the nursery suite. He must find his wife before one of the Bollivers did. She had a pistol. Surely she would be all right.

Surely, surely…

Suddenly the sound of a light footstep issuing from an intersecting corridor interrupted his mantra. Persephone! But wait— That did not sound like her tread. Leo eased in the direction of the sound, bringing his back up against the wall at the corner.

Celeste Bolliver, pistol in hand, came hurrying past. Quick as a striking panther, Leo leaped away from the wall. He locked his left arm around the woman's throat, the hook pricking her skin. "Do not make a sound, Celeste. I will rip your throat out in an instant."

She drew a deep breath, opened her mouth, gasped— And remained silent.

"Very wise. If you will now drop your weapon, I shall reunite you with your husband." She did as he demanded, and Leo pulled her backward down the hallway to the linen closet. Without releasing her completely, he instructed her to open it.

Expecting a charge from Hubert Bolliver, he kept his pistol trained on the door. But no such attack was forthcoming.

Lionel Bolliver tumbled out of the closet and sprawled on the floor. A red blotch over his heart revealed a dagger wound.

"My God in heaven." Leo could not believe his eyes. "You seem to have lost a father-in-law as well as a husband."

Celeste laughed. "One fewer obstacle."

The woman made Leo shudder. "You do not really believe you will get away with this, do you? Rather than ascending to the marquessate, you will all ascend to the gallows."

She laughed again, and Leo let his gaze search for Hubert. He might be right behind him. He kicked the elder Bolliver gentleman out of the way and thrust Celeste inside. This time he would damn well keep the key.

Just as he shoved it into a pocket, all hell erupted.

"Well, well, well. And who have we here, cowering in a corner? A pair of little mi— Ow!"

Phona had kept her horse at the ready. She swung it now with all her might. It glanced off Maximilian's shoulder and struck his ear. He howled and grabbed the stick, twisting it out of her hands.

"You little bitch!" He flung the toy across the hallway. "I shall greatly enjoy teaching you some manners." He seized her hair and dragged her out of the alcove.

Mama, her eyes wide with fright, spun around, took a hesitant step forward, then stopped. Maximilian pulled Phona closer to him, her head bent back, his hand twisted cruelly in her hair. He put his knife to her throat, and a thin thread of blood started trickling down her neck.

"Come, Lady Pointeforte, fight me. Give me more reason to punish you." He moved the knife to the top of her breast, and another bead of blood appeared. "These would be so much lovelier with a bit of decoration. A scar here—" He moved the blade to the other side. "And there. I would enjoy your body all the more."

Phona gritted her teeth. She'd be damned before she would plead with the monster. She must stay alert. If she could get away only for a moment...

Her captor laughed under his breath. "Perhaps I shall cut off a hand, so that you are a match for your beloved husb—"

Suddenly a banshee screech rent the air. "You beeeaast!"

Mama exploded out of the alcove, striking Maximilian in the center of his chest. He tried to twist away, but his feet were too close to Phona's. As they became entangled, Mama's weight bore him over backward onto the floor.

"You beast! You beast! You—" She followed him down, fists pounding, nails flashing, teeth seeking a hold.

Phona perforce went down with them. As she fell, she turned so that she landed on all fours. Maximilian had let go of her hair, and was trying to fend off Mama. As soon as she hit the floor, Phona scrambled to her feet and made for the stick-horse.

"Beast! Beast! Beast!" Mama struck his face, clawed at his eyes. His nose was bleeding.

Maximilian was trying to free his knife hand, which was trapped between his body and Mama's. He grabbed her arm with his other hand. Phona saw the knife go up. Saw it come down.

Mama!

She scooped up her weapon and raced toward them, her heart in her throat. A well of blood blossomed on Mama's back. The knife rose again. Phona swung. Maximilian roared as the horse smashed into his fingers. The blade sailed off down the hallway.

"Beast. Beast. Beast." Oblivious to the gush of blood, Mama continued to tear at Maximilian's battered face. He now grasped her hair, trying to dislodge her. He drew back his fist.

"What in the name of—" The door of Lisette's bedchamber crashed open. "Dear God!"

Phona threw herself onto Maximilian, desperate to stop him from hurting her mother any further. She wound herself around his arm, letting her weight bear it down. She felt more than saw Lisette dive onto the pile of bodies, trying to control the man's other arm.

Mama continued her assault. Although with slightly less vigor. Blood welled through her lace.

"Beware! Give me room." Phona glanced up to see that the authoritative voice belonged to Lady Aldborough. Leo's mother stood over Maximilian's head with a large vase, poised to strike.

As Phona tried to obey the command, another voice, a man's voice, drawled, "I believe that will be enough, ladies. I really do not care which of you I kill first."

A quick peek showed her a man she had only seen once before. The man who, on the day Hades had taken her, had asked hopefully, "Is she dead?"

Hardesty. He carried a pistol in one hand, and a knife in the other. Lady Aldborough adjusted her aim and hurled the vase at his head.

He sidestepped, laughing. "Oh, good try, my lady. Now if you will all just step away from my elder brother?"

He stepped in and pulled Mama away from Maximilian. She tried to strike again, but could not. He tossed her at Phona's feet, and Phona tried frantically to stanch the blood.

"Keep that harpy off me!" Maximilian shook Lisette loose and stood, dabbing at the scratches on his face. One eye had swelled shut, the lid of the other was torn and bleeding.

Hubert roared with laughter. "Have you been in a cat fight, brother?"

Maximilian dug out a handkerchief and held it to his bloody nose. "I hope the witch dies and rots in—"

The report of the pistol took them all by surprise. All except Hubert. Maximilian looked startled for a heartbeat. Then a large red stain flowered in the center of his white shirt. He stood for another beat, then folded at the waist and fell to the floor. They all gazed at Hubert's smoking pistol, horrified and bewildered.

"Now I am the eldest." Hubert tossed the empty pistol away and shifted his blade to his right hand. He took a step toward Phona. "And now, if you please, Lady Pointeforte— the present Lady Pointeforte, that is—you will come with me. The rest of you, stay where you are, or I will slit her throat here and now."

"Don't move, Persephone!"

Phona had never heard such a welcome voice. She looked up from Mama to see Hades, flanked by his stepfather and her Papa, all wielding pistols.

Hubert whirled around. Cocked his knife arm to throw.

A thunder of shots filled the corridor. Hubert Hardesty Bolliver collapsed atop his dead brother.

Equally dead.

Dawn had risen before they got it all sorted out, and he and his bride had returned to their rooms and carried Grand-mama back to hers.

Another dawn. Another night of danger and death. Leo heartily hoped it was the last one he ever would see. He had stood with his arm around his sobbing lady while Dr. Ha-verstance stitched up the knife slash in her mother's back.

Lady Hathersage proved surprisingly stoic, weeping only over the fact that she feared she would have a long scar on her back. As the doctor worked, her white-faced husband gripped her hands and whispered reassurance into her ear, but she continued to wail, "But it will be ugly!"

Leo shook his head in wonder. She had come within an inch of losing her life, yet all she could think of was her famed beauty.

But never mind that. She had very likely saved Persephone's life. The lady had brought down an adversary twice her size, and was well on her way to battering him into submission. As far as Leo was concerned, his mother-in-law could be as frivolous and vain as she wished. He would never say another word against her.

He chuckled to himself. Never again would he doubt the strength and resolve of the ladies of his family. If—God forbid—he ever needed an army again, they would be his first recruits. And he would use his father-in-law and stepfather to help hold them back.

Those two gentlemen had joined forces in the kitchen, where they found Mrs. Oglethorpe searching for her keys and Arthur eating cakes. When the situation had been explained to her, she had whisked the boy and the cookie jar into her rooms and barricaded the door.

Now at last, Leo could take his wife in his arms and wipe the blood away from her wounds. Kiss the marks left by Maximilian's knife. He leaned back against the headboard of his bed and cuddled her on his lap, kissing the red line on her neck. "Does it hurt?"

"Only a little." She lifted her face to him.

Leo kissed her gently. "My only regret is that it was not I who killed Maximilian Bolliver."

She stroked his beard. "At least none of your wicked cousins will be able to harm you again. That is all that matters to me. What will happen to the women?"

"They will either be transported or hung. I don't care which." He lowered his lips to the marks on her breasts. She sighed and arched into the kiss. Of their own accord, his arms tightened around her before he remembered himself. He loosened his hold. "I am a cad. You need to rest."

"Perhaps not just yet." She smiled up at him.

"Oh. Well, then…" Leo shifted them around and leaned down to pull off his boots. She slid off the bed and gave them a tug, tossing them over her shoulder as they came off. Then she got up and went to work on the buttons of his britches. He stood to give her better access, his shaft straining at the fabric.

When the britches were in a pile on the floor, she began to unfasten his shirt. Reflexively, Leo grasped her hands. She gazed up at him seriously. "Please, my lord. Allow me this." She grinned. "Unless, of course, you want to make love with your hook on."

"No! Ye gods, no." Startled, he released her hand. She went back to work on the buttons. Leo closed his eyes. He must become accustomed to her hands, her gaze on his injury. It was part of him, and he wanted to give every part of himself to her.

But, God help him, it was damnably difficult.

She patted his cheek. "It will be all right, my love."

Together they undid the buckles and dispensed with the straps. He eased the hook off and threw it toward a corner. She slipped the silken tube off and stood looking into his eyes. "I love you, my lord."

"Oh, Persephone. My brave Persephone." He wrapped his arms around her and pulled them back into the bed. "My love. My wife." Leo couldn't wait for her buttons. He jerked her dress, and they popped and flew in all directions. "I love you. How I love you. I never knew how much until I realized I might lose you. I thought I would go mad when—"

Suddenly he couldn't get enough of her. Her gown ripped. Her shift followed it. He covered her face with kisses, then moved down her body. She sighed and moaned, gasped and arched.

When he could stand it not another second, he entered her warm, comforting body. He remembered nothing else until they were lying sated in one another's arms, murmuring softly in the warm afterglow.

It was the first time since she had removed the tube and gazed at him with so much love in her eyes that he had thought of his truncated wrist.

The wrist was still empty, but his spirit was filled.

With love and promise for the future.

Epilogue

"Truly, Mama, there is no need for you to go about swathed like a nun."

Phona and her mother were walking slowly through the gardens of Hathersage Hall. It had taken a worrisomely long time for Mama's wound to heal. She walked slowly and spoke without quite the energy she had enjoyed before, but the doctor assured them that, in time, she would again be the belle of the ball.

But she would not go to balls. "Phona dearest, I do not want anyone to see it."

"I understand that, Mama. Pointeforte is the same about his lost hand."

Mama shuddered. "Oh, the poor dear. How does he stand it? He is so brave."

"And so are you, Mama." Phona placed a light kiss on her mother's cheek. "You saved me."

Her mother brightened. "Yes, I did, didn't I?"

"Indeed, and I shall tell everyone in the *ton* when we next go to London. You will be quite the heroine and the center of attention."

"Oh, I don't think… I do not think I will be seen in

London again." She gazed at the ground, once again crest-fallen.

"Certainly you will. Do not be foolish. You and I shall go to Madame's, and she will design you the most ravishing gowns that do not show a single peek of the scar."

"Truly, dearest? Do you think she can—"

"Of course she can. Madame LeBlanc is a genius." Phona took her mother's elbow as they climbed a few steps.

Mama looked encouraged. "That's true, you know. And your Papa gave me the *loveliest* tissue shawl recently." She actually blushed. "He does not seem to mind that…"

Phona hid a smile. "There, you see. We shall contrive. We will utterly defeat that tiny scar."

"It is a very large scar, dearest. But do not repine. To help you I would do it again…and again and again. I love you very much, Phona. I am very proud of you."

Tears prickled behind Phona's eyelids. "I know, Mama." And she did know. Had always known. "I love you, too."

"Oh, Phona, dearest. Do be careful. You are getting mud on your boots. You don't want to stain your good half boots."

Phona chuckled. "Yes, Mama."

No, Mama would never change.

But Phona had.

Author's Note

Well, dear readers, are you asking yourselves, "What the heck is that myth she is talking about?" It is a Greek myth that was adopted, as was much else, by the Romans. And as with many myths, it is an explanation of why our world is as it is—specifically why we have winter and summer. You may find an interesting interpretation of it on the Web at http://www.mythicarts.com/writing/Persephone.htm.

In the Greek version the names were as they appear in this book—Demeter, Persephone and Hades. In the Latin version they are Ceres, Proserpina and Pluto. But I couldn't call the hero Pluto, now could I? Shades of Walt Disney! Actually, the story was inspired by the discovery that the name *Demetra* is derived from *Demeter*. Well, obviously. But who knew?

The myth, as well as this book, has embedded in it the theme of how the relationship between mother and daughter changes as the daughter becomes an adult. And how the daughter changes as she takes her place in the adult world.

Also, this book has embedded in it the theme of family and the importance of family loyalty as well as the wonder of falling in love. Not to mention that of the unexpected power of women. Surprise, guys!

I hope you enjoyed the book. Until the next one—be happy!

* * * * *

Love Inspired
HISTORICAL

*Powerful, engaging stories of romance, adventure
and faith set in the past—when life was simpler and faith
played a major role in everyday lives.*

See below for a sneak preview of
HIGH COUNTRY BRIDE
by Jillian Hart

*Love Inspired Historical—love and faith
throughout the ages*

Silence remained between them, and she felt the rake of his gaze, taking her in from the top of her wind-blown hair where escaped tendrils snapped in the wind to the toe of her scuffed, patched shoes. She watched him fist up his big, work-roughened hands and expected the worst.

"You never told me, Miz Nelson. Where are you going to go?" His tone was flat, his jaw tensed as if he were still fighting his temper. His blue gaze shot past her to watch the children going about their picking up.

"I don't know." Her throat went dry. Her tongue felt thick as she answered. "When I find employment, I could wire a payment to you. Rent. Y-you aren't think-ing of bringing the sher-rif in?"

"You think I want *payment?*" He boomed like winter thunder. *"You think I want rent money?"*

"Frankly, I don't know what you want."

"I'll tell you what I don't want. I don't want—" His words cannoned in the silence as he paused, and a passing pair of geese overhead honked in flat-noted tones. He grimaced, and it was impossible to know what he would say or do.

She trembled, not from fear of him, she truly didn't believe he would strike her, but from the unknown. Of being forced to take the frightening step off the only safe spot she'd known since she'd lost Pa's house.

When you were homeless, everything seemed so fragile, so easily off balance, for it was a big, unkind world for a woman alone with her children. She had no one to protect her. No one to care. The truth was, she'd never had those things in her husband. How could she expect them from any stranger? Especially this man she hardly knew, who was harsh and cold and hardhearted.

And, worse, what if he brought in the law?

"You can't keep living out of a wagon," he said, still angry, the cords still straining in his neck. "Animals have enough sense to keep their young cared for and safe."

Yes, it was as she'd thought. He intended to be as cruel about this as he could be. She spun on her heel, pulling up all her defenses, and was determined to let his upcoming hurtful words roll off her like rainwater on an oiled tarp. She grabbed the towel the children had neatly folded and tossed it into the laundry box in the back of the wagon.

"Miz Nelson. I'm talking to you."

"Yes, I know. If you expect me to stand there while you tongue lash me, you're mistaken. I have packing to get to." Her fingers were clumsy as she hefted the bucket of water she'd brought for washing—she wouldn't need that now—and heaved.

His hand clasped on the handle beside hers, and she could feel the life and power of him vibrate along the thin metal. "Give it to me."

Her fingers let go. She felt stunned as he walked away, easily carrying the bucket that had been so heavy to her, and quietly, methodically, put out the small cooking fire. He did not seem as ominous or as intimidating—somehow—as he stood in the shadows, bent to his task, although she couldn't say why that was. Perhaps it was because he wasn't acting the way she was used to men acting. She was quite used to doing all the work.

Jamie scurried over, juggling his wooden horses, to watch. Daisy hung back, eyes wide and still, taking in the mysterious goings-on.

He is different when he's near to them, she realized. He didn't seem harsh, and there was no hint of anger—or, come to think of it, any other emotion—as he shook out the empty bucket, nodded once to the children and then retraced his path to her.

"Let me guess." He dropped the bucket onto the tailgate, and his anger appeared to be back. Cords strained in his neck and jaw as he growled at her. "If you leave here, you don't know where you're going and you have no money to get there with?"

She nodded. "Yes, sir."

"Then get you and your kids into the wagon. I'll hitch up your horses for you." His eyes were cold and yet they were not unfeeling as he fastened his gaze on hers. "I have an empty shanty out back of my house that no one's living in. You can stay there for the night."

"What?" She stumbled back, and the solid wood of the tailgate bit into the small of her back. "But—"

"There will be no argument," he bit out, interrupting her. "None at all. I buried a wife and son years ago, what was most precious to me, and to see you and them neglected like this—with no one to care—" His jaw ground again and his eyes were no longer cold.

Joanna didn't think she'd ever seen anything sadder than Aiden McKaslin as the sun went down on him.

* * * * *

Don't miss this deeply moving story,
HIGH COUNTRY BRIDE,
available July 2008
from the new Love Inspired Historical line.

Also look for SEASIDE CINDERELLA
by Anna Schmidt,
where a poor servant girl and a wealthy merchant prince
might somehow make a life together.

Lawyer Audrey Lincoln has sworn off
love, throwing herself into her work
instead. When she meets a much younger
cop named Ryan Mercedes, all her logic
is tossed out the window, and Ryan is
determined that he will not let the issue
of age come between them. It is not until
a tragic case involving an innocent child
threatens to tear them apart that Ryan
and Audrey must fight for a way to
finally be together....

Look for

TRUSTING RYAN
by Tara Taylor Quinn

*Available July
wherever you buy books.*

HIGH-SOCIETY SECRET PREGNANCY

Park Avenue Scandals

Self-made millionaire Max Rolland had given
up on love until he meets socialite fundraiser
Julia Prentice. After their encounter Julia finds
herself pregnant, but a mysterious blackmailer
threatens to use this surprise pregnancy and ruin
his reputation. Max must decide whether to turn
his back on the woman carrying his child or risk
everything, including his heart....

**Don't miss the next installment of
the Park Avenue Scandals series—
Front Page Engagement
by Laura Wright—
coming in August 2008
from Silhouette Desire!**

Always Powerful, Passionate and Provocative.

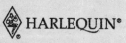

MADE IN TEXAS

It's the happiest day of Hannah Callahan's life
when she brings her new daughter home to Texas.
And Joe Daugherty would make a perfect father
to complete their unconventional family. But the
world-hopping writer never stays in one place
long enough. Can Joe trust in love enough to
finally get the family he's always wanted?

LOOK FOR

Hannah's Baby

BY

CATHY GILLEN THACKER

*Available July
wherever you buy books.*

LOVE, HOME & HAPPINESS

REQUEST YOUR FREE BOOKS!

Harlequin® Historical
Historical Romantic Adventure!

2 FREE NOVELS PLUS 2 FREE GIFTS!

YES! Please send me 2 FREE Harlequin® Historical novels and my 2 FREE gifts (gifts are worth about $10). After receiving them, if I don't wish to receive any more books, I can return the shipping statement marked "cancel". If I don't cancel, I will receive 6 brand-new novels every month and be billed just $4.94 per book in the U.S. or $5.49 per book in Canada, plus 25¢ shipping and handling per book and applicable taxes, if any*. That's a savings of 20% off the cover price! I understand that accepting the 2 free books and gifts places me under no obligation to buy anything. I can always return a shipment and cancel at any time. Even if I never buy another book, the two free books and gifts are mine to keep forever.

246 HDN ERUM   349 HDN ERUA

Name	(PLEASE PRINT)
Address	Apt. #
City	State/Prov. Zip/Postal Code

Signature (if under 18, a parent or guardian must sign)

Mail to the Harlequin Reader Service:
IN U.S.A.: P.O. Box 1867, Buffalo, NY 14240-1867
IN CANADA: P.O. Box 609, Fort Erie, Ontario L2A 5X3

Not valid to current subscribers of Harlequin Historical books.

Want to try two free books from another line?
Call 1-800-873-8635 or visit www.morefreebooks.com.

* Terms and prices subject to change without notice. N.Y. residents add applicable sales tax. Canadian residents will be charged applicable provincial taxes and GST. Offer not valid in Quebec. This offer is limited to one order per household. All orders subject to approval. Credit or debit balances in a customer's account(s) may be offset by any other outstanding balance owed by or to the customer. Please allow 4 to 6 weeks for delivery. Offer available while quantities last.

Your Privacy: Harlequin Books is committed to protecting your privacy. Our Privacy Policy is available online at www.eHarlequin.com or upon request from the Reader Service. From time to time we make our lists of customers available to reputable third parties who may have a product or service of interest to you. If you would prefer we not share your name and address, please check here. ☐

HH08R

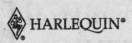

COMING NEXT MONTH FROM

HARLEQUIN®
HISTORICAL

- **THE DANGEROUS MR. RYDER**
  by **Louise Allen**
  (Regency)
  Those Scandalous Ravenhursts!
  He knows that escorting the haughty Grand Duchess of Maubourg to
  England will not be an easy task. But Jack Ryder, spy and adventurer,
  believes he is more than capable of managing Her Serene Highness.
  *Join Louise Allen as she explores the tangled love-lives of this
  scandalous family in her miniseries.*

- **THE GUNSLINGER'S UNTAMED BRIDE**
  by **Stacey Kayne**
  (Western)
  Juniper Barns sought a secluded life as a lumber camp sheriff to escape
  the ghosts of his past. He doesn't need a woman sneaking into camp
  and causing turmoil....
  Watch sparks fly as Juniper seeks to protect this vengeful beauty.

- **A MOST UNCONVENTIONAL MATCH**
  by **Julia Justiss**
  (Regency)
  Initially, Hal Waterman calling on the newly widowed Elizabeth
  Lowery is just an act of gentlemanly gallantry. Hal is enchanted by the
  beautiful Elizabeth and her little son—but it is a family he knows he
  can never be a part of....
  *Follow Hal's quest to win over Elizabeth's heart—and the approval of
  the ton—so he can take her as his bride....*

- **THE KING'S CHAMPION**
  by **Catherine March**
  (Medieval)
  Troye de Valois, one of the king's own élite guard, has long lived in her
  heart and dreams. Dreams that are shattered when he reveals his anger
  at their forced marriage and the emotions Eleanor is reawakening in
  him....
  *Drama and passion collide in this stirring Medieval tale of a forced
  marriage.*

HHCNM0608